A FORCE

TO BE

RECKONED

WITH

An icy detective goes against the tide in this slick mystery

LINDA HAGAN

Published by The Book Folks

London, 2021

ISBN 978-1-913516-76-5

www.thebookfolks.com

A Force To Be Reckoned With is the third novel in a series of standalone murder mysteries set in Belfast and beyond. More details, plus a list of characters, can be found at the back of this book.

Chapter 1

She thought she would have been tired enough to sleep but she was wrong. Again. Eventually she slipped out of bed not wanting to wake Seb. It was past 3am and now she was sitting in the dark looking out of the floor-to-ceiling window in the living room, hunched up in an old corduroy-covered armchair, head resting on her drawn-up knees, her body tired but her mind still whirring incessantly. She couldn't still her thoughts; couldn't find any peace from her doubts about herself, her life, her future. The dark room enclosed her making her feel safe and offering some sense of comfort. Outside the moonlight shone down creating a searchlight effect on the golden strand in front of their rented holiday apartment. It was almost like a theatrical experience, she, the audience waiting for curtain-up, for the performance to begin, the golden sands the set. But no actors on stage.

She could hear Seb turning over in the bed in the next room and snoring loudly. He would never believe her that he snored. But she didn't mind. He had spent nights cradling her in his arms when the nightmares came back. So she could forgive him a bit of snoring. She could forgive him many things. He had become her rock; the anchor to her life, wildly pitching like a tiny rowing boat in a vast ocean. The internal review into her actions during her last case had exonerated her of any blame but it hadn't eased her sense of guilt.

She shivered. They hadn't bothered to light the log burner. Now it was chilly sitting out in Seb's flimsy old T-shirt, which she liked to wear. It still carried the lingering fragrance of his aftershave. She reached across and grabbed her dressing gown from the armchair and wrapped it tightly around her.

Her mind was wandering back to a far different sandy scene when her attention was caught by a movement on the beach in her peripheral vision. Two silhouetted figures were moving near the water's edge. At first they seemed ghostly, ephemeral. They were leading a horse and cart. It all seemed so implausible and for a moment she thought she must be dreaming or maybe hallucinating. That had happened once or twice in the early days after she had got back from Afghanistan and had been on heavy meds but not for a long time now. She gripped the arms of her chair, feeling its ribbed covering with her fingers, trying to get a grip on reality; feeling the swirls and worn dips in the material for reassurance. Were the figures really there?

She watched mesmerized as they moved at a leisurely pace across her view until, when they were almost directly in front of her – she couldn't help thinking centre stage – they stopped. They turned and walked unhurriedly hand in hand towards the sea. Their movements were slow, fluid, almost balletic in their grace, adding to the dreamlike experience for Gawn. She allowed herself to speculate about what was happening. Were they young lovers having a secret tryst? Or a couple enjoying a romantic stroll to end their evening?

The figures moved slowly, almost as if they were floating above the sand, not making contact with the earth at all. Both were dressed all in white like the ghostly apparitions of her childhood reading of *A Christmas Carol* or the angels in the illustrated book of Bible stories her grandmother had read to her. She thought that one was male and the other female but had no good reason to think that. Their flowing robes concealed their bodies. She watched fascinated as they paused and embraced briefly. Then they turned away from her again and began walking into the surf. Both shed their robes as they walked slowly into the tide. Now she could make out their naked outline against the black of the night and the silver moonbeams playing on the surface of the water. One was a girl. Gawn could see her slight build, her youthful breasts in profile, her shapely hips – child-bearing hips, her mother would have called them – the outline of long dark hair falling down over her shoulders. The other was taller, bigger, broader, a man. Skinny-dipping, of course. Gawn smiled. Now she understood. A bit of harmless daring. She smiled again.

She watched them walk out until the water was up to their waists and then strike out swimming even further away from her and the shore. When the moon went behind a cloud, she lost sight of them for an instant only to have them reappear further away. And then her voyeuristic fascination turned to horror. The couple seemed to be struggling. Their arms were flailing, the waves splashing over their heads. Were they in difficulties? Had they developed cramps? She didn't think the current was particularly strong here but maybe they were battling some kind of undersea eddy that was dragging them down.

Gawn found herself carried back to the night when she had been the one floundering in the waves, gasping for air, struggling to keep her head above water. She felt she had to do something to help but while she was still watching and before she had had a chance to move she saw the taller figure hit the other and push her down under the waves.

'Seb! Wake up! For God's sake. Quick!' Shock and urgency sounded in her voice.

'What?' A sleepy reply issued from the bedroom. He was only half awake. He raised himself up on one elbow in the bed and tried to focus his eyes to see her in the darkness of the living room.

'Phone 999. Hurry, for God's sake! Something's happening.'

'What's happening?' he managed to ask.

By the time he had turned on the bedside light and found his mobile, she had seen the taller figure stride back out of the water grabbing the floating robes as he passed them, climb up into the cart and set the horse in motion. Meanwhile she was struggling to throw on some clothes, almost overbalancing as she thrust her legs into her tight jeans and grabbed her shoes, putting them on as she rushed to the door.

'I'm gonna help. Tell them there's someone drowning.'

'Christ! Be careful, Gawn.' His words followed her as she flung the front door open, careered out into the night and, without looking to left or right, ran across the road. She jumped the low concrete barrier which separated the roadway from the shore and ran down the sandbank to the beach, the deep sand sucking at her feet and threatening to trip her up at every step. The cart and its driver were already far along the strand and almost out of sight.

As she reached the water's edge, she cupped her hands in front of her mouth and yelled, 'Hello!' She yelled again and then listened for any reply, her eyes desperately searching the dark waves. 'Anyone there?' There was no answering call for help, no shout, no scream, only the swish of the incoming tide, the waves washing up on the beach. Gawn ran along the line of the sea, becoming increasingly agitated, scanning the dark waters for any sign, any movement. There was nothing. Suddenly Seb appeared at her side, shoeless, wearing only a pair of jogging bottoms. She could make out the goosebumps on his skin.

'Can you see anyone?' she asked.

He looked first at her, then at the vast expanse of water. Here there was no land, just the Atlantic Ocean before them as far as the eye could see.

'No. There's nothing.'

Her distress made her voice shrill. 'But they were there.'

'It's OK.' He tried to put his arms around her to comfort her but she pushed him away.

'No it's not. Someone just drowned. I think he killed her.'

'What? What are you talking about?' He couldn't help a note of disbelief creeping into his voice.

'There were two people in the water. I saw two people.' She was speaking quickly, her agitated movements mirroring the anxiety in her speech. 'One hit the other and then pushed them under the waves. Then he drove away in a cart.'

'A cart? Are you sure about what you saw?' He tried to hide any trace of scepticism in his voice. He knew she had been having more nightmares recently. It was hardly surprising after all she had been through. That was why he had suggested they have time away on the North Coast to give her a break.

'I know what I bloody saw, Seb.' She was angry. She wasn't crazy. The tide was coming in more quickly now. They had to move further up the beach back towards the road.

'Look.' She pointed to a set of cartwheel tracks and the marks of a horse's hooves just before the water washed over them.

'I don't see anything.' He hadn't been looking in the right spot. Now the only evidence she had was gone; washed away.

While they stood facing each other, neither mindful of how cold it was, a police car pulled up and two officers jumped out. They ran down to the beach and confronted Gawn and Seb. The younger one looked a little wary, not sure what to expect from these two half-naked characters on the beach in the middle of the night.

'We've had a report of people on the beach acting suspiciously,' the older policeman said, eyeing them up and down, taking in their state of undress and Gawn's agitated expression.

'Yes. I phoned it in,' Seb explained.

'There were two but one drowned and the other has gone,' Gawn added quickly, annoyed at their lack of urgency. Did she sound a bit crazy? By the look in the PC's eye, she thought he suspected she might have been drinking or maybe taking drugs.

'And you are?'

'I'm Detective Chief Inspector Gawn Girvin, Serious Crime Squad, and I'm telling you I've just witnessed a murder.'

Chapter 2

While the two policemen took a perfunctory look around the beach, Gawn and Seb had gone back to the apartment. Apart from anything else, they were freezing. Seb had donned an old sloppy jumper – ripped at the neck and cuffs and bearing a cartoon drawing of a cannabis plant and the logo "Free Willy" – which he had bought during his student years in California. Now he kept it for slouching around at home. He poured them both a glass of brandy, his drink of choice at the minute. Shortly after they had taken their first sips, the policemen arrived at the door. Seb invited them inside and they walked in, carrying the cold night air with them on their uniforms. Gawn watched their eyes scanning the room and taking in their unpacked luggage sitting in the corner; the bottles of brandy and their month-long supply of wine which Seb had carried in from the car but never got beyond the living room. They began asking questions. Gawn had the immediate impression that they were just going through a routine without any enthusiasm, not convinced that anything had actually taken place.

At first it seemed that they still didn't believe her at all, didn't even believe she was who she said she was, until she produced her warrant card. Perhaps they thought she was in the habit of impersonating a police officer. Then they suggested she might have been dreaming and merely imagined she saw something – a trick of the moonlight, perhaps. She still suspected they thought she might be drunk. She must look dishevelled. She had thrown her clothes on when she'd rushed out. She looked down now and noticed she was wearing two different shoes. Her thin T-shirt was clinging to her body emphasising her braless breasts, her nipples rigid with the cold, and she felt vulnerable in front of these two young men. Her skin was out in goosebumps. Her hair must be a sight and, as Seb had handed her a glass of brandy as soon as they got back to warm her and stave off the shock, they could probably smell the alcohol on her breath. All in all, she had to admit to herself she probably didn't look the most convincing witness. And Seb's sweatshirt didn't help either.

'We'll pass the report on, ma'am. There's no point getting anybody out of their beds at this time of night. There'll be nothing to see until the morning. The tide will have washed anything that was there away, and we can't exactly cordon off the sea, now can we? They'll send someone out to speak to you in the morning.' He smiled in what he hoped was a reassuring manner but it only served to infuriate Gawn.

Seb glanced quickly across at her, afraid she was going to explode. He knew the signs.

'I don't need to be told how an investigation is run, Constable, and I don't need your sarcasm either. I look forward to seeing your superior officer first thing in the morning.' It was clear she was dismissing them.

The younger of the two constables – he couldn't have been more than twenty – looked embarrassed and nervous.

He wasn't used to dealing with angry Chief Inspectors in the middle of the night or at any time really. Nor with suspected murders, come to that. It all seemed a bit weird and he just wanted to get back into the safety and warmth of the patrol car and get away. She must be some boss to work for. Thank goodness Inspector Cairns isn't like that. It'll be somebody else's problem tomorrow, he thought to himself.

'Thank you, Constable. We'll wait to hear from someone in the morning.' Seb sounded so reasonable as he accompanied them to the front door.

Gawn didn't trust herself to speak. Someone had just been murdered. She had seen it. She was sure of it. Or was she? She mustn't start to doubt herself. Her mind had played tricks on her in the past but not for years. She was off all her medication. She was happy. The insomnia, when she couldn't sleep and the nightmares when she could, had started again recently but she thought she knew why and she just needed time to sort it out in her mind. But what had happened here tonight was no nightmare. She was sure.

'That's them gone.' Seb sighed heavily. He gulped down the rest of his brandy and poured himself another glass. He held the bottle up to her offering a top-up. She shook her head. He flopped down into the chair at the window where Gawn had been sitting when she saw the two on the beach.

'You believe me, don't you, Seb?' She stood straight in front of him in an almost confrontational pose. There was a pleading tinge to her question which annoyed her. She shouldn't have to explain herself to anyone, especially not to him. He knew her. She knew what she'd seen. No matter what anyone else believed.

'I believe you think you saw something.' He chose his words with care and spoke hesitantly for he knew she would be disappointed that he didn't agree with her unreservedly. She would understand he wanted to support her but he couldn't be sure and wasn't going to lie to her just to keep her happy. She wouldn't thank him for doing that.

'I don't *think* I saw something. I did see something, Seb. I saw one human being kill another right in front of me.' She balled her two hands into fists in anger. She couldn't stop tears of frustration slipping down her face.

'Come here, darling.'

He set his glass down on the table and held out his hand to her. She looked at it and hesitated but then took it and allowed him to pull her gently down onto his knee. She snuggled into his shoulder and he hugged her tightly to his chest and stroked her hair. Then he ran his finger backwards and forwards over the knee of her jeans, tracing the line of the scar from the incident when her car had been run off the road. He thought he had lost her that time. But here with him was her safe place. Here she could be herself. Nobody but Seb knew how fragile and vulnerable she could be. To the outside world she was the Ice Queen, that hard-nosed bitch of a Chief Inspector who led from the front, didn't tolerate anything other than total commitment from her team and never accepted failure.

'It'll be alright. I promise. They'll come back in the morning. They'll find some evidence or a body on the beach or something and then we can enjoy the rest of our stay here and leave it all up to the local cops.' He stroked her hair again as he spoke. If only he felt as confident as he sounded.

Chapter 3

They had both managed to get a little sleep. In the end it was Seb who woke first and slipped out of bed leaving

Gawn snuggled down under the duvet. He made himself a coffee and settled down at his laptop in front of the picture window. The justification for their two-month let of the apartment was to give him time to work on his next mystery novel. It was to be the fourth in his series of *Inspector Darrow Investigates* and he was struggling to get started. He had a deadline looming when he needed to have something to show his literary agent and the publisher in Hollywood who had paid him a sizable advance.

He was still facing a blank screen and an accusatory flashing cursor when Gawn emerged from the bedroom behind him. He heard her and turned to watch as she walked across barefooted to where he was sitting. He loved looking at her first thing in the morning when her hair was all fuzzy and sleep was still in her eyes. She looked at her most vulnerable and sweet then, not at all like the intimidating police officer she appeared as most of the time. Even he could find her a little daunting sometimes when she was in Chief Inspector mode.

Gawn reached over, took the mug of coffee from his hand and helped herself to a sip from it. She closed her eyes and exhaled slowly, then handed it back to him.

'I needed that. Hot and strong.'

'Just like me,' he joked and smiled up at her.

'I don't know about the strong but you're certainly hot this morning, Dr York.' She paused, then added, 'I can do cheesy, you know.' A smile spread across her face too. It was like old times. Gawn seemed almost like her old self. They both laughed and he was about to pull her into an embrace when the doorbell rang.

'Who could that…' he started and then asked, 'Do you think that's our friends from last night?'

A fleeting look of horror passed across Gawn's face as she glanced down at what she was wearing.

'I better get some clothes on. I can't meet anybody dressed like this.' She looked down at Seb's old Oxford

University T-shirt which she liked to sleep in. It didn't leave a lot to the imagination barely reaching the tops of her legs and clinging suggestively to the curves of her breasts, and she certainly couldn't be seen in public in it. It had been bad enough last night but at least it had been dark then and she'd had jeans on to hide the ugly scar on her knee.

'Don't worry. I'll see who it is and let them in. You go and get dressed.'

Ten minutes later Gawn emerged from the bedroom dressed in a pair of tight black jeans with a faded denim shirt tucked into the waistband. Its top three buttons were left undone. Seb noticed that the top of the scar on her chest was just visible between her breasts. She had taken time to apply a light touch of make-up and to sweep her hair up into her signature chignon. She found Seb chatting with a middle-aged, balding man who was sitting opposite him on the second armchair in the room. The two were drinking coffee like a pair of old friends. From behind, the man looked and sounded like everyone's favourite uncle. Avuncular was the word that came into Gawn's mind. When he heard her coming in, he turned round and immediately stood up. His puffy blue anorak reminded her of Monsieur Bibendum and she smiled at the thought. He was tall, slightly taller than her but not as tall as Seb. His broad shoulders exuded strength and stability. She imagined he would be good in a crisis. Probably used to calming distressed little old ladies and now neurotic Chief Inspectors too, she thought cynically, as he introduced himself.

'Chief Inspector, I'm DI Cairns. Thomas Cairns.'

She was impressed with his firm handshake. She was aware that his eyes were scanning her face, appraising her. She wondered what sort of report the two constables had come back with last night. What had he been expecting to find? A neurotic fantasist? A cop who had succumbed to the pressures of the job and turned to drink or drugs? A drama queen with an overactive imagination? Would he come to this investigation with an open mind? Would he even take it seriously as something requiring investigation?

'You've read the report from last night?' She asked the question but knew that, of course he had read the report, why else would he be here? And sending an inspector was to show that they were taking her claims seriously or at least they wanted to give that impression. She didn't offer her first name but merely motioned for him to sit back down. With no other chair available, she perched on the arm of Seb's seat. 'Well, Inspector?' She waited to hear how he wanted to play this.

'We've got men searching the beach now, ma'am. Though, to be honest, we don't really expect to find very much.' When he saw her raised eyebrow, he hurried on. 'The tide's out this morning and anything there might have been last night will more than likely have been washed out to sea. There are some caves a bit further along and we'll check those too of course, just in case. I've got some men on a door-to-door to see if anyone else saw anything but it's still quite early in the season. Most of the holiday rental properties are still vacant and it was the middle of the night so there won't have been many people up and about. But, who knows, maybe we'll get lucky.'

'What about missing persons?'

'None reported.' He paused then added, 'We've a general alert out to shipping and we've contacted the coastguard both here and in Scotland and they'll be keeping a look out too. Other than that, there's not much we have to go on. Until a body turns up or someone's reported missing, that's really all we can do.'

'What about the cart?'

'The cart?'

'Yes, wasn't it in the report that the two arrived in a cart and the man drove off afterwards in it?'

The inspector looked a bit bemused. Gawn was sizing him up too. Was he sent to placate her or were they really going to take this seriously and investigate her report?

'Yes. It was but we can't exactly rush around the countryside examining every cart. What kind of cart was it, ma'am? Can you be specific? Was it a jaunting car for example?'

Gawn had to admit she wasn't sure. She wasn't even sure what a jaunting car looked like. She didn't really know anything about carts other than that they were pulled by horses.

'It wasn't particularly big. I think it would only have held the two of them and it was pulled by just one horse.' This was the best she could do and even to her ears it sounded less than useful.

'Well, we'll obviously keep an eye out but again if we don't have a body, there's little more we can do.'

With that, for now, she had to be content.

Chapter 4

Gawn and Seb had watched a gaggle of figures in uniform stretched in a more or less straight line making a desultory search of the beach over the next three hours. At first Seb had tried to concentrate on his novel and get something, anything, down on paper to appease his agent but Gawn was so agitated that he had to give up trying. Even she had to admit that there must be hundreds of pieces of detritus washed up on beaches along this coastline every day. It was probably a thankless task. Impossible even. You would either find far too much – all irrelevant to what Gawn had seen – or nothing at all. And it seemed that 'nothing at all' was the case here. Around midday, Cairns returned.

'Not much to report, I'm afraid, ma'am. They found the usual stuff you would expect – a dead seagull, a man's leather shoe, rubbish left over from picnics on the beach, a child's doll. That sort of thing. They've collected it all and bagged it but no white gowns.' He didn't seem too surprised or too disappointed. He had followed protocol, not dismissed her report out-of-hand. There could be no come back on him.

'Thank you, Inspector. We appreciate it.' Seb, ever the diplomat, nodded to show he understood the position Cairns was in.

'So, what happens now?' Gawn asked and it was clear from her tone she was challenging the local policeman. She had known they wouldn't find any gowns, the male figure had taken them away with him, but she had hoped there was some trace of what had happened.

'We wait. You know how it works, ma'am. We have quite a lot on our plate at the minute including a spate of burglaries and an outbreak of anti-social behaviour. We don't have the manpower or the budget to go gallivanting all over the place without evidence of a definite crime.'

Gawn's face showed what she thought of Cairns' comments and his use of the word 'gallivanting', as she walked to the other room.

'Like a body,' Seb added helpfully. He appreciated the inspector's predicament and in her more rational, less personally involved and less 'whatever the hell was going on with her at the minute' mode, Seb was sure Gawn would have done so too. 'Thank you, Inspector.'

The two men shook hands at the front door and Seb was surprised to see a look of sympathy in Cairns' eyes.

'Take care of yourself and take care of your–' There was a moment's hesitation before he added, 'wife.' He obviously couldn't bring himself to refer to a senior officer who was sharing this man's bed as his girlfriend.

Cairns was clearly on the traditional, not to say old-fashioned, side of morality and Seb thought he sensed a whiff of disapproval about their relationship. He was reminded of his grandfather in dark suit and stiff white collar heading off to the local mission hall on a Sunday morning.

'I've done a bit of homework about her, you know. She's quite the hero, isn't she? It can't be easy to come to terms with all she's been through,' Cairns said.

'She's fine. We're just having a few days away. Everybody needs a bit of a break sometimes.'

'Indeed, sir.'

They shook hands again and with that he turned and left. Seb closed the door thoughtfully behind him.

What was the inspector implying? Yes, she had been wounded in Afghanistan, but that was years ago. Last year she had been stalked and then she was injured investigating a criminal gang from Eastern Europe. She'd lost her sergeant around the same time but Gawn had never told him all the details about that although one time, late at night, when she'd had another one of her nightmares, she'd said it had been her fault. Any time he had tried to bring the subject up since then, she had closed him down, and he didn't want to push her too hard. But he had been worried about her for some time. There was something playing on her mind but she wouldn't talk to him about it, whatever it was.

She still wouldn't agree to move in with him although he kept asking her to and she had not invited him to share her apartment on a permanent basis. So, he had come up with the idea of this time away together. He needed to get on with his novel. His agent and publisher were getting anxious. He had taken a sabbatical for a term from the university to work on it. He suggested she could come with him as she was on sick leave anyway. At first, she had rejected the idea out of hand. When he changed where he would do the work to the North Coast area of Northern

Ireland instead of the South of France, he had managed to convince her to come for a few days and then if she really didn't want to stay, she could travel up at weekends or whenever she could fit it in. He would be there for two months. The apartment was small, only one bedroom but perfectly positioned right on the beach with a glorious unobstructed view of the ocean. He had imagined long romantic walks hand-in-hand by moonlight but that hadn't happened. Yet, he thought hopefully to himself.

He was surprised, when he returned to the living room that Gawn was nowhere to be seen. He was even more surprised when she appeared from the bedroom with her coat over one arm and carrying her Louis Vuitton overnight bag.

'Where are you going?' He didn't really need to ask, of course. He knew by the look on her face she had made her mind up and there would be nothing he could do about it. She was leaving.

'You need to get on with your novel. I'm only holding you back. I'm a distraction.'

'Yes, but what a distraction!' He tried to keep it light, make a joke of it. But the situation was anything but a joke to him. He moved across to embrace her, but she sidestepped him.

'Seriously, Seb, you need to work and so do I.' It was obvious her mind was made up and trying to argue her out of it wasn't going to do any good. If anything, it might only exacerbate whatever crisis he sensed they were heading towards. He wanted to put that off for as long as possible. Maybe if she did go back to work, she would snap out of whatever this was. He had to hope that anyway. He didn't want to think about the alternative.

He moved across to take her bag and carry it out to the car for her. She let him, relieved that he wasn't going to try to argue with her. She knew this was best for both of them. They needed a bit of space between them. She needed space. If she hung around, God knows what would end up happening. What she might say or do. She needed time away from him to set her mind straight.

'Drive carefully, darling.' He didn't ask her to phone him later or let him know she was safely home. He didn't want to crowd her; to come across as needy. He went to kiss her goodbye but she turned her mouth away from him, so he contented himself with a tender kiss on the cheek and then she climbed into her car and drove off. Just like that, she was gone, and he was alone.

Chapter 5

The apartment seemed so empty and so quiet after three weeks with Seb constantly by her side. They had left it in a mess when they had set out on Saturday morning, knowing Martha, her cleaning lady, would be there on Tuesday to tidy up. Their breakfast dishes were still stacked beside the sink. Seb's clothes had been discarded on the bedroom floor rather than placed with hers in the laundry basket, something which infuriated Gawn but Martha excused as 'just what boys are like'.

Gawn checked her answering machine. The light was flashing so she knew she had at least one call. In fact, she had two. The first was from her friend, Jenny Norris, the pathologist.

'Hey there, Gawn. Long time no see. Have you disappeared down a black hole or something? I've been trying your mobile but it was switched off. Give me a ring. We need to catch up. Bye.'

Gawn deleted the message and made a note to herself to phone Jenny, just not right now. She had kept her mobile switched off not wanting to talk to anybody and she needed a few days yet before she could face her friend's cheery chatter.

She pressed to hear the second message. There was a pause before a man's deep voice came on the line. She recognised it straightaway. It was her godfather, Assistant Chief Constable Norman Smyth.

'Gawn, I just wanted to check how you're doing. I tried your mobile but it went to voicemail. Phone me, my dear.'

He sounded tired. She knew his work made all kinds of demands on him and he carried a heavy burden of responsibility. He knew all that she had been involved in; what had happened to her and about her sergeant. She wouldn't need to explain anything to him. She could just talk and that was what she needed to do. She couldn't talk to Seb. He was a civilian. He didn't understand all the demands her work made of her. She couldn't share some of it with him, with anybody really. But she couldn't face talking to Smyth tonight. She decided to leave it, to sleep on it.

* * *

On Monday morning she spent a bit of time tidying up but she knew she was just trying to put off phoning Smyth. Eventually, she could postpone it no longer. She looked down at her hands while she waited for him to answer. Her palms felt sweaty. Was he going to tell her that her career was finished? The internal inquiry might have found no fault but the top brass might have different ideas. They didn't like loose cannons who couldn't be trusted to follow orders unquestioningly.

'Norman Smyth.'

'It's Gawn.'

She heard him sigh.

'I'm so glad you phoned, my dear. Are you at home?'

'Yes.' He had known she'd intended to spend some time up at the North Coast.

'What about your friend? Didn't it work out for you?'

'No.' She knew she was being monosyllabic but couldn't bring herself to try to be more forthcoming. Smyth knew about Seb but had never met him.

'I heard about your murder mystery.'

'My what?' Her mind obviously was a bit slow. It took her a second to realise he was referring to the scene on the beach. 'How? Stupid question. I suppose you've had someone keeping an eye on me.' She tried to be outraged but couldn't manage the energy that would require of her.

'Not at all. I just happened to be chatting to the Chief Superintendent for the district. He mentioned it. It's not every day, or should that be every night, they get a call-out from a Chief Inspector who's witnessed a murder.' She could almost hear the smile in his voice.

'I think they thought I was drunk or maybe delusional.' She tried to laugh as if she couldn't understand why anyone would possibly think that.

'I can't speak to that. I only know they looked into it as far as they could with no other evidence. It's still on their books. If anything turns up they'll follow it up. You can be sure of that.' He paused as if he was trying to work himself up to say something. 'That's not actually why I wanted to speak to you, my dear.'

She held her breath. Was this it? Was he going to tell her that she was being side-lined to some desk job?

'What are you doing for dinner this evening?'

'Probably takeaway pizza. I don't think I've got much in the fridge.' She sounded impossibly cheerful for a simple comment about pizza but relief was flooding through her. She didn't think he would do something so serious as essentially ending her career out in a restaurant. He would do it by the book. She would have been called to his office at Police Headquarters.

'Let me take you to dinner.'

It didn't take her very long to decide to accept his invitation.

* * *

Later that evening she was sitting opposite her godfather in a popular inn on the outskirts of Holywood almost directly across the lough from her home in Carrickfergus. Smyth had suggested it as it was near his house in Cultra and, as he explained, more or less his home from home. He ate there frequently and they all knew him. That was obvious from the speedy service they received. They had met up in the foyer and walked in together. Smyth didn't have to say anything. They were expecting him and the two were immediately escorted to a quiet table in a corner of the room where they would be able to talk undisturbed.

Gawn had spent the afternoon at the hairdressers. At first she had been delighted that they were able to fit her in at such short notice. Now she was sitting feeling rather conspicuous with a new short haircut. She felt as if everyone was looking at her although she knew that wasn't the case. No one else would even know, or care, she thought to herself, that she had had her hair cut.

Her godfather had reacted with surprise when she had walked in from the car park. 'Goodness me. I almost didn't recognise you, Gawn. The last time I saw you with hair that short you must have been about three years old.' He had kissed her on the cheek and squeezed her arm in greeting.

She wasn't sure how she felt about the new look yet. She just knew she needed to do something to make a change in her life.

They took a few minutes to look over the menu. Gawn wasn't hungry. Smyth selected sirloin steak but she knew she wanted something lighter. The homemade fish and chips would be tasty and she went for that. To drink, they both chose sparkling water, neither wanting to risk running foul of the Traffic Branch with all the aggro that would entail.

'You said you wanted to speak to me, sir.' She never used his Christian name although she would never forget the kindly man who had brought her a lovely doll which she had immediately named Mabel. That doll had become her constant companion for years after her father was killed.

'For goodness sake, we're not in uniform now. I haven't asked you to dinner as the Assistant Chief Constable.'

'Why have you asked me, Norman?' She had paused before adding his name. It sounded strange on her tongue. She held her breath suspicious now about what ulterior motive he might have.

Before he could answer, a waiter arrived with their water and a basket of artisan breads.

'First of all, I wanted you to be the first to know, I'm retiring.'

She hadn't expected that. It was so out of the blue that she wasn't sure what to say.

'It'll be general knowledge in a couple of days anyway, but I wanted to tell you first. Word travels fast and they'll be queueing up to put in a bid for my job.'

She was genuinely sorry to hear this. It wasn't just because it had been good to feel she had someone at the top on her side but also because she knew he was a sincere and caring man. He had always wanted to make a difference, like her. Whoever replaced him would have a lot to live up to.

'I'm sorry to hear that, Norman.'

'You can only keep doing the things we do for a certain length of time, and I've reached my limit. I want to be able to enjoy my retirement; have a few good years to do all the things I haven't been able to do.'

'Well, here's to your retirement.' She lifted her glass of water in a toast.

'Thank you, my dear. But that brings me on to something else. Where you fit in.'

'Me?' Again, her stomach did a flip. Was he going to suggest she should retire too?

The waiter appeared with two plates of food and a selection of side dishes to compliment the steak. Gawn sprinkled salt and vinegar over her fish and chips. If she was going to splurge, might as well make a good job of it. Smyth smothered his food in brown sauce.

'I see you still like your sauce, Norman.'

'You remember that? Just like your father. I remember in the early days your mother used to make your father Daddies Sauce sandwiches for his lunch. We laughed about it but that's how I got my taste for the stuff. A meal isn't complete without the old brown sauce.' He smiled at the recollection. He cut a mouthful of the steak and chewed it before continuing, 'I'm setting up a special team.'

So this was business after all.

'You'll know of course about the work of the Legacy Investigation Branch.'

She did. It dealt with homicides and security-forces-related deaths arising from the Troubles.

'Most of its work is focused on the Troubles but its remit also includes unsolved non-Troubles-related deaths. Now there's some thought of extending that to include all kinds of unsolved cases, not just murders, in fact specifically not murders. And I want to run a test case.'

'And?' She thought she could see where this was going.

'You need to get back to work. We need you to get back to work. The Standards boys cleared you. You know that. You're too good a police officer to sit at home twiddling your thumbs, Gawn. But I don't think you're quite ready to get back to leading the Serious Crimes Team,' – he saw the look on her face and rushed on – 'at least not yet.'

Gawn bit her lip. Smyth knew her well. He knew her confidence had taken a battering and he was right, she didn't think she was ready to lead the team again yet either. She hoped it was something she could get over. She wondered if he had come up with some little scheme just to ease her back to work or if there was something more.

'What aren't you telling me, sir?' She hadn't used his name as she realised he was speaking now as ACC. This was business.

'Every police officer, if they're in the job for any length of time, will have one case, one victim, one victim's family that they can never forget.' He paused and looked off into space. She knew he was remembering. 'Mine's Jason Sloan. It was 1999 and I'd just been promoted to detective sergeant. The boy went missing. I think we did our best with what we had at the time. I hope we did. But I'd like you to go over it. Come to it with a new eye. No preconceptions.'

That sounded like a strange word to use. What 'preconceptions' had others come with, she wondered.

'Don't make up your mind straightaway. I'll have a file with the basic details of the case sent to you tomorrow. Read it. Think about it and if you decide it's something you could spend a week or two looking into, let me know.'

'A week or two?'

'I'll be away by the end of the month. If you turn something up before I go, great, but, if not, then it'll just have to remain my unsolved case.'

They talked no more about it. Gawn had lots of questions, but she realised Smyth wasn't going to answer them. She wondered if that was just another way of sucking her in; whetting her appetite to find out more.

Their meal ended pleasantly. The food had been good but the company and the reminiscences about her parents had been even better.

'By the way, I love the hair, Gawn. But you know, you can change the look but that doesn't change the person inside, and you don't need to change, my dear. You will always be someone who'll step up. No matter what.'

He kissed her lightly on the cheek in farewell and she watched as he got into his Mercedes and drove off. He had used Seb's mantra. That phrase, 'no matter what', was what Seb had said to her. He meant he would always love her no matter what she did; no matter how she treated him. She wanted to believe that, right now she needed to believe that. But if she kept pushing him away, she wondered how long that would be true.

Chapter 6

A large brown envelope was lying on her mat the next morning. It had been slipped under her front door. All mail was delivered to post boxes in the foyer of her apartment block. No one should be able to access the floors without a security code, but she guessed if you were the ACC that wasn't a major problem. She lifted it and carried it to the countertop in her kitchen. It could wait until she'd made some coffee. The weather had brightened, and the sun was shining this morning. She opened the French doors onto her balcony and let the fresh air and the noise from the marina below come in. Gawn liked the sense of constant movement which living beside the water gave her. She could hear voices where some people were already working on their boats. A middle-aged man and woman, arm in arm, walked underneath her balcony with two little dogs on leads. She noticed a large container ship lying moored in the lough almost directly opposite her window waiting for a new cargo.

Coffee was ready and she poured it into her favourite oversized mug. She placed the envelope on the table and then sat down in front of it. She had eschewed the temptation to google the name Jason Sloan last night. No preconceptions, she smiled to herself. She picked the envelope up and hesitated for a minute. Seb always used a letter opener. He hated it when she merely ripped a letter open. One of his little foibles. Then she ripped it, as carefully as possible.

It contained only three A4 pages. Smyth wasn't giving her much to go on. But she was sure there would be boxes of evidence and witness statements to plough through if she took this on. She read the first page. Jason Sloan had just turned nineteen when he went missing after a night out in Belfast city centre on Saturday 17th April 1999. He was last seen leaving a nightclub in the Ormeau Avenue area of the city around midnight and getting into a car with two friends. He was the son of a single mother. His father had been Jamaican and his dark skin had made him an easily recognisable figure in the still predominantly white East Belfast of his day. She read his home address and immediately recognised it as the same public housing estate where Seb had grown up. They had been roughly the same age – Jason a couple of years older – so the chances were Seb had at least been aware of him.

Gawn turned to the second page. It was a witness statement from a bouncer at the Starlit nightclub. Ray Totten stated that he had seen Jason and two other boys leave the premises just after midnight. They had been drunk and, although he hadn't had to throw them out, he had been on the verge of it. They were making a nuisance of themselves, picking arguments and harassing some of the female clientele. He had watched them walk off arms around each other's shoulders, laughing and singing, in the direction of Ormeau Road, but before they had reached the end of the street a car had pulled up and the boys had got in. It had then turned left and driven off towards Cromac Street. He couldn't give them a registration but was able to tell them it was a dark-coloured saloon car which was too general a description to be of any use.

The final page was a list of people who had made statements or been questioned as part of the investigation.

Some of them would need to be re-interviewed if they were still alive and still in the country. Most of them would have forgotten all about the case either because they had got on with their lives or because they chose not to remember. Her eyes scanned down the page and came to rest on the very last name on the list; last alphabetically. Jacob York. Seb's full name was Jacob Sebastian York. He had been named after his grandfather. So Seb's grandfather had been questioned. Norman Smyth had known about that connection. Of course he had.

Chapter 7

Things moved quite fast after that. Two days later she found herself driving under the raised barrier at a suburban police station in East Belfast. She was not surprised to see Paul Maxwell, her erstwhile sergeant, now Inspector Maxwell, waiting for her at the front door of the building. His face showed some surprise at first and she realised he was seeing her new hairstyle for the first time. Keeping it professional, he made no comment about it.

'Good morning, ma'am. We were told to expect you today and I knew you would want to be first here.'

'Good morning, Inspector.'

She smiled. She was pleased to see him. It was good to see at least one friendly face. She wasn't sure how she would be regarded here and what kind of welcome she would get. She expected that an outsider investigating a cold case on the premise that the original case had been bungled in some way or at least something had been missed, would not be particularly welcome. Invisible barriers would come up, ranks would be closed, even though this was not the station where the case had first been investigated and she was sure none of the original officers would be here. Few of them would even still be in the service. But Northern Ireland was a small place. Everyone knew everyone else or knew someone who knew them. The tradition of policing ran in families, as she herself was proof of, and it was possible a son, or a daughter she reminded herself, or even a grandson or granddaughter could be here.

'We've allocated you two rooms. We're a bit tight for space so it's not exactly the penthouse, I'm afraid.' He smiled apologetically. His superintendent had ranted about having to find accommodation for them at all. If he'd had his way they'd be in a leaky mobile in the car park but Maxwell had tactfully pointed out that ACC Smyth had phoned personally to make the request so perhaps it would be a good idea to be as helpful as possible and, anyway, it was only for a couple of weeks.

Maxwell led her down a corridor towards the back of the building, their footsteps echoing off the tiled floor. It was still early. Few others were around. They could hear voices from elsewhere in the building but they didn't pass anyone as they made their way to what would be her base for the next two weeks. He pushed open a set of double doors and switched on fluorescent lights illuminating a room packed with two desks, a set of filing cabinets and a whiteboard on wheels. A stack of boxes, no doubt containing the documentation to do with the case and any exhibits, stood to the side. That was all that could be fitted in. Facing them was another door and he opened it to reveal what Gawn suspected might once have served as a large store cupboard. It was smaller than her en-suite and had no natural light. The single desk, which she presumed was meant for her, took up virtually all of the space. She thought to herself that if she spent more than a few minutes in that room, she would end up having a panic attack.

Maxwell sneaked a glance at her and then felt he had to apologise again. 'Sorry.' He shrugged.

'I've been in worse. It's not your fault, Paul. Anyway, I doubt we'll be spending too much time in the building. We'll need to get out and talk to the original witnesses.'

She could have added 'before they all die' but didn't. She wasn't sure whether anyone here knew which case they were looking at and that could be a reason to be viewed with even greater suspicion. There might be one or two guilty consciences around who would be fearful it was something they'd been mixed up in. That was why she was keeping things close. Her new team, whenever they arrived, would be ordered to keep everything to themselves too. She wasn't even going to tell Maxwell, although she trusted him.

As if on cue, they heard voices outside in the corridor and the doors were pushed open to reveal two newcomers. First through was a young woman. Gawn had read up their personnel files and knew who Smyth had selected to help her. It had made interesting reading but the reality was fast becoming even more interesting than what had been written.

The young woman was Josephine Hill. Detective Constable Jo Hill. She looked even younger than the twenty-four Gawn knew she was. She could pass for late teens, a useful asset for an undercover cop. Her blond hair was cut really short and shaved at the sides, hinting at a skinhead connection. She was not wearing any make-up but her hands were festooned with rings. She was dressed in a pair of faded jeans which Gawn thought looked as if they might have been used to do some painting evidenced by the splatters of red paint down the front. A black leather biker jacket and a pair of black DMs completed a look which Gawn suspected might be her attempt to project a tough image. She knew the girl had put in a complaint about sexual harassment in her last post and had asked for a move while a review and investigation were taking place. With the complaint still pending she was no doubt sensitive to any comments about her appearance; perhaps being deliberately provocative to see how far she could push it. She wondered how the young woman regarded her, whether as a potential ally in the battle of the sexes or just another senior officer who would give her a hard time and try to sweep her complaint under the carpet.

Behind her came a tall distinguished-looking man. It would have been hard to conjure up a starker contrast than these two. His salt-and-pepper hair, his crisp pink shirt, neatly knotted tie and navy suit were so different to the girl's outfit. He could have stepped from the pages of one of those clothing catalogues her mother had pored over. Man about town for the over fifties, she thought to herself a little ungenerously. He was obviously fond of aftershave for its fragrance preceded him and filled the room. It covered the slightly musty smell which Gawn had been aware of but she felt it would quickly become overpowering in such cramped conditions. This must be ex-Detective Sergeant Walter Pepper. He had been providing administrative and logistical support at Police Headquarters and undertaken some investigative duties since his retirement on health grounds. She noted his walking stick. He had been knocked down by a joyrider and his leg had been badly smashed leaving him with a permanent limp. This then was her team. Thank you, Uncle Norman, she thought to herself, sarcastically.

'Good morning. I'm DCI Gawn Girvin. I'll be SIO for the duration of our time here.'

She shook hands with the two newcomers.

'I'll leave you to it. I'll get someone to bring you a kettle and some tea and coffee to get you started.' Maxwell spoke as he moved over to the door. He smiled and nodded to Gawn and then to the others.

'Thank you, Inspector.'

Once he had closed the door, Gawn turned to her new team. The two were an unlikely and mismatched pairing.

Hill, petite for a police officer – she must have just passed the height requirement – standing side by side with the solid bulk of all six feet of Pepper. She wondered how they would get on with each other and how she would get on with them both. She decided to give them the benefit of the doubt. Norman Smyth must have seen something in them, in their files, in their previous work, to make him think they could do a good job. He was giving her another chance to prove to herself that she could still do this job. Maybe this was their second chance too.

'OK. Down to business. We need to hit the road running.' Then her eye caught Pepper's walking aid and she was about to apologise but then didn't. She couldn't pussyfoot around these two for the duration of the investigation. If she was going to accept them as they were, they would have to accept her too. 'We've no time to work ourselves in slowly. We have two weeks to go over this case and come up with a result. I take it you've read the notes I sent you?' She paused long enough for them both to indicate by a nod of the head that they had. 'Right, the boxes with all the evidence and the witness statements are here.' She pointed to the four boxes stacked precariously. 'I need you, do I call you Walter or Walt or what?'

'Walter's fine, ma'am.'

'OK, Walter. They tell me you're an organisational genius. You can get all the documents into order for us. Then we'll need to go through them, one by one and prioritize what we need to follow up on. Let's all try to find somewhere to sit. That's our first issue. Then some coffee and then we'll go through the facts of the case.'

It was a full fifty minutes later before all three of them were sitting clutching cups of tea or coffee and ready to start. A PC had brought the promised kettle, three mugs, a packet of teabags and a jar of instant coffee. No milk. Gawn didn't suggest that Jo Hill get the milk in future. She didn't want to be accused of gender stereotyping. She would bring it herself, even though she didn't take milk in her coffee. This investigation was going to be like walking on eggshells for so many reasons.

Chapter 8

'OK. Take us through the case, Jo.' Gawn had already read through most of the case notes of course, but she wanted to make sure the other two were up to speed and to discuss what was most relevant for their inquiry.

'Jason Sloan was nineteen when he went missing. He lived in Belfast with his mother and older brother, Keith, who was twenty-one. Jason had left school at sixteen, done a lot of short-term jobs but he'd finally got a permanent one working in a garage with an apprenticeship as a car mechanic. He had no official police record although he'd had a few run-ins for minor things according to the local PC – graffiti on the local shops, breaking a window playing football, causing a disturbance with his mates, that sort of stuff. On the night of Saturday 17th April 1999, he was with two unidentified friends at the Starlit nightclub on Ormeau Avenue. About midnight, the three were asked to leave by one of the security staff. They were being loud and a girl had complained about them harassing her. She said, quote, "He grabbed my arse." The last person to see them was that bouncer. His name was Ray Totten. In his statement he said that he only knew it was Jason because one of the others had called him by name and because he was Black – which he wasn't, he was mixed race but that made him stand out – and when he was shown a photograph Totten did identify Jason. The three got into a dark-coloured car at the end of Ormeau Avenue where it meets the Ormeau Road and they drove off in the direction of the city centre. He didn't see the driver of the car. He said he couldn't even be sure if it was a man or a woman. He couldn't give the registration or the make. Jason's mother reported him missing on Tuesday the 20th.'

Gawn had been nodding as Hill had gone over the details, pleased that the constable had summarised the salient points clearly. Then she asked, 'Why the delay?'

'His mother told the desk sergeant that she knew he'd been going to the Starlit but then thought he was staying with his mates over the weekend. That was something he did sometimes, so she hadn't been expecting him home and hadn't been particularly worried. When he still hadn't appeared on Tuesday and she checked with his work and found he hadn't been there on Monday either, she got worried and reported it. He's never been seen since.'

'I see the investigation was led by an Inspector Jack Forbes. Do you know of him, Walter?'

'No. He must have been before my time. But it doesn't seem to have been a very big team – just him, a sergeant and a couple of constables. I think things were probably a bit stretched just then.'

'We'll see if we need to try to chase up any of the team who are still around but we'll leave it for now. We don't want to ruffle any more feathers than we have to. So, what progress did they make with it?'

'It was a busy time, ma'am. As I said it was a small team. The Good Friday Agreement had been signed the previous year but there was still a lot of trouble. You had the whole Drumcree stand-off and a solicitor had been blown up by a car bomb a few weeks previously. Tensions were running high in several parts of Belfast and outside the city too. Police officers were being deployed all over the place to cover for others hurt in rioting and they still had to be incredibly careful. You'll know all about that, ma'am.'

So Pepper had done his homework about her as she had about them. He knew her father had been blown up in his car on his way to the station one morning. She also suspected he was paving the way to telling her that not a lot had been achieved by the investigation.

'They tried to identify any other clubbers, but it was a thankless task. Apart from occasionally ID'ing a few underage kids trying to get in, they didn't keep a record of their patrons. And they didn't have a trove of credit card receipts to help them. The few they did trace claimed they hadn't even seen Jason so they were no help at all. Plus, CCTV wasn't the big thing it is now, either inside the club or outside. Nowadays we'd be able to follow the car that picked them up wherever it went. Not then.'

'They did house-to-house in the estate where Jason lived?'

'Yes, they did, but they couldn't get any of his friends to admit to being out with him that night. They all had alibis provided by their family or girlfriends or they'd been playing football together at the local community centre. So they never traced the other two men who were with him. Totten was shown photographs of some of Jason's friends but he couldn't identify any of them as being with him that night so they remained a mystery. And they were never able to trace the driver of the car either. They did carry out a search of the Lagan but nothing showed up to suggest he'd gone into the river. And they put out a general appeal on TV but nothing useful came from it either.'

'Did Jason have any enemies, anyone he'd clashed with?'

'Not that they could get a sniff of. No, ma'am. Total blank.'

'And no paramilitary involvement?'

'Nothing in the reports indicates that. It was a quiet estate. They didn't have much trouble. The local policeman went in and out of the houses, played football with the kids, helped the old dears with their shopping. I get the impression, ma'am, if I'm allowed to say this, that they didn't try too hard. He was nineteen. There was no indication of foul play. If he wanted to clear off and not tell his mother then so what? Boys do that sort of thing all the time. Sometimes they come back; sometimes they start a new life in England or Australia or God knows where. And there was no indication of any violence against him. He had just disappeared. Reading between the lines I think they believed he had run off. He was considered a low-risk misper by the team at the time.'

'Seems cruel on his mother. Was there anything to say he was having any trouble at home, that he had problems with his mother?'

'No, ma'am. The officers who interviewed her seemed to see her as a nice ordinary woman. The sergeant on the case put a wee comment in the margin of his report about how distressed she was and his recommendation that she get medical support.'

'And he had no trouble at work?'

'No. His boss said he was doing well. He was pleased with him.'

'OK. Keep digging through the statements. I'm going to speak to Jason's mother. She needs to be told we're having another look at this just in case she gets wind we're re-interviewing witnesses. I don't want to get her hopes up. There's precious little to go on.'

Chapter 9

She had decided to make this trip alone. It would help her get her bearings, some sense of what the place was like where Jason had grown up and lived even though she knew it would probably have changed considerably in the intervening twenty years. But she knew too that change in Northern Ireland could sometimes be incredibly slow so she expected if Jason were able to walk back to his own front door he might still recognise much of what was around him. The models of the cars would have changed and there would be many more of them in the narrow streets but it would be behind the venetian blinds and net curtains that life would be so very different.

She had driven around the outer road taking time to look over the city below from her vantage point in the Castlereagh Hills. Her eye was caught by Samson and Goliath, the two giant yellow cranes, iconic in their position dominating the cityscape and pointing to an industrial past long gone. The shipyard still remained but its work had changed so there were no huge liners being built on the slips today to catch the imagination of the youth of Belfast dreaming of an escape to exciting exotic destinations. Now, they, like their counterparts elsewhere, dreamed of fame and success on reality TV shows and online channels.

She had driven into the housing estate and followed the bus route through it, meandering its way along the narrow streets which had never been designed for the number of cars they now had to deal with. Some householders had sacrificed part of their small front gardens to provide a space to get their car off the roadway. Others chose to park half on the road and half on the pavement blocking the way for wheelchair users and young mothers with their prams. Gawn noted the neat gardens. This estate was well-kept. The houses were cared for. These people had pride in their homes. She had made a few enquiries and found there was a very low rate of turnover among tenants. Some had lived here twenty and thirty years. Like Louise Sloan. She had come as a new bride with her ex-soldier husband over forty years ago and still lived in the same house today, no doubt fearful of moving in case Jason ever came calling. Gawn had come across that before. Usually parents but sometimes husbands or wives who couldn't bring themselves to leave their homes after a loved one went missing or was killed.

Gawn noticed that many of these houses must be privately owned now, evidenced by "For Sale" signs and that made her think of Seb. He still hadn't told her he was selling his house. It might even already have been sold for all she knew. She had come across it with its "For Sale" sign when she was driving past. At the time they were going through a rough patch and she hadn't brought the subject up with him. More recently when they seemed to have managed to get their relationship onto a better footing she didn't want to do or say anything which might cause conflict so she'd chosen to ignore it. But always, at the back of her mind, it was eating away at her. She wondered when he was going to tell her and what it meant for them that he was doing it at all.

The bus she was following turned right and headed up a steep hill towards the terminus but her sat-nav told her to keep straight ahead. Within a few yards, the voice announced she had reached her destination. She could see the number 14 on a helpful plaque to the side of a red front door. She got out of the car and took a moment to look around. In the distance she could see a church and in front of it an open green space where some children were playing football. A large flag flew in the breeze from a lamp-post at the street corner. She turned around and looked up the hill the bus had climbed as part of its route to a row of identical grey houses. She tried to work out which would be number 3. She had checked knowing she was going to be here. That was where Seb had grown up. That was where his mother still lived. For all she knew Angela York could be watching her from behind her curtains. Gawn turned back to face number 14. Half its garden had been paved and now served as a parking space. A brand-new Hyundai sat there. The front of the house boasted a fancy stone porch extension. It seemed Jason's mother had managed alright on a widow's pension and a job as a canteen lady at the local school.

She rang the bell. The door was flung open almost instantly by a woman dressed for painting. Her hair was held back in a scarf. She wore a pair of dark blue slacks teamed with a plain navy sweatshirt splattered with a variety of paint colours. Gawn immediately thought of Jo Hill. Perhaps she should have brought her along. The clinching piece of evidence was that she was clutching a paintbrush in her hand. She looked and sounded flustered.

'Oh, sorry. I thought you were someone else. I'm expecting my son with some more paint.'

'Mrs Sloan. I should have phoned ahead. Sorry. I'm DCI Gawn Girvin.' She held up her warrant card. 'I wonder, could I have a word with you?'

The colour drained from the woman's face.

'Nothing's happened to Keith, has it?'

'No. No. Nothing like that. It's about Jason.'

* * *

Louise Sloan had insisted on changing out of her painting clothes and then making a cup of tea before she would sit down and listen to what Gawn had to say. Gawn had spent the time alone in the living room, while the woman was upstairs, having a look around. You could learn a lot about a person from their home.

Louise Sloan's home was tastefully and, Gawn thought, quite expensively furnished. It was not cluttered. There were no china figurines or other ornaments which Gawn would have dismissed as dust gatherers. There were shelves to the side of the fireplace which contained two rows of books. Gawn scanned them to see what Louise's reading preferences were. Most were fiction, light romantic, a few classics including of course *Pride and Prejudice*. But there were some autobiographies as well and a number of cookery books. She picked up a copy of the latest cookbook from one of the celebrity chefs Seb raved about and opened it. Gawn was stunned to read a Merry Christmas message from Norman Smyth. So, he had kept in touch with the woman all these years. That explained why he wanted her son's case looked at one more time. She hastily returned the book to its place on the shelf as she heard Louise Sloan moving in the hallway.

The door opened and Louise backed in carrying a tray on which were two cups and saucers, a milk jug, a sugar bowl and a plate of chocolate biscuits. She set it down on a side table and offered a cup to Gawn.

'Sorry. I never even asked if you'd prefer coffee.'

'Tea's fine. Thank you.'

'Would you like more milk? Do you take sugar? Would you like a biscuit?' The plate was held out. The woman was gabbling away, putting off hearing whatever she was to be told.

Gawn shook her head.

'No. Thank you.'

When she had exhausted all the mundane topics and could delay no longer, she blurted out, 'Have you found his body then?'

'No. Sorry. We haven't.' She watched the other woman's face and tried to interpret what she was seeing. It was a mixture of disappointment and relief.

'I've imagined the day someone would come to the door and tell me that he'd been found. But that was in the early days. The first four or five years. Then you just try to get on with life but it's always there. It never goes away. Not completely.'

First four or five years. Gawn realised the agony this woman had been living through. Life had moved on for everyone else but she couldn't. Not fully.

'I used to envy that girl's parents. I know she had an awful death but at least they had a body. They could bury her and have a place to go to visit her.'

Gawn didn't know what she was talking about.

'Girl?'

'Karen Houston, I think her name was. A lovely-looking girl.'

'Who was she, Mrs Sloan? A girl from around here?' This name was new to Gawn.

'No. She didn't live around here. I think she came from Newtownards or somewhere over that direction. She was the girl they found lying in a ditch murdered up the Craigantlet Hills just after Jason went missing.'

'When exactly?'

'I'm not sure exactly but it was just a few days after my Jason went missing, I think.'

There was nothing about this girl in any of the documentation Gawn had seen. But then why should there have been? The two cases would not have been handled by the same officers. The girl was a murder victim while Jason was a missing person and he had gone missing before the girl was killed. She knew even today young men especially went missing all the time. They probably expected him to turn up. They had had no evidence to suspect foul play and, she presumed, nothing to link the two cases although that was something she determined to check.

'Well, if you haven't found his body, is it because of Scotty Alexander that you're here?'

That name Gawn did recognise. Scott Alexander had been interviewed at the time as one of Jason's friends although he hadn't been with him on the night he went missing.

'What about Scott Alexander?'

'Well, what he said at John's funeral.'

'Who's John?' Gawn interrupted.

'My brother. He died a couple of weeks ago and Scotty – he doesn't live in Belfast anymore – but he'd heard about John and he came to the funeral.'

Gawn waited. What had Scott said? Was he there on the night Jason went missing and he'd just revealed this to Louise or something?

'He said he saw Jason.'

'Where? When?' Gawn knew she sounded eager but this might be the early breakthrough they needed.

'At the funeral. At John's funeral at Dundonald Cemetery. He said he was standing beside a tree, kind of half behind it, as if he was hiding; keeping out of sight. Jason and John were always very close. John was like a sort of father to him after his own dad was killed at work. But I thought Scotty had just imagined it. He's not been very well and I thought it was just his imagination. If Jason had been there he'd have come over and spoken to me. He wouldn't have been hiding behind a tree, not from me.'

Gawn knew exactly what it was like for others to doubt what you had seen. She thought of the figures on the beach and wondered if anything had turned up yet. Like a body.

Chapter 10

Gawn could feel eyes watching her as she got out of her car and walked into the building although no one was in sight. She passed a couple of PCs in the corridor but both were careful to avoid making eye contact with her. Gawn was getting some idea of what it must be like to work for the Discipline and Anti-Corruption Branch. Two heads bobbed up from their work when she opened the door of their allocated broom cupboard, as Hill had dubbed it. She noted the picture on the whiteboard and Jason's name carefully printed where Pepper, she presumed, was starting to collate their evidence.

'Any use, boss?' It was Hill who had managed to make herself at home in her new surroundings.

Gawn remembered from her personnel file that up to the time of the complaint the young woman had been an exemplary officer with glowing appraisals. Her desk was covered now with papers but she seemed to have a system to deal with them, much of it involving coloured stickies. Pepper, who had divested himself of his jacket and rolled up his sleeves, was also facing a pile of papers but at the minute he was focusing on his computer screen.

'I'm getting more questions than answers,' Gawn said. 'We need to trace Scott Alexander. He was a friend of Jason's and he told Mrs Sloan he had seen Jason at her brother's funeral two weeks ago. If he was lying to her, it seems very cruel and it's hard to know what he would gain from a lie like that. On the other hand, he should probably be able to identify his friend even after twenty years. Can you find him, Walter? When you do, we'll go to him. I don't want to start having to ask favours to use interview rooms here. I'd rather keep under everyone's radar as much as possible. We also need to chase up all the other friends who had convenient alibis. Apparently, they were all playing football at the local community centre. And, Jo, can you contact Belfast City Council for any CCTV at the cemetery and also get the footage from any traffic cams on that stretch of road? It would be good if we could identify who it was Alexander actually saw.'

She then told them about Karen Houston.

'It may be just coincidental, but I'd like to look over the case notes. Can you chase them up for me too, please, Jo?'

'On it, boss.'

Gawn then withdrew into her inner cupboard within the 'broom cupboard', as she would forever think of it now. A pile of notes sat on her desk. Jo had put together a list of the people interviewed during the original investigation – only those who were still alive and could be questioned again. Her eye went to one name – Jacob York. Seb's grandfather was dead, she knew. It could only mean one thing. The person who had been interviewed about Jason's disappearance was not his grandfather but Seb himself. For one second she contemplated whether she should phone Smyth and let him know about her connection to a witness. She thought he would still want her to go ahead; that he would trust her to do her job, and she wanted to carry on. Seb had been a neighbour of the Sloans', nothing more. He would not be able to add anything to her investigation but she realized at some point he would have to be re-interviewed. She could delegate it to one of the others. It didn't have to be her, but she knew really it did and she wondered how he would react to that.

A knock on the door frame – she had left the door open, no way could she endure sitting closed in here – and Hill walked over to the desk holding out a folder.

'I printed this off for you.'

'Thanks. It's been a long first day. You and Walter should head off home now. We'll start fresh tomorrow morning.'

'I'll bring the milk tomorrow, shall I, boss?'

'Only if it suits you.'

'It's fine, ma'am. I'm not a serial complainer, you know.' The young woman smiled.

'I didn't think you were.'

'I was always a team player but some of the old boys didn't want a woman on their team.'

'You know I can't discuss this with you, don't you, Jo? But, as far as I'm concerned, we three are a team, for the next two weeks anyway. We all pull our weight. No matter who we are.'

'Yes, ma'am.'

The girl turned to leave.

'And, Jo.'

She turned back.

'Yes, ma'am?'

'Maybe something a little less appropriate for a heavy metal concert and scaring off all comers?'

The girl smiled again. 'Yes, ma'am.'

Chapter 11

Pepper had managed to chase down Scott Alexander. He was living in a duplex apartment in Groomsport, a village in County Down on the shores of Belfast Lough. Nowadays it was a sleepy little place, more peaceful than its bustling neighbour, Bangor, whose relentless encroachment threatened its existence.

Alexander's apartment was in a converted former gentleman's residence, sitting in its own manicured lawns complete with a tennis court. It was right on the seashore and within sight of the Copeland Islands. Gawn remembered that her brother had gone through a phase of birdwatching in his early teens and had spent weekends at the bird sanctuary on the island. So, Alexander had done well for himself. Pepper had filled her in on the journey from Belfast. The man had started out with a market stall setting up daily in towns around the country and now owned five shops selling ladies' clothes. They were quite well-known and even advertised on local TV and radio. Perhaps she had seen them? Not her sort of clothes, she thought to herself. He had never married and had never been in any trouble with the police other than the odd speeding ticket.

Gawn had seen a photograph of a young Alexander taken about the time of Jason's disappearance. He was in a group of five young men sitting on a wall smoking. Jason was one of the others easily picked out by his swarthy complexion and wiry black hair.

She knew Alexander would have aged but he was only a couple of years older than Seb so she was shocked when an emaciated-looking man, who seemed more like a sixty-year-old than someone not yet in their forties opened the door to them.

'Mr Alexander? DCI Gawn Girvin and this is my associate Walter Pepper. You spoke to him on the phone.'

She held up her warrant card. Before he could respond, Alexander broke into a fit of coughing. They waited until it had subsided.

'Come in.' His voice was raspy.

They followed him as he shuffled into a large bright lounge-cum-dining room with a small kitchen annex. It was furnished with dark wood panelling and a huge purple velour-covered sofa. A circular mahogany dining table and four ornately carved chairs sat in the corner at a window which looked out over the garden and down to the beach. Photographs were scattered over the table, some of them black and white. Alexander must have been refreshing his memory before talking to them. A spiral staircase led up to a second floor. This place wouldn't have been cheap. The man really had done well for himself.

'Take a pew.' Alexander indicated the sofa with a feeble wave of his arm.

He sat on one of the hard dining room chairs with his back to the window while they sat side by side on the sofa opposite him. Alexander extracted a handkerchief from his pocket and wiped his mouth. His eyes were rheumy and his fair hair was thin and wispy. His clothes hung on him as if he had bought them two sizes too large. He had the unmistakable look of a man who is seriously ill.

Gawn started the questioning. 'Mr Alexander, as my colleague told you on the phone, we're reinvestigating the disappearance of Jason Sloan. We believe that you told Jason's mother that you'd seen him in Dundonald Cemetery at his uncle John's funeral. Is that correct?'

'Correct that I told her or correct that I saw him?' He laughed at his own cleverness but that only brought on another prolonged bout of coughing.

'Did you see Jason, sir?' Gawn wasn't really in the mood for semantic games.

'At the time I thought I did. But I'm on a lot of medication and sometimes it makes me a bit…' He sought the right word. 'I can imagine things that aren't there.'

'So you're saying now you didn't see him?'

'The truth is I'm just not sure. I saw someone… in the distance. I thought it looked like Jason, like what Jason would probably look like now,' he corrected himself. 'I suppose I've been thinking about Jason and John a lot recently.' His eyes strayed to the photographs lying haphazardly over the table beside him. 'They were always very close. After Jason disappeared, John kind of took me under his wing. He helped me get a start. Everything I've achieved is because of him. I guess I thought if Jason was still alive he'd want to be at his uncle's funeral. I suppose I wanted it to be Jason…' After a pause he added, 'To ease my conscience a bit.'

'Your conscience about what?'

'Whatever happened to him.'

'Do you have something to feel guilty about?' Gawn asked gently and then just waited. It would be too easy if he broke down and admitted to some part in his friend's disappearance.

'We all have things to feel guilty about in our past, don't we, Chief Inspector?' His eyes moved between the two police officers seeking their agreement but neither responded.

'And when was the last time you actually saw Jason for sure, Mr Alexander?'

'On the night he disappeared.'

'Had he been playing football too before he went to the nightclub?'

'Football? No, I mean I was there at the club. With him.'

'You were with Jason Sloan at the Starlit nightclub? That's not what you told the police at the time, sir.' Gawn couldn't help excitement sounding in her voice. This was better than she had expected.

'No. Well, I knew to keep my mouth shut then, didn't I? Now it doesn't matter. They're probably all dead and I will be soon too.' He laughed and that brought on another bout of coughing.

Gawn found herself wondering who the 'they' were.

'Can I get you a drink of water or something, sir?' Pepper asked and then glanced across at the DCI in case she was annoyed at the interruption.

She nodded almost imperceptibly. Alexander couldn't even catch his breath to answer. He just pointed to the kitchen area. Pepper walked across the room and returned with a glass of water. He handed it to the man. Gawn noticed how shaky Alexander's hands were as he clutched it.

'Mr Alexander, Scott, tell us about the night Jason went missing.'

Alexander sat back into his chair. He didn't respond straightaway but experience had taught Gawn to wait, not to rush. This man wanted to talk. She could sense that. He wanted to set the record straight while he still could.

He took a deep breath as if steeling himself for what he was going to say. 'We went to the Starlit to put in a bit of time. See if we could pull. But we knew we were going on to a party anyway. It was all arranged. Someone would pick us up and take us.'

'Who?'

'We didn't know until we saw the car. That night it was Jakey – Jacob York.'

Chapter 12

Gawn felt the room start to move away from her. It was as if she were underwater. She could hear Scott Alexander speaking but his voice was coming from a long way away. She deliberately dropped her pen on the floor and took time bending over to pick it up. By the time she was upright again, her head had started to clear a little but her heart was pounding.

'Are you alright, ma'am?' Pepper had noticed her reaction. He didn't know about her relationship with Seb so he hadn't made the connection with the Jacob York Scott was talking about.

'Yes. I'm fine. Thank you. Just a bit of a stomach upset. Something I ate last night.' She glanced down at her notebook to give herself time to gather her thoughts.

'Where did York take you?' she eventually managed to ask. She was surprised at how normal her voice sounded.

'To the party. We'd been before. They happened most Saturday nights but you didn't always get invited. Not every time. You really hoped you'd get to go again.' Now that he had started, it seemed Scott Alexander wanted to get it all out in the open. His words came out in a rush as if he was racing against time to let someone else know what he knew.

'It was a lot of older men, professional people, men with money and young women and guys our age. It was pretty much do whatever you wanted. Open house. There was as much booze as you could drink. Not cheap stuff either. There were usually drugs of some kind, just for the taking. All free. It was great. The girls were usually pretty wasted and you could take your pick. Sometimes some of

47

the men came on to you and you went along with it. It wasn't our thing but hell you didn't want to rock the boat and not get invited back. Sometimes some of the older guys liked to watch you either with a girl or a boy. Our mates were all at home counting pennies to see if they could afford a packet of fags and a fish supper and maybe shag a wee girl up an entry, if they were lucky.'

He paused for a second and took a deep breath before continuing. He probably hadn't spoken so much to anyone for a long time. A smirk crossed his face as he started talking again, as he remembered. 'We had whatever we wanted. We had the run of the house. As many girls as we wanted. Threesomes. Whatever. Money in our pockets at the end of the night. Most times you couldn't remember what had happened after the first half hour. Somehow you'd get home. You'd wake up in your own bed or maybe at a mate's house. It was exciting. Of course, you couldn't tell anybody. You knew if you did, you'd regret it.'

'You were threatened?' Pepper asked.

'Nobody needed to threaten you,' he said disdainfully. 'These men were powerful people. That was bloody obvious. You knew just from the way they talked and their clothes and their cars, they had money. They could buy and sell you. And who was going to believe the likes of us if we said anything against them? I remember one wee fella sitting crying one night claiming he'd been raped. They took him outside. We never saw him again. Maybe he just didn't get invited back. Maybe something happened to him. You didn't ask. You didn't want to know.'

'Did you know any of the others at the parties? Any of the other young people who were brought along?'

'No. I think maybe a few were from the country.' Before they could ask how he knew, he added, 'They had country accents. They didn't sound like they were from Belfast. But we weren't all sitting around chatting, you know, making polite conversation.' He laughed at the thought. 'We were making the most of our opportunities.'

He laughed again and the coughing took his breath for a minute.

'Where was this party?'

'I don't know exactly. I just sat in the car and got out when we arrived. It was somewhere between Holywood and Bangor but I don't know better than that. I've driven that road a thousand times since then but I couldn't tell you where we turned off or what the house was like. We always went late at night. We never arrived before midnight. It was always dark. I don't know what the outside of the house was like.'

As he'd been speaking, Alexander's voice had been getting weaker.

'I'm getting really tired. I get tired easily these days. It's these damned tablets. The doctors say they're all that are holding me together but they knock the stuffing out of you.'

'Maybe we could come back on Monday, ma'am?' Pepper had a softer heart than Gawn. She really wanted to carry on with the questions now they had got him talking. These young men had been involved in something criminal and it may have led to Jason's disappearance. Alexander must know what had happened to him. Her instinct was to press ahead, keep questioning him, get answers for Louise Sloan but she knew she really wanted answers for herself too. Just how was Seb involved in all this?

Reluctantly, Gawn agreed. 'Of course. Would that be alright, Scott?'

He nodded. It seemed the effort to speak was beyond him.

'We'll see ourselves out, shall we?' asked Pepper.

They left Scott Alexander sitting by the window. His skin was almost colourless. His eyes didn't follow them as they left the room. That would have required too much of an effort.

Outside, Gawn turned to Pepper.

'When we get back I want you to start a search for any callouts, any disturbances, any reports of noisy parties, basically anything suspicious in the Cultra area on Saturday nights in 1999-2000. If there's nothing then expand the area to take in Holywood and as far as Bangor West.'

'There could be a lot, ma'am.' The man was about to complain.

'You can discount burglaries or car thefts or anything like that. At least to start with. It's noisy parties or disturbances we're looking for. There shouldn't be too many of those in nice respectable Cultra with all the judges and barristers and big businessmen who live there.'

'Not to mention the odd Chief Constable or two.' Pepper laughed.

Chapter 13

She had left Carrickfergus just before dawn, eager to hear what Seb had to say about all this. She headed out along the coast. Today she barely noticed the amazing scenery and spectacular views as she drove along. The traffic was light and most of it was going in the opposite direction, heading towards Belfast. The sun had risen and was beginning to poke through the early morning clouds bringing the promise of a good day as she pulled into the parking space alongside Seb's car and let herself into the apartment. Her sense of anticipation was growing but so too was a sense of dread. She hadn't seen him for nearly a week; they hadn't even spoken on the phone. She wanted to see him, but she knew interviewing him about Jason Sloan was going to be tricky. This was not the ideal scenario for getting their relationship back on track.

As she entered the flat, she noticed the smell straightaway. She would have recognised it anywhere. Seb had once joked, during their very first dinner together, that he had enjoyed smoking cannabis when he was in Amsterdam but the topic had never come up again and she had assumed it was something that had happened once or twice in the past, not something he was still engaging in. She looked across and spotted a half-smoked spliff on the fireplace. This was decision time. Cannabis was an illegal substance although a small amount for personal use would result in no more than a warning, a rap on the knuckles, but she was a police officer. She knew many people, Seb included, argued that a little cannabis never hurt anyone; that it was harmless, no worse than smoking a cigarette. But it was still illegal. What should she do? It was a moral dilemma. This was not something she had experienced very often. Issues were usually black and white for her; it was either right or wrong, legal or illegal. What were her choices? She could ignore it, pretend she hadn't noticed, but that wasn't really an option. She could take the coward's way out – destroy it and then never mention it. Or she could confront Seb about it. And, of course, she knew right away which one she would choose.

She walked across to the bedroom door and reached out to turn the handle. But then pulled back. Were there any other nasty surprises waiting for her? He wasn't expecting her. Once before in her life she had found the man she believed loved her, in bed with another woman. She couldn't let that happen again. Better to walk away without knowing. She knew she loved Seb and until yesterday she had thought she knew him and that he loved her. But he was an attractive man. She knew he had had many girlfriends before her and he was an experienced lover. She saw the way other women looked at him even when she was with him. She was about to chicken out and leave, planning to phone him and arrange for Pepper and Hill to interview him when the door burst open. Seb, wearing the silly blue and red Superman pyjamas she had bought him as a joke for Christmas and dared him to wear, appeared in front of her, yelling and brandishing a heavy book. The serious look on his face dissolved into a huge smile of relief when he saw her.

'You scared me half to death. I thought I was being burgled.'

'And you were going to defend yourself with a book? I know they say that the pen is mightier than the sword but that's taking it a bit far.'

'It was the only thing that came to hand.' He dropped the book to the floor and instead grabbed her.

'I'm so glad to see you, darling. I've missed you.' He kissed her. Gawn breathed deeply in his aftershave and felt the security of his shoulder as she laid her head against him and snuggled in.

'I've missed you too, Seb.'

He moved her back and looked at her.

'Where's Gawn and what have you done with her?'

'Do you like it?' She was afraid, seeing she had never even mentioned to him that she was thinking of having her hair cut, that he would be annoyed.

'Of course I like it. It's lovely.' And he reached out and stroked her hair running his fingers through it. 'It'll be like making love to another woman. Let's make up for lost time.' He smiled and eagerly took her hand to lead her into the bedroom but she pulled back. His brow furrowed. Something was obviously wrong, and he had no idea what was coming next.

'Do you want to make love to another woman?'

'For goodness sake, Gawn, lighten up. That was just a joke.'

'Well, drugs aren't. How long have you been using?'

'Using?' He didn't know what she was talking about or at least he was making a good job of pretending he didn't.

Her head turned in the direction of the fireplace. 'The cannabis?'

His eyes followed hers. 'Oh, wow. I thought he'd got rid of it.' A sheepish look passed across his face.

'Who's he?'

'Peter. My literary agent. You've never met him. He's been worried about the lack of progress with my book and he came up yesterday to give me a bit of a giz up. He was smoking it. Not me. Sorry. Not guilty, gov.' He held out his two hands as if for handcuffing.

'It's not a joke, Seb. What if Cairns had arrived here instead of me?'

'He'd probably have overlooked it, you know. It's not the big deal it used to be. I believe it'll be legalised within a few years.'

'And you'll be using it then? Is that what you're telling me?' Gawn was aware that her voice was becoming shrill and she knew it wasn't really because of the cannabis that she was annoyed. It was down to the heavy feeling of dread in the pit of her stomach over how he would react when she questioned him about his involvement with Jason Sloan's disappearance and what she might learn about him.

'No. No, of course not. I won't be and I didn't. I would never do anything to compromise your work, Gawn. I respect what you do. You know that. Look, let's get rid of the evidence and forget about it. OK?' He didn't wait for a response but walked across, lifted the joint, carried it into the bathroom and she heard the flush as he got rid of it. Taking her hands again he smiled. 'You missed an opportunity to handcuff me there, Chief Inspector.' His eyes twinkled.

'You're incorrigible, Sebastian York.' She knew she shouldn't but she'd missed him. She knew it was cowardly. She was only putting off the inevitable but she allowed him to lead her into the bedroom glad to put off their confrontation even for only a little while.

Chapter 14

Gawn woke up with a start. She'd fallen asleep with her head on Seb's chest but now he was nowhere to be seen. Then she heard noises from the other room. He was singing some pop song she didn't recognise. The aroma of freshly ground coffee wafted into the bedroom through the half-open door. She picked her clothes up where they lay scattered over the floor and dressed quickly. She was still tucking her shirt into the waistband of her trousers when she opened the door fully and emerged into the main room. Seb was standing in front of the cooker turning bacon in a sizzling frying pan. He was wearing a full-length apron emblazoned with the word "Chef".

'I'm just making us some breakfast. I hope you're hungry. You've given me an appetite.'

'Lovely look. Very trendy apron. Is it the latest from Paris?'

'I don't want to get my new shirt splashed.' He indicated the floral shirt he was wearing.

'You'll make someone a lovely wife,' she teased.

He balled the tea towel up and threw it at her, deliberately missing. Then his face turned serious. 'Talking about lovely wives,' he began but she cut across him, not allowing him to get any further.

'Seb. I need to talk to you. It's serious.'

He could see from her face that it was and wondered what was coming next.

'I need to interview you.'

He was stunned. 'Interview me? Are you serious?'

'Yes.'

He turned around and switched the gas ring off from under the pan before turning again to face her.

'Is this still about the bloody hash?' His face was crumpled in disbelief.

'No. It's about my case.'

'Your case? You came up here to interview me for your case?' He couldn't take in what she was saying.

She nodded in response. Now he was astonished, and it showed in his voice. He snatched his apron off angrily and flung it into the corner.

'What was that that just happened between us? Is that how you normally prepare for an interview?' He didn't understand what was happening. He just wanted to lash out and hurt her because she had hurt him. He felt used again as she had used him in her last case. As he looked at her he saw not the beautiful, vulnerable woman who loved to lie in his arms but almost a stranger. Her face was set. 'Are you going to read me my rights? Should I have a solicitor present, *Chief Inspector*?'

'Seb, please. Don't make this more difficult than it has to be. I just need to ask you a few questions.' But this was difficult, bloody difficult. There was no easy way to do it and she knew she shouldn't have allowed him to make love to her, but she had needed to feel that closeness to him. Now the strain of what she might find out about him was playing on her mind.

He moved across the room and stood directly in front of her. He looked angry, as angry as she'd ever seen him.

'Couldn't you have just asked me over the phone?'

'No.' She needed to be able to look at his face when he answered her, to see if he was telling the truth or hiding something. She thought she would know. But she couldn't tell him that, couldn't let him know she had any doubts about him.

'Jason Sloan.'

She saw a look of instant recognition and a certain wariness cross his face. He turned away from her and sat down on an armchair, and that told her a lot.

'Yes?' he said.

'You knew him?'

'If it's Jason's disappearance you're investigating then you know the answer to that.' He wasn't going to make things easy for her.

'How well did you know him?'

'Not well. We were neighbours. I saw him about. He was a bit older than me. We didn't hang around together or anything. We weren't friends.'

'On the night he went missing, you were playing football with a group from the church in the community centre. Is that right?'

'No one ever asked me that. I was asked if I'd gone to the club with him; if I was one of the three men thrown out. I told them I wasn't. I was only seventeen. They'd never have let me into that club.'

Gawn already knew all this. She had read and reread all the reports. Buried deep within a lot of irrelevant interviews from a door-to-door on the estate was a note reporting that it was Seb's mother who had explained that her son was at the local community centre and didn't know anything about where Jason had gone. When questioned, Seb had stated that he had not been at the Starlit club with Jason Sloan, that night or ever.

As she looked at this man she loved, she thought that he didn't want to lie to her but he had avoided answering her question directly and that made her instantly suspicious.

'So, were you playing football, Seb?' she persisted.

Gawn hadn't even noticed before this moment that there was a clock in the room. Now its tick sounded thunderous as she waited for his answer.

'I didn't do anything to Jason Sloan.'

'That's not what I asked you, Seb.' Her voice was cold now. She needed answers, not just for the case, but for herself.

He slumped forward in his chair. His head went down. He seemed to be studying his hands, turning them over to examine the backs. She sat down opposite him, saying nothing, just waiting. The wait seemed to go on forever and with every passing second she became more fearful of what he was hiding.

'No. I wasn't.' He was speaking so quietly she could barely make him out.

'Where were you?'

'I was… I… it was difficult. Most of the people in the estate were great. Just ordinary decent people. But there were a few and you just knew to keep out of their way. I knew anyway. I'd passed my 11 plus got into a good grammar school. I knew that was my ticket to the kind of life I'd always dreamed of. But I knew I had to work hard to get to the top.' He was watching her face closely as he spoke, his eyes pleading for understanding.

What he was saying might or might not be relevant to her investigation but Gawn let him go on. He obviously needed to tell her in his own way.

'I was just about to leave for Oxford. I'd got offered a scholarship but I still needed to get the grades. The other boys, the ones I'd gone to primary school with, I didn't really hang around with them anymore. I was studying most of the time. But that night I was sent for.'

'Sent for? By whom?'

'Big Sam. Everybody knew Big Sam.'

This was the first time she had heard mention of a Sam in relation to Jason's disappearance. He hadn't featured in any of the reports. He had never been questioned. She was sure.

'Everybody knew not to mess with Big Sam. I don't know whether he had a criminal record or anything, but the word was he was The Man. If you wanted someone roughed up, he could arrange it. If something fell off the back of a lorry, it fell into his arms. He sent for me.'

'And you went?' She couldn't help a note of surprise sounding in her words.

'I wanted to keep my kneecaps so, yes, I went.' His voice was harsh but when he looked up she could see how difficult this was for him. 'I'm not proud I was such a coward, Gawn. I could have said no and maybe nothing would have happened.'

She wasn't going to give him any kind of absolution for what he had done. She just needed answers. 'This Big Sam.'

'Sam Legget.'

'Sam Legget, what did he want you to do, Seb?'

There was another long pause. Her heart was beating faster, pounding so hard she imagined he would be able to hear it. What revelation was coming?

'He gave me his car keys and told me to go and pick up three guys in Ormeau Avenue.'

'How were you to contact them?' Now they were getting to the crux of the matter. Just how involved in all this had Seb been?

'I wasn't to. I just had to wait outside until they came out.'

'You knew them?'

'Yes. It was Jason and Albert Wright and Scott Alexander.'

'Where did you take them?'

'I don't know.'

'You don't know?' She didn't even try to hide the scepticism in her voice.

'Yes.' He was almost shouting at her. Then his voice dropped as he continued. 'I know it sounds stupid, but they knew where they were going. They gave me directions. It was somewhere on the way to Bangor but I'm not sure exactly where. I was concentrating on driving. I'd only had my licence for a couple of weeks. I'd worked really hard for nearly a year to save up for driving lessons. We didn't have a car and I hadn't driven much, especially at night, so I was just trying to get us there, in one piece.'

'Where?'

'I told you. I don't know exactly. They were talking in the car. They were going to a party. They'd been there before. They said it was great. They were boasting. All the booze they could hold down and girls for the taking. I thought they were probably making most of it up just to impress me, to be "big men". They asked me if I wanted to go too. They could get me in. They knew the top man, they said. But no way did I want any part of it, whatever it was. You do believe me, Gawn, don't you?'

He looked up but this time she didn't meet his eye. She didn't speak. She thought she believed him. She wanted to believe him. God knows she needed to believe him – that she hadn't misjudged the most important man in her life, but she knew he liked women and he liked sex. There was a lot about her past she had never told him and now she realized there was a lot about his past she didn't know either.

'They made fun of some of the older men who would be there.'

'Did they mention any names?'

'If they did, I wasn't listening. I didn't want to hear. I can't remember any names. I swear, Gawn.' He looked up at her again and met her eyes trying to judge if she believed him. 'I would tell you if I could.'

'Can you describe the house?' Keep it business-like, she kept telling herself. Don't let him see how much this is tearing you apart.

'It was twenty years ago. It was dark and I was shit scared. I was worried I was going to end up in a ditch.'

Instead of which, it was Karen Houston who ended up in a ditch that weekend, Gawn couldn't help thinking.

'Did you hit anything… anyone when you were driving?'

'Hit? You mean like, have an accident?'

She nodded.

'No. Nothing,' he said.

'How did you get back home?'

'I was told to leave the car there. I thought I was going to have to walk home but some guy I'd never seen before gave me a lift back to Belfast. It was nearly three before I got home.'

'And your mother wasn't upset?' Her intonation rose in disbelief.

'She'd gone to bed. They'd sent her a message that I was going to stay with my friends so she thought that was OK.'

'And what did you think had happened to Jason?'

'Nothing. At first. I didn't even know he was missing until the next week. I told you. I didn't hang around with him. I was busy doing my A levels. I was hardly out of the house.'

'And when you did hear he was missing?'

'I didn't know anything had happened *that* night. I hoped he'd decided to go off somewhere. If he was mates with Big Sam he'd maybe wanted to get away. Lots of the fellas in the estate went over to England for work. I thought maybe he'd gone too and then I got a message from Big Sam to keep my mouth shut.'

'And that's what you did.' There was a weary disappointed quality to her voice now.

'I didn't lie. When I was asked, I answered the questions truthfully, but nobody asked the right questions. I was seventeen, Gawn. We can't all be bloody heroes like you.'

She could hear the plea for understanding in his voice but she offered no encouragement, no word to show she understood what it had been like for him; that she understood why he had done what he had. Instead, in a monotone voice she said, 'You're going to have to give a formal statement.' She had almost said 'sir' but then added, 'Seb. You can come to Belfast or I can send my people to meet you at the local station here.'

'Not you?'

'I think it would be better not.'

He nodded that he understood. 'OK. I'll come to them.'

'I'll get them to phone you and arrange a time to suit.'

She didn't know what more to say. She couldn't make light of it. He may have been an accessory to serious criminal activity, even if it was twenty years ago.

'Seb, I–'

'Don't say anything. Please, just go.'

She stood up and looked at him. He was sitting with his head in his hands. He seemed so unlike the confident, bouncy man who had buoyed her up when she was down. But he had been a scared seventeen-year-old who felt he didn't have a choice. She thought she knew him well enough to know this would have weighed heavily on his conscience. But the truth was, she just wasn't sure; wasn't sure about so many things anymore. She knew there was nothing she could say right then and anything she might say could make everything worse. They would both need time to figure out what his revelations meant for both of them.

Chapter 15

Gawn felt sick on her drive back. She had to stop the car by the side of the road and wait until the wave of nausea had passed. A cold sweat sat on her brow – a reaction to finding out about Seb's involvement in Jason's disappearance. She didn't understand how he could have kept the secret all these years. Obviously she had thought she knew him better than she did. He had secrets. She had expected that. So did she. So did everyone, of course. But she had never thought of something like this. Past girlfriends, maybe an illegitimate child tucked away somewhere. But she had skeletons in her own past too.

When she eventually threw her jacket and bag down on the sofa and plonked herself down beside them, she was feeling sick again and slightly light-headed. She gave herself a moment to recover and then phoned Pepper at home apologising for disturbing him over the weekend but she wasn't going to be in the office straightaway on Monday morning and wanted him to get started on arranging Seb's interview to get it done as soon as possible. She didn't want it hanging over him. And over her. She gave him Seb's mobile number so he could sort out the details for a formal interview under caution. She didn't want to be there; within a hundred miles of it. She gave him Albert Wright's name too and asked him to trace the third man if he was still alive. She couldn't remember if he had been on the list Jo had given her. She wanted to interview Scott Alexander again on Monday and asked Pepper to make the arrangements for the two of them to go back to Groomsport and see what else they could learn. She was sure Alexander knew more than he had told them so far.

By the time Gawn had finished talking to Pepper and explaining all she wanted him and Hill to do, she was exhausted. She thought it was probably a physical reaction to all the emotional trauma she was going through. The past couple of months had been tough but Seb had been her rock through it all. Now to discover that he was not the person she had thought he was, had hit her hard.

Gawn couldn't face coffee. Even the thought of it was enough to bring on another wave of nausea so she poured herself a glass of water and settled down to look over some of the files she had brought home, hoping that having something to concentrate on would take away her queasiness. She opened the first folder and the face of a pretty girl, smiling for the camera, seemed to glare back at her accusingly. This was Karen Houston. She was just twenty, just a few months older than Jason Sloan. She had been a medical student at the local university. The report detailed how on that Saturday evening she had been visiting a friend's house in one of the avenues opposite the gates of Stormont Castle on the outskirts of East Belfast. She had left at ten o'clock to catch a bus back to her home in the countryside outside Comber, a market town about ten miles away. The bus driver swore that he had picked no one up that night in that area and the assumption was that she had accepted a lift home with someone passing on the main Upper Newtownards Road. Probably someone she knew. Please, God, not Seb, Gawn couldn't help herself thinking. She texted Pepper asking him to make sure to question Seb to see exactly when Sam had given him the car keys and if he had driven the car anywhere else before picking the boys up. She also wanted them to question him thoroughly about the route he had taken and hoped it would not include the Upper Newtownards Road or Dundonald where Karen would have been waiting earlier in the evening. At this rate Pepper would regret coming out of retirement and she would be joining the list of his wife's least favourite people.

Next, she read the details of the girl's post-mortem. Karen had died on the Saturday but her body had not been found until the following Tuesday when a dog walker had discovered her in a ditch at a local forestry site in the hills between Belfast and Bangor. Her parents had been away on holiday and had not reported her missing. Yet Gawn was surprised her body had lain undiscovered for so long. She was sure it would have been a popular spot, yet it seemed no one had seen anything.

Karen had a high level of alcohol in her system. Her friend admitted that they had had a few drinks but only a few, which suggested she had been drinking later in the evening. Toxicology tests had shown traces of Rohypnol in her hair roots. At the time, awareness was growing of roofies, the date rape drug, but this was its first recorded use in a crime in Northern Ireland. Karen's body showed signs of recent sexual activity. It was assumed the man – or men, it seemed likely – had used condoms. She had also been sodomised with a wooden object and partially strangled but the actual cause of death was multiple organ trauma resulting from being run over by a car. Gawn's blood ran cold as she read how the girl's injuries and detailed analysis of the road markings where she was found had shown she had been run over twice. The car had reversed and run over her a second time. Bastard. No accident then. My God, what this girl had gone through. Roofied, for much of the time, she would have been conscious and totally unable to do anything to protect herself. What kind of animal or animals had done this? She couldn't bring herself to think of Seb being involved with these people in any way.

Chapter 16

Although he really needed to be concentrating on his novel and getting some more words down on paper, Seb couldn't settle to write. It was impossible. When Gawn had shown up, he had really thought they were in a good place, at last. He had been on the point of proposing to her; he had the ring in his pocket and then she had dropped the bombshell. Jason Sloan.

He hadn't thought about Jason Sloan for years. When she said the name, it had all come flooding back. He hadn't really known Jason. They didn't go around in the same group. And Jason was older. He didn't think he'd particularly liked him. He could be a nasty wee bugger when he was with his mates. He'd seen them giving one of the younger kids a hard time once, but he hadn't done anything about it. Another instance of not getting involved.

But, of course, he had never forgotten that night. He'd been up in his bedroom revising for his first A levels exam. His mum had called him, and he'd come down to see Alan from across the street and wee Jock, the local community policeman. Alan was OK. A bit of a quiet lad like himself. Jock was Mr Jolly to all the adults. He was always charming to the women and old ladies, one of the guys with the men, but he knew he'd taken some of the more troublesome boys round the back of the community centre and given them a hammering. Anti-social behaviour rates in the area had dropped and all the oldies thought the sun shone out of his ass. Jock had told his mum there was a football game and they needed another player to make up the numbers. She was always worried he was working too hard, and she'd encouraged him to go.

He'd gone but he'd only intended to stay for half an hour to please everyone. He'd hardly got through the door before he saw Big Sam and two of his sidekicks standing nonchalantly in the hallway, leaning back against the noticeboard looking as if they owned the place. Sam threw something at him and he caught it, a reflex action to stop it hitting him in the face. It was a set of car keys. He'd been told to pick the three boys up and take them wherever they wanted to go. This was a 'favour' to Big Sam. He knew what that meant, had known straightaway he didn't really have any choice. They didn't threaten him. They didn't have to.

Looking back now he realised he had been quite excited. He was going to get driving. He'd saved so long and hard for his lessons to pass his driving test but his mum would never be able to afford a car so opportunities to drive were few. Here he was with the chance to drive a big shiny BMW, far out of his league. He'd had his lessons in a Renault Clio with about as much go in her as a tractor. He wasn't stealing the car. He couldn't get into any trouble for that. It was Sam's car. He drove it all the time but not tonight. Tonight it was Seb's and he'd felt great as he drove down the Castlereagh Road into Belfast city centre. He could pretend he was that successful writer he so wanted to be, dreamed of being some day.

The three boys had already been well pissed when he'd picked them up. They were making all kinds of claims about what they were going to do. They were acting silly like drunk people often do. Laughing at things that weren't even funny. He could see they were excited. They invited him to come to the party with them. Was he tempted? He thought, if he was being honest, maybe… for just a second, but even then he'd been Mr Sensible not Captain Fantastic like Gawn seemed to expect of him all the time. He needed to get back to his studies. He couldn't afford not to make the grades in his A levels. Getting to Oxford was more exciting for him than getting drunk and shagging a few girls, risking getting caught with drugs and having a police record, which would stop him studying in America some day, another dream of his. So, he had left them off and got out of the car. He had wondered what he was supposed to do then. He didn't have enough money for a bus or train. He wasn't sure where there was a train station nearby and anyway, the trains would have stopped running by this time. He couldn't afford a taxi and it was at least fifteen miles to his home. He had been seriously considering walking and hitchhiking although there wouldn't be many cars on the road and fewer that would stop to pick up a young man at this time of night, when an older man opened the door of the house to let the three boys in and spotted him.

'You the driver?' He had smiled in a half-friendly manner.

'Yeh.'

'How are you getting home?'

'Walking, I guess.'

'I'll give you a lift part of the way back to Belfast. I'm leaving anyway.'

He remembered being a little reluctant to go with this man. He could smell alcohol on his breath and thought if he'd been at the party he might have been doing drugs as well, if what the boys had said was true, but he needed to get home. The car was a small white sports car. He'd had to squirm his way in, his long legs barely fitting. His knees seemed to end up somewhere around his ears. It had been very uncomfortable. Made more uncomfortable by the fact the man didn't introduce himself or say anything very much.

He took a turn off the main Bangor Road. Seb didn't know his way around that area then. Now he knew it had been over the Craigantlet Hills, a country route between Belfast and Bangor avoiding the main road. They were travelling at speed through the countryside. It was a pitch-black night. Clouds covered the moon and there were no lights on in any of the houses Seb could make out in outline as they sped past. He remembered being nervous, wondering what he would do if the man stopped the car and tried anything on. He thought he'd be able to fight him off. Eventually the road began its descent and round a bend Seb was relieved to see the lights of Belfast set out below him. When they reached the main Upper Newtownards Road, just near Stormont Buildings, the man stopped the car.

'This is as far as I can take you.' He seemed to be about to close the door behind Seb as he slithered his way out of the passenger seat and practically fell out onto the pavement when he added, 'My advice? Don't ever go near that house again.' And with that he had driven off.

Years later Seb had come across him again. He had seen his face in the newspaper when he was being knighted by the Queen for his services to industry in Northern Ireland.

Chapter 17

All these thoughts had been going through his mind as he drove along. He wasn't headed anywhere in particular. He just wanted to get out of the apartment after she had driven off leaving him and to put off phoning his mother which he knew he would have to do.

Maybe he would take a walk on the beach. He needed to get a bit of perspective. He hadn't done anything wrong. So why did he feel so guilty? Such a failure? Because that was how Gawn saw him. He knew he always judged himself against her. What would she think? What would she do? He suspected it was thinking that way that had got her sergeant killed.

It was a pleasant day. The weather had picked up and the sun was out. Only two weeks until Easter and then the trippers would descend on this area filling the guesthouses and cafés, leaving their litter all over the white sands, spoiling its beauty and its peace. The caravan parks would fill up with families escaping the narrow streets of Belfast to sit in narrow rows of mobile homes. Noisy groups of young men and women out for a good time would be bused into the area to seaside nightclubs. But, for now, the roads were mainly empty. Then he rounded a bend in the road and found himself held up by a line of cars trying to make their way into a makeshift car park while others were manoeuvring to exit. What was this place? He saw a sign for the Sunshine Wholefood Farm Shop. He loved food and he loved cooking. Tonight he would cook. He would go in and buy the best produce he could find and rustle himself up something tasty and exotic and forget all about bloody Gawn Girvin.

It took him several minutes to make his way into what was basically a field with some stones thrown down to help cars get traction in wet weather. It was a popular spot. He noticed young families emerging with bulging bags and children sucking on colourful lollipops. The shop was packed, and he spent time browsing. The produce looked fresh and he selected a huge T-bone Dexter steak at a meat counter manned by a teenage boy with alarming acne. He teamed it up with some asparagus. He knew he had potatoes and the ingredients for a good sauce and plenty of wine to wash it all down back at the apartment. He was paying at the checkout when he noticed a sign pointing to a café area. A cup of coffee and a scone or muffin would be good, he decided. Something to cheer him up.

The café was not as packed as the shop had been. He chose a table near the window overlooking the farmyard. A quick glance at the menu was enough to show him they had a range of coffees and some blueberry muffins so when a rather pretty waitress came up to the table he knew what he wanted.

'Ready to order?'

'Yes. I'll just have a filter coffee please – the Ethiopian blend – and a blueberry muffin.'

He smiled at her and she smiled back. She turned and walked back to the counter to get his order. His eyes followed her. He noticed her tight jeans and the way her hips moved as she walked. It was a long time since he had even looked at another woman. It seemed almost like a betrayal to be admiring her body and then he thought to himself that he was never going to measure up to Gawn's exacting standards no matter how hard he tried. So why not? Might as well just stop trying.

Staring out of the window as he waited for his order, Seb watched mesmerized as an older man moved slowly past him sitting on a cart drawn by a chestnut horse. It was like watching a programme on television. Had he known it, it was not unlike the detached feeling Gawn had experienced watching the figures on the beach, as if she were merely an audience to some dramatic performance. He almost did a double-take not trusting his own eyes for a second. He couldn't help but think of Gawn's story of a murderer in a cart and of that night only a week ago. His eyes met the eyes of the man. He noticed their unresponsive grey coldness. There was no spark of recognition or of acknowledgement.

'Here we are, sir.'

He was whisked back to reality at the sound of the waitress' voice. He looked up and the girl was beaming down at him. He guessed she was no more than mid-twenties, not much older than his students. He caught the aroma of her scent, light and fresh making him think of fields full of flowers in early summer. He had a flash of fantasy of her lying among the flowers waiting for him.

'We're having an open house tomorrow night. I wondered if you'd be interested in coming along.'

'Sorry. We? An open house?' He felt like an idiot, like he had missed something obvious.

'Oh, I thought you knew about the commune. Every now and then we have an open night so visitors can come and see how we live. There's one tomorrow night. If you'd like to come.'

She made it sound like a personal invitation but Seb knew from his time living in California how these sorts of communes worked; how they recruited new members. He didn't think his charms were so great that she had fallen for him at first glance. She probably got extra credit for bringing someone along.

'That's very kind but I'm afraid I'm busy tomorrow night. Maybe some other time.'

She seemed a little disappointed but accepted his excuse and turned to serve a new couple who had just seated themselves at a nearby table.

Seb looked out the window at the retreating cart. The man didn't look back. Seb turned his attention to his coffee and muffin. Both were good and he enjoyed them. He knew he couldn't put off phoning his mother for much longer. Gawn would be sure to send someone to interview her and check out his story. He was not looking forward to the conversation. Just as with Gawn, he didn't want to be a disappointment to his mother. As he made his way back along the corridor towards the exit he passed some sepia photographs on the wall – without stopping to look at them. If he had, he would have seen groups of young people but one or two featured the older man he had seen too. They were all dressed in long flowing white robes.

Chapter 18

Gawn was not looking forward to this. She had put it off as long as possible. But no matter what she had tried to do on Saturday, she couldn't concentrate and she couldn't shake off the waves of nausea she was experiencing in anticipation of the coming ordeal. Interviewing Seb had been awful. She expected this to be as bad, if not worse. So on Sunday morning, with the bells of the local church at the top of the hill sounding as if knelling her to her doom, she climbed out of her car in front of Angela York's house. She wasn't expecting a warm reception. She had only met the woman once, in the early hours of the morning, in Altnagelvin Hospital with Seb lying in the intensive care unit. And it had been her fault he was there. She had put him in danger; her work had.

There was little different about this house to make it stand out from all the others in the terrace. It was a boxy grey house in a line of boxy grey houses. The only touches of colour came from the yellow front door and the bright curtains at the front window. She rang the bell, stood back and waited. It didn't take long until the door was opened and she was face-to-face with Seb's mother. The woman's face looked familiar, the same wide set eyes and generous mouth as her son.

'Mrs York, I don't know if you remember me—'

'I remember you,' the woman interrupted her. Her voice was neutral, neither welcoming nor challenging.

'May I come in? It would be better than talking out here where all your neighbours can see.'

'I have nothing to hide from my neighbours... or anybody,' she added. She opened the door slightly and stepped aside leaving just enough room for Gawn to walk in past her. 'Straight ahead.'

Gawn noted that this house had the same layout as Louise Sloan's. Stairs to the right, front room to the left and the lounge straight ahead. An unlit wood burning stove dominated one wall of the living room, a basket heaped with logs sitting beside it. A huge television filled one corner and an L-shaped sofa faced it. Some cartoon show was playing on the TV, sound turned down. There were toys and books scattered over the sofa and the floor.

'You just missed Helen and the children,' the woman said, feeling the need to explain the untidiness.

Gawn knew Helen was Seb's older sister. Her children, Charlie and Murphy, were often at his house and she had seen photographs of him with them, although she'd never met them. 'Uncle Seb' was a great favourite. Spoiled them rotten.

'Mrs York, I need to ask you some questions,' Gawn began. She noticed there were no cups of tea and plates of biscuits being offered today.

'I know what it's about. Seb phoned me last night. You'd better sit down.' Her voice was still flat, non-committal, but she obviously found it hard to be ungracious and had offered the seat as she would to any visitor.

Gawn wondered if Seb had arranged with his mother what she should say when he had phoned her and then berated herself. He wasn't a criminal cooking up an alibi.

'You told the police at the time of Jason Sloan's disappearance that Seb was playing football the night he went missing.'

'Yes.' The woman wasn't going to go out of her way to help her. She would protect her son.

'But he wasn't, was he?'

'I didn't know that.'

'Is that what he told you, what he told you to say?'

'No, to both of those, Chief Inspector.' Now there was a note of bitterness in Angela York's voice. 'He did not tell me to say that either then or now. When we spoke last night he warned me someone would be coming to talk to me. He didn't say it would be you.' She managed to put a lot of meaning into that small word, *you*. 'All he said last night was I should tell whoever came all I know, which isn't a lot.'

'If he didn't tell you he was playing football, how did you know?'

'Because they called for him.'

'They?'

'Alan Turner, the wee boy that used to live across the street, and Jock.'

Gawn knew there was a Jock involved with the case. Only he wasn't a local resident. She remembered seeing the name of Jock Irvine, the local community policeman.

'Do you mean Jock Irvine?'

'Yes. He used to organise games for the boys. He was always trying to keep them all out of trouble. Not that Seb needed keeping out of trouble. He was a good boy. He worked hard at school. That night, he was up in his room as usual. I practically had to force him to go out with them.'

'Did Jock normally call for Seb?'

'No. I told you Seb was busy working.'

Gawn changed tack. She would have to get Pepper to see if he could find Alan Turner and Jock Irvine and have a chat with them. The policeman or probably retired policeman should be able to give them lots of useful background information.

'Did you know someone called Big Sam, Mrs York?'

'I didn't know him. I knew *of* him, but only what was common knowledge; what everyone knew or heard. We never had anything to do with him. He lived at the other end of the estate. He had a bad reputation. I knew that alright. I would never have allowed Seb to have anything to do with him. Anyway, he had more sense than to get involved with Big Sam.'

Obviously he still hadn't told his mother about this man's involvement that night and his part in it all.

'So Big Sam never came to the house?'

'No. I told you we had nothing to do with him. If he'd come here, I would have sent him packing.' She was getting annoyed now at the continuing questions.

'Seb didn't come home until the early hours of the morning. Was that normal?'

'No. It wasn't. He didn't go out much. Usually only with his friends from school. He never stayed out late without letting me know. He knew I was a worrier. He was considerate that way.'

'But you weren't worried that night?'

'No. Jock called back here later and told me the boys were all going to stay over at someone's house. I can't remember who, before you ask. I didn't really know them all. But Jock said they were having a good time, they had ordered pizza and Seb might even sleep over too.'

'And you were happy enough with that?'

'I was happy he wasn't running the street getting into trouble like some of the boys did. I was happy he was having a bit of a break. Sometimes I worried about him working too hard.'

'What about the next day, Mrs York, what did he say to you about what had happened?'

'Nothing.'

'Nothing?' Gawn was doubtful the woman was telling her the truth. She was sure Seb's mother was the type who would have kept a tight leash on her children and would want to know everything they were doing. She couldn't imagine she hadn't asked.

'Nothing. It was a knockabout football session in the local hall, not exactly the final of the World Cup. What was he going to say? I probably asked if he'd had a good time. I'm sure I would have but whatever he said I don't remember.'

Gawn realised she wasn't going to get anything more out of Angela York and the lead about Jock Irvine was a useful one. Irvine must have known Seb wasn't playing football and certainly wasn't sleeping over at any other boy's house. If he had come back and given her that story, it meant he was involved in some way. She stood up.

'I'm not the enemy, you know, Mrs York. I want to help Seb. He could be in trouble.'

'The only trouble he's ever been in is because of you.'

Gawn saw a spark of anger in the woman's eyes even though her voice was still calm and controlled.

'He's crazy about you. Gawn this and Gawn that. It's all I hear every time he phones me or calls in. Last night when he phoned he sounded like a different person. I hardly knew him. All the life had gone out of him. That's what you've done to him so don't tell me you're not the enemy. And now please, leave my house.'

After the front door had been closed firmly behind her, Gawn sat in the car for several minutes. She had to work very hard not to burst into tears. It had been even worse than she had feared. She made a note on her iPad that they needed to trace Alan and Jock Irvine as soon as possible. The policeman must have known what was going on in the estate and he should be able to tell them more about Big Sam. But he knew more than that. He, at the very least, had turned a blind eye to some of the goings-on but it was even possible he was part of it all.

Then she put the car into drive and moved off squealing the tyres in her desire to get away as quickly as possible. She hadn't noticed Angela York watching her from behind her upstairs curtains, the tears streaming down her face.

Chapter 19

She had spent the rest of Sunday, after her meeting with Seb's mother, moping about the apartment. She hadn't slept well and she was tired. On Monday morning she made a detour to the chemist on her way to the office and was now later than she had intended. She was hoping that Pepper and Hill might already have got some results from their enquiries. She was travelling past CS Lewis Square with its bronze sculptures of the Narnian characters so beloved of generations of children when her mobile rang. She pulled the car over to the side of the road to answer it. When she looked at the number she didn't recognise it.

'Girvin.'

'Good morning, Chief Inspector. It's Thomas Cairns, Inspector Cairns from Causeway Division.'

'Inspector.' She couldn't hide a trace of surprise in her voice. She hadn't expected to hear from him. She had almost forgotten about the events on the beach with everything else that had happened.

'Dr York gave me your number.'

'Yes?' She didn't elaborate, just waited to hear what he had to say.

'We've found a body. I expect he's already told you.'

If the policeman was fishing, she wasn't going to rise to the bait.

'Where?'

'It was washed up only a couple of miles along from your apartment into one of the caves. Female. Naked, as you said, and with long hair and a bruise on her face as if she'd been hit. The doctor said it could have happened post-mortem on the rocks or something but it could also be the result of a punch as you described.'

Gawn was ashamed that she was pleased to hear of this girl's death. It meant she had not been hallucinating but it also meant a girl had been murdered. That was nothing to be pleased about.

'Have you identified her yet?'

'Yes. We were in luck there. Her name is Magda Gorecki. She hadn't been reported missing but her parents in Poland were concerned that she hadn't been in touch with them for several weeks and they were worried. They phoned the Polish Consulate General in Belfast and his office contacted us because she was known to be living in this area. When the body turned up we were able to get dental records and a passport photo from Poland. Her parents are arriving today to identify her but I don't think there's any doubt.'

'I see. Do you have anyone you like for it?'

'Well, she was living in a sort of New Age quasi-religious commune up the coast a bit. They run a wholefood farm shop – it's quite good actually. My wife shops there sometimes.'

Gawn coughed pointedly. She didn't need to hear about his domestic arrangements.

'Yes and a holistic centre as well,' he continued. 'They offer classes in the use of crystals and all sorts of weird things. Sorry, ma'am, if that's your type of thing.'

Gawn couldn't help smiling at the idea of her being into communal living with a group of hippies.

'It's not,' she said very definitely. 'So what did these people have to say for themselves when you questioned them?'

'We couldn't go at them too hard, ma'am. The girl lived there alright but we don't know if anything happened to her there or that anyone there was involved in her death. In fact they all claim Magda left over a week ago. On good terms. They said she told them she was going back home to Poland.'

'And you believe them?'

'That was their story. They all stuck to it and we've no evidence to the contrary but we've no evidence she did leave either so we're doing checks on them all. There's three males living there including the leader. Moon Happiness he calls himself. He's an American, from San Francisco.' His words and the tone of his voice suggested that explained everything. 'The fact that the commune members sometimes wear white gowns might be coincidental, it could be someone trying to implicate them, or it could have been someone else from the commune with her that night. And, before you ask, they do have a cart on their farm. I'm waiting for a search warrant and we'll go over the whole place. The trouble is, of course, she lived there so there's going to be lots of traces of her. What we need is her belongings still there to prove she didn't leave and some proof of violence against her but, as you witnessed the attack at the beach, and, from what you said, they seemed to be on very close terms immediately before the attack, it's very unlikely we'll find anything like that on the farm. We're going to ask for DNA samples from the men but at this stage they would have to be agreeable and I don't know if they will be. Anyway, we think this new attack proves that the murderer is definitely still in the area.'

'Attack? Has someone else been attacked?'

'On the car, ma'am.'

'What car?'

'Your... partner's.'

'His car was keyed and the tyres were slashed on Saturday night. I thought he would have told you. The officer there yesterday morning thought it was probably just some drunken yobs on their way past from the pub but there was a note left on the windscreen. I take it you haven't been speaking to Dr York.'

'What did it say?' She wasn't going to explain herself to him.

'Stay out of it or else.'

'Stay out of what? You think it could have something to do with the girl's murder? But how would anyone even know about us or about what I saw?'

There was a pause and Cairns cleared his throat. 'I'm afraid my young officers were a bit loose-lipped, ma'am. I've spoken to them, and they've had it recorded against them on their personnel files. I'm sorry, ma'am. They thought it was funny and they shared it with a few friends at the pub and obviously it's got round.'

'I see. Thank you for keeping me up to date, Inspector. I'd appreciate it if you'd keep me in the loop and… and if you'd keep an eye on the apartment. I'm on a case in Belfast at the minute so Dr York is there by himself.'

'Of course, ma'am. We'll keep a lookout.'

Chapter 20

Gawn could almost feel the waves of energy and excitement flowing from the broom cupboard as she walked up the corridor. Maybe it was just her. She wanted to find whatever had happened to Jason Sloan for his mother and for Norman Smyth. As soon as she opened the door, she could see that both officers were busy. They didn't break off what they were doing when she entered and closed the door behind her. Pepper was speaking on the phone and merely waved in greeting. Hill finished what she was writing before looking up and speaking.

'Morning, boss.'

Gawn looked at the whiteboard and saw that it had been populated by several new photographs. There was Jason and Scott. They had been joined by another young man. Underneath was the name Albert Wright and "Died 10th February 2002" written in black marker pen. So they wouldn't be able to interview him then. A dead end. Literally. There was a picture of a young man in army uniform with "Alan Turner" written below it and another of a man in police uniform staring seriously into the camera – Jock Irvine. An official police mugshot of Samuel Legget, their Big Sam, finished the row of pictures.

'I see you've been busy.' She inclined her head towards the board. 'And I see we can't interview Mr Wright.'

'Yes, nor Alan Turner. He was killed in a training exercise on Salisbury Plain. But Wright's daughter still lives in Belfast. I've got an address for her if you want to speak to her.'

'What age is she, Jo?'

'Twenty-two.'

'Then she wouldn't know anything about it. She was only a baby when Jason went missing and still a child when her father died. How did he die anyway?'

'Car crash. He'd stolen a car and was joyriding.' She glanced across at Pepper who seemed unaware of their conversation as he listened to whoever was on the other end of his telephone call. She lowered her voice slightly before continuing. 'He wrapped it round a tree and killed himself and his passenger. His girlfriend.'

'The girl's mother?'

'No.'

'Thanks for that. Bye.' Pepper replaced the receiver. 'Good morning, ma'am. Good weekend?'

She knew he was just being friendly but she was feeling a bit defensive about her weekend.

'Great. Thanks. Now what have we lined up for today?'

'Jo and I are going to see Jacob York at noon at Oxford Street station. Do you want to be there, ma'am?'

'No. You two deal with it. But make sure to put him over the routes he took there and back with the three men and on his way back with the older man. He may have remembered something useful. I'm sure he's been thinking about it over the weekend.' She knew she had been. Every time she'd determined not to think about it anymore, it had come back to her. She couldn't get it out of her mind.

'Then we have another interview with Scott Alexander lined up for three,' Pepper said.

'That should fit alright. What about you, Jo?'

'They've sent over the footage from the entrance gate at Dundonald Cemetery. We're in luck. There is only one entrance so at least we don't have to watch multiple camera feeds. I thought I'd make a start to see if I could spot our Jason lookalike.'

'Good. Any word on disturbances in Cultra?'

Both detectives shook their heads.

'Still waiting for the info, ma'am,' Pepper said.

'OK. Have we got an address for Jock Irvine?'

'Working on it.' Pepper could have added, there's only two of us, you know, but he didn't.

'Good work. Both of you. I know I'm asking a lot of you but we're up against the clock. I appreciate what you're doing. Meantime I want to have a chat with Karen Houston's family.'

Chapter 21

It was only a few miles as the crow flies from the estate where Seb and Jason and the others had lived but it might as well have been a thousand. When Gawn had first read the address she had assumed it was a farm. Instead, as she approached the house down a winding country lane, she saw a set of solid wooden gates hanging on six-foot-tall grey brick pillars blocking her way. When she reached to within ten feet of them, they started to swing open slowly. So not only were they electronically controlled but someone was watching and had been monitoring her arrival to open the gates for her without her having to announce herself.

She still couldn't see a house. Then, she rounded a bend and a sprawling hacienda-type single-storey building appeared before her. It was huge. Two cars were parked outside on the circular drive – a trendy Mini, complete with what Gawn had always called 'go-faster stripes', and a Range Rover. It looked like a scene from an American soap or a setting for a glossy magazine photoshoot.

As she pulled on the handbrake and turned off the ignition, the front door of the house opened. Gawn was surprised to see a woman of about her own age standing in the doorway. She was casually, but to Gawn's knowing eye, expensively dressed.

'Chief Inspector Girvin?' The woman extended her hand in greeting. 'Please come in. My mother's in the kitchen. I hope you don't mind. We have a wee snug there and it just seemed like a more casual place to meet.' Then, as an afterthought, she added, 'I'm Julie, Karen's older sister.'

Now that she had said that, Gawn could see the resemblance to the victim's photograph in the file. They had not put her photo up on the board for she was not part of their official investigation into Jason's disappearance. And for some reason, which Gawn couldn't really explain even to herself, she didn't want any casual or nosy visitor to their office to know they were looking into Karen Houston's murder.

Julie led her into a large kitchen with a full wall of glass looking out over the County Down countryside. Today it was sunny, and the view was breath-taking towards Scrabo Tower and in the distance the waters of Strangford Lough. The kitchen was pristine, every surface sparkled. It was hard to believe that any actual cooking went on here. There was probably a good cleaning lady. Then Gawn smiled to herself. Who was she to judge? She had a cleaning lady for her postage-stamp-sized kitchen, and she definitely didn't cook – except when Seb was there.

'Mrs Houston, thank you so much for agreeing to see me.' Gawn walked towards the older woman. She could see the family resemblance.

'Excuse me for not getting up, Chief Inspector.' The woman didn't offer to shake hands and Gawn noted the twisted arthritic fingers. 'Would you like some tea or coffee? We were just about to have some.'

Valerie Houston fulfilled the lady of the manor role perfectly. Gawn expected it was one which she had held for many years. A background check had revealed that the Houstons had been a well-known couple in Ulster's social circles and linked to lots of charity events. They had opened their gardens for an annual party to fundraise for a local children's hospital and Martin Houston, having retired after a successful career in business, had sat on committees and boards of trustees of several major local charities until his death. He had been one half of Houston and Patterson Engineering, a major employer.

'That's very kind. Thank you. I never turn down a cup of coffee.' While Julie went off to make the coffee, Gawn looked out of the window. 'You have a beautiful home and a fabulous view, Mrs Houston. It must be lovely to watch the seasons go by from here.'

'Yes. I've been very blessed in so many ways. Thank you, my dear.'

Julie set a large cup with a special handle down beside her mother and then turned and handed a cup and saucer to Gawn, who recognised the Casa Bugatti Milla design of the china she had always admired.

'Except in one very important way,' Mrs Houston continued. 'You never get over losing a child. You forget sometimes. For a short time, and then something brings it all back. You hear a piece of music. Or one of Julie's wee ones is running across the lawn and she looks just like Karen at that age. It can be anything and it comes at you just when you're not expecting it. Do you have any children, Chief Inspector?'

Gawn had not been expecting the personal question.

'No. No, I was never lucky enough.' She had almost said yes but thought it better not to go there. This wasn't about her. It was about this frail old lady. With all her money and her beautiful home, Gawn felt sorry for the woman. She was no different to Louise Sloan who was still trapped in that one day and the loss of her child.

'Please, help yourself to milk and sugar.'

'This is fine as it is. It's very good of you to talk to me.'

'I have no problem talking about Karen. In fact, I love to. A lot of my friends now never knew her, and I think the ones who did don't like to bring the subject up. I think they're embarrassed, or they're scared of upsetting me or they've simply moved on with their lives.'

Valerie Houston, like Louise Sloan, had not; could not.

'You were away when Karen was found.'

'Yes, we were having an early holiday in Tenerife.'

'And Karen hadn't gone with you?'

'No. She was at university. It was term time. She had exams coming up. She could have come if she'd wanted. We'd have loved her to, but she wanted to stay at home by herself.'

'You weren't here either, Miss Houston?'

'Mrs Patterson,' the woman corrected her, 'but please call me Julie. No. I was away working in America for a year out after uni.'

Gawn nodded. She had already known that. She turned back to the older woman and asked, 'You weren't concerned about leaving Karen here by herself?' Gawn's eyes looked around assessing the size of the place and its isolation.

'The house wasn't as big then as it is now. We've extended several times since then. After Martin – my husband – died, Julie and her family moved in with me and we've future-proofed the house as well for whenever I have to use a wheelchair.' Mrs Houston smiled ruefully. 'And there used to be a couple of other properties on this lane where we knew the families and she could have got help if she needed it. But there was no suggestion anything happened here. She wasn't attacked here.'

'No. Of course not. I'm just trying to get to know your daughter better. Did she drive?'

'You're wondering why she didn't drive to her friend's house that night? She had my car but she'd had a wee accident earlier in the week. She'd just backed into a bollard in a car park. It was nothing major, just a bump, but she wanted to have it repaired before we got back so she'd left it at the garage where we got all our work done.' Almost as an afterthought, Mrs Houston added, 'I got rid of that car. I couldn't bear to be in it. I wouldn't have been annoyed that she'd damaged the car. Accidents happen. If she'd had her own car that night, she might still be alive.' There was a slight tremble in her voice.

Gawn hurried on with her questions. 'But she'd have been happy enough walking back from the bus to the house at night by herself?'

'Yes. If there'd been a problem, if it was heavy rain or something, she'd probably have phoned one of her friends in town and got them to run her up from the bus stop. But she was very independent.'

'What about boyfriends?' Gawn asked and looked at both women. Sometimes sisters knew more about each other's love lives than they shared with their mother.

Valerie Houston spoke first. 'There was nobody serious. She'd gone out a few times with some of the boys she met on her course but that was all. She was young. It was all fun for her. She didn't want to settle down. She had her whole life in front of her… or so we thought.'

Gawn turned her head to look straight at Julie encouraging her to respond. The woman seemed unable to meet her eye. Eventually, unwillingly it seemed, she answered.

'She'd been fairly serious about Andrew but they split up long before whenever she started university.'

'And where was this Andrew when she was killed? Do you know?'

'In New York with me. Andrew's my husband. We married the year after Karen was killed when I got back from America.'

Mrs Houston cleared her throat and Gawn wondered if this was a touchy subject; if she wasn't happy that her older daughter had stepped into the shoes of her younger one and was enjoying the happy married life Karen had never had the chance to have. 'We were told Karen must have taken a lift with someone when she was waiting for the bus,' she said. 'I know she would never have gone with a stranger. I told the police that. She was too sensible. Too careful. The police questioned all our friends and all her friends at the time but there was nothing to suggest they had anything to do with her murder. At least that's what we were told. Why are you investigating again now, Chief Inspector? Has something new been found?'

Gawn didn't want to get the woman's hopes up.

'We haven't re-opened the case, I'm afraid, Mrs Houston. I'm looking at another case from around the same time. I wondered if there were any links.' She saw a look of disappointment cross the woman's face and hastily added, 'You can be sure, Mrs Houston, if I find anything which links to your daughter I will follow it up.' Gawn stood up. 'Thank you for your hospitality and your willingness to help me.'

Julie led her out into the hallway. They passed a lighted display cabinet and Gawn stopped to admire the silver trophies in it.

'Dad was a very keen golfer. It was his passion, that and fast cars.' Julie laughed.

There were photographs on the wall beside the cabinet. One was of a famous local golfer with two older men.

'That's dad on the left. And this is dad and my father-in-law when they got their first big contract.' She was pointing to an old photograph of two young men both standing proudly in front of sleek sports cars. 'They owned Houston and Patterson and they were always great rivals on the golf course and on the road.'

Next to it was a picture of the whole family. It was a posed studio photograph but, although it looked rather formal and Mr Houston seemed slightly old-fashioned among the three females in their fashionable clothes and stunning jewellery, they looked a happy group. Mrs Houston was wearing a fabulous emerald necklace which Gawn was sure must have cost thousands. But their money hadn't guaranteed their happiness and she guessed

Mrs Houston would give it all up to have her daughter back again.

Gawn thanked Julie for their help. It was a beautiful home but not a totally happy one. The spectre of the loss of Karen hung over it and it would not have helped to have Julie married to Karen's ex. Gawn was mulling over all this as she drove away.

Chapter 22

Gawn returned to the police station anxious about what Pepper and Hill might have to tell her about their interview with Seb. Her first surprise was when they began by saying he had come with a solicitor in tow.

'Did he refuse to answer any of your questions? Did the solicitor try to block you from asking anything?'

'No, boss. We gave him the usual caution but Dr York seemed very keen to be as helpful as possible. He answered everything.'

'Did you ask him if he had gone anywhere else in the car before he picked the others up?'

'Yes. He says he didn't. He drove straight to the Starlit.'

'Did you take him over the route he travelled with them?'

'Yes. He explained all about the journey. On the way he drove mostly on the main road from Belfast through Holywood. He wasn't a very confident driver at the time, he told us, so he wanted to keep to the main road until they told him to turn off to the left somewhere about Cultra. He couldn't be specific about exactly where but he remembers it was after he had passed the Folk Museum. He remembered he'd once been there on a school trip so he recognised the bridge over the road from one part of the museum to the other.'

That was new. He hadn't mentioned that to her. So he had been thinking about it.

'Then on the way back to Belfast, the man took him by a country road. He didn't know where he was at the time but he has driven in that area many times since and he says he's sure it was the road out of Holywood over Craigantlet coming down into Dundonald Village.'

Pepper could see Gawn working out if that would have put him past the spot where Karen Houston's body had been found.

'That would have been too far up the road for them to have passed the Houston girl at the bus stop and anyway that would have been long after she was there. Then they would have had to turn off that road to be anywhere near where the girl's body was dumped, ma'am.' It was as if Pepper had been reading her mind. 'So, if he's telling the truth, he wasn't anywhere near anything.'

If he's telling the truth, she thought. She was angry with herself for even thinking that.

'Did you believe him?'

'I must say I did, ma'am. That's my gut instinct for what it's worth.' He paused and then added, 'He did provide one other useful bit of information, not for us so much, but if they're ever looking at the Houston girl's murder again.'

'What?'

'He gave us the name of the man who brought him back to Belfast. He didn't know him at the time but he says he recognised him years later when his picture was in the paper. He didn't have any reason to come to the police with the information then for Jason was safe and well when they had left the house so he didn't connect the man with his disappearance. He thought the boys had just been exaggerating to impress him about the drugs and girls and, anyway, the man had left so he wasn't going to blacken his reputation by connecting him with some sexual irregularities, as he put it, if there even were any, if it wasn't all just talk. When we suggested that it might have been more than irregularities, a girl might have been murdered, he seemed genuinely horrified that the information he had could have helped the police investigation.'

That she could believe.

'Who was it?'

'Sir Philip Patterson. You know, from Houston and Patterson. We have a connection, ma'am.'

Gawn was stunned. Philip Patterson had been Martin Houston's business partner, was Julie's father-in-law and a well-known local figure in business and political circles. If she thought she had been treading on eggshells up to now, it was nothing compared to how she would have to take this forward.

'Right. We can't do anything with this information just now. It's not our case. It's not anyone's case at the minute as far as I know. Leave it with me. I need to think about what we do next and, both of you,' – her eyes moved from one to the other to make sure they were both listening – 'keep this to yourself. It goes no further than these four walls. For now. I'm not burying it but we need to move carefully. So, for now, let's concentrate on Jason Sloan.'

Gawn's mind was working overtime. She wondered if Norman Smyth had any idea of what he was starting when he asked her to look into this.

'Walter, you and I have to see Scott Alexander again.'

'Yes, ma'am. I phoned to double-check with him. I couldn't get a reply so I asked a friend to check in on him for me. I thought he looked really bad when we left him on Friday. Apparently, he was taken ill over the weekend. They moved him to the hospice.'

'What are the chances of being able to speak to him there?'

'I thought you would ask that, ma'am. I phoned. He's conscious and they said as long as he was willing they could allow it but he wouldn't be fit to talk for long. He's very weak apparently.'

'Right, let's go then. Jo, any joy on locating PC Irvine yet?'

'No, ma'am. I'm working on it.'

'And the CCTV?'

'On it too, ma'am.'

'Right, we'll be back soon. Maybe you'll have had some luck by then.'

Chapter 23

The car park at the hospice was quite full. Gawn had never been inside the building before although she had driven past it many times. It was just across the road from Police Headquarters. Her first impression was of colour and laughter; not what she had expected at all. The walls were brightly decorated with children's drawings and colourful paintings. The atmosphere was not the sombre one she had anticipated. They were greeted by a smiling receptionist who directed them to a room towards the back of the building. On the way down the corridor they passed a ward. Gawn glanced in and saw some patients lying on top of the beds fully clothed, reading, listening to music, chatting with visitors; others were sitting in armchairs. There was even one man with a pet dog sitting at his feet. Music was coming from some of the other rooms, and laughter.

The door to Scott Alexander's room was slightly ajar. Gawn pushed it slowly open. A nurse was sitting by the side of the bed, holding Alexander's hand. Gawn was immediately taken back to the night at Altnagelvin Hospital when she had witnessed Angela York sitting like that with her son. No one should be alone at times like these. She was glad the nurse was there for Scott no matter what he might have done in the past.

'You're here to see Scott?' the nurse asked in a nasally voice.

'Yes.' Gawn flashed her warrant card.

'He's very weak. Try not to tire him too much. He wants to talk to you. Maybe it will help him find some peace if he can.' She stood up. 'I'll be back in a wee minute, Scott.' She patted his hand, checked his drip and walked out of the room.

The two detectives positioned themselves on either side of the bed. They both pulled up chairs and sat down.

'Not so well today, Scott?' asked Pepper in a kindly voice.

'I've been better,' he wheezed and then fell into a paroxysm of coughing.

'You were telling us about the party in Cultra but you didn't get to the end of your story. What happened, Scott? What happened to Jason?' Gawn asked, keeping her voice soft and calming but wanting to get to the point of their visit as fast as she could. She was sure the nurse would be back soon to cut their interview short. She needed answers quickly.

'I don't know what happened. I was totally wasted. Out of my head. I woke up in my own bed the next day. I didn't have a clue how I got there. But Albert told me what he and Jason had done.'

Gawn sat forward in her seat. The dying man's voice was weak, and she had to strain to hear him. She didn't want to miss anything he might say.

'They were reasonably sober, well, the best of us anyway. One of the top men got them to help him. He had a girl he needed help to carry out to his car. She was unconscious. He told them he was going to take her home but he couldn't manage her by himself. But on the way he stopped and turfed her out of the car. Then he ran over her and left her. Albert told me he'd never forget the girl's face. It was really pitch black but the moon had come out from behind the clouds and the moonlight shone down on her lying in the ditch. She was naked. He said she'd been lovely. He was still shaking when he was telling me the next day.' A single tear had escaped the side of Scott's eye and slid down his cheek.

'He ran over her?' Gawn wanted to make sure Scott was telling them the truth.

'Yes. He ran over her and then he reversed and did it again.'

Now she knew he was. The medical evidence had shown that.

'Why didn't Albert go to the police? Or Jason? Or you?'

He looked at her as if she were mad.

'Are you joking? Some of them probably *were* bloody police. Anyway, I hadn't seen anything. Not really. I was never more glad of anything in my life. I didn't want to see anything. Albert was all for running away. He was bricking it. But Big Sam came round and told him it would all be alright. They had it covered. He just had to keep his mouth shut. He gave him money. He gave me some money too.'

Gawn wondered what Sam's comment had meant. How had they 'had it covered' and who had done the covering?

Scott paused and pointed to a glass of water sitting on the bedside cabinet. Pepper stood up and reached across for it. He helped him take a sip.

'Thanks. The money didn't do him much good, poor bugger. He sucked most of it up his nose or shot it into his arm. I used mine. I told everyone that John helped me get my business started. He did help me but it was only with advice. I got the money for my first stall from Big Sam.'

'And what about Jason?'

'Albert said Jason did a runner. When the man drove the car over the girl, Jason made off into the woods. They didn't go after him. Albert had already wet himself, he was so scared and he wasn't going to start chasing after Jason in the woods in the dark and the man was wasted, couldn't run the length of himself. Albert and I only talked about it one time ever. We both wondered if they'd caught up with Jason and got rid of him like the girl or whether he'd got away. We didn't know. Better not to.'

He paused and looked at them with sad eyes. 'I hope he got away.'

It was Pepper who asked the next question and they both waited for the answer, almost holding their breath.

'Who was the man, Scott, the driver?'

'I don't know his name. Never did. Everybody just called him "the judge". I don't know if he was really a judge or it was just a nickname. He was bloody scary anyway. I know that. No one argued with him. You knew not to cross him. He was a vicious bastard. I'd heard stories of him with some of the girls, what he'd done to them.'

Scott's voice was getting weaker, and just as Gawn was hoping that she'd not been eavesdropping, the nurse returned.

'I think that's about enough, don't you? Scott needs his rest.' She smiled as if they had a choice but they all knew she was ordering them out.

Gawn would have liked to ask if Scott knew the names of any of the others at the party but she knew she had lost the chance.

'Take care, Scott,' Pepper said as they walked out.

They didn't think they'd be questioning him again.

Chapter 24

Gawn and Pepper barely spoke the whole way back to the office. Both were lost in their own thoughts. Eventually, when they had been forced to stop by a red traffic light, Gawn turned to the older man. She could see he was as uneasy as she was.

'If he's telling the truth, we've a whole conspiracy here; a real can of worms.'

'Why would he be lying now? He's nothing to gain by lying, ma'am. Like that nurse said, he's trying to make his peace.'

A judge, policemen, pimping thugs, some kind of cover-up. It was as bad as anything she had come across at the Met. Fleetingly she wondered if Norman Smyth had had his own suspicions about Jason's disappearance; if perhaps he had realised there was a link with Karen's murder but had never felt able to do anything about it until now when he was retiring. He had needed someone he could trust who would follow the evidence wherever it led so he had come to her. She had thought he was doing her a favour by easing her back into work. Now she thought he had landed her right in the middle of a major scandal. For one fleeting second she thought about walking away from it all. Having Seb involved, even if he had only driven them to the party and was no more than a taxi driver, was awkward. She could claim a conflict of interest and withdraw but then she remembered the promise she had made to Valerie Houston. She would just have to keep Seb out of it. She recognized the irony that she was prepared to suppress his involvement, manipulate the evidence so that she could continue with the case. If she felt like a hypocrite, it didn't last long.

Once back in the office, they closed the door and filled Hill in on what Scott had told them. Her face went through a range of emotions as she listened open-mouthed.

'Shit!' The girl realised what she had said and added, 'Sorry, ma'am.'

'So, where do we go from here?'

'The pub for a good strong drink?' Pepper suggested only half-jokingly.

'Jo, any luck with the disturbance reports from Cultra?'

'Yes. They came through eventually. I asked for Cultra and Craigavad and as far as Helen's Bay. I hope you don't mind. I just thought it would be better to get them all. Then if nothing shows up in Cultra we'll have the others without having to request them and wait again.'

'Good idea. Well done.'

'I got a map of the area and I've marked where there were a number of disturbance complaints, not just one-offs.' The girl indicated the map she had pinned to the board. There were only three ringed zones. 'As you see, it's a very law-abiding area. Very few complaints. But these three properties did have some. This one' – she indicated a circle on the map – 'had several over the course of a long weekend but I read the reports and it seemed that parents were away and the boys in the family were taking the opportunity for some partying, so although there were three complaints, it all related to the same period of time and it was young people who were spoken to.'

'OK. What about these other two?' Gawn pointed.

'This one had several complaints. All on Saturday nights. Not every Saturday night or anything but, over the period we are interested in, a total of six. Most related to the noise of car doors being banged, and shouting as people were leaving in the early hours of the morning.'

'Who lived in this house at the time?'

'The registered owner was an American mining company, Revere Consolidated. They used it for their executives to stay when they were based here so there may have been more than one person or family in the house over that period of time. I would need to contact the company in Texas and ask for names. I didn't know whether you would want me to do that.'

'Let's hold back on that one for now. What about the other property?'

'The owner was called Paul Esdale. He was a barrister.'

Barrister – judge, Gawn wondered to herself.

'I know that name, ma'am,' Pepper said. 'It would have been before you came back to Northern Ireland, when you were with the Met. Mr Justice Esdale was on the bench here. He was a tough cookie. I remember as a young constable having to give evidence before him. He was a hard man. Renowned for his stiff sentencing.'

'It couldn't be a coincidence, could it?' Gawn asked, not really expecting an answer. Then she seemed to realise what time it was. 'Right. It's getting late. You've done a lot of good work today, you two. Go home. Relax. We'll pick this up in the morning when we've had time to mull it over for a bit. We mustn't jump to any conclusions. And please, don't mention any of this to anyone. I don't know if you have partners, husbands, wives or whatever but not even to them. Please.'

When the other two had gone, Gawn sat on. She stared at the board. She decided she needed the wise counsel of Norman Smyth but what she really needed, what she really wanted was Seb. She knew she couldn't tell him any of this, she just wanted to be with him, but she knew that was impossible. He would want nothing to do with her, she was sure. And even if by some chance he did, she could compromise the case if she contacted him. Instead, she phoned Smyth. She gave him a brief outline of what they had discovered so far, leaving out all mention of Seb's involvement, and then asked to meet him. Just as with Seb, she wanted to be face to face with Smyth when she spoke with him so she would know if he was telling her the truth.

Chapter 25

Smyth had seemed reluctant at first but had then suggested they meet somewhere outside of the office. He named Albert Mooney's, a popular bar and restaurant at Ballyhackamore and, even though the place held bad memories for her, she'd agreed. He had arrived first and was already ensconced in a suitably shabby chic tan leather wingback armchair on the raised area at the front of the pub when she walked in. It was busy and noisy which was good. There would be little chance of being overheard, but she was acutely aware of how exposed they were. She remembered being followed here once before.

'Hello, my dear. You sounded a bit harassed on the phone.' He stood up and kissed her lightly on the cheek.

'It's been a busy day.' She smiled as she flopped down into the squishy armchair opposite him.

'I got you a glass of white wine. I hope that's alright. It's very busy in here tonight and I thought it would speed things up if I had a drink ready for you. I'm afraid I have a meeting at 7.30 so I can't stay long,' he explained by way of apology.

If he was in a hurry, then she would cut through the pleasantries and get straight to what she wanted to know.

'Why did you ask me to look into Jason Sloan's disappearance?' She had decided that she wanted to get a few things out in the open. She had had her suspicions for a while that Smyth had been less than straight with her.

'I told you. It's the case that got to me.'

'Why?'

'Does there have to be a why? We all have them. If you don't yet, you will someday.' He took a sip of his drink.

'It wasn't because you wanted someone to look into Karen Houston's murder and you couldn't just re-open the case with no new evidence?'

By the guilty look on his face, she could see that she had hit home.

'You're quite right, my dear. There's no way I could get that case opened up again.'

'But you must have suspected that Jason's and Karen's cases were linked. Why?'

'I thought it even at the time.' He saw her look of surprise and hurried on. 'I was a lowly detective sergeant then, Gawn, and hadn't even been that for very long and the Houston murder wasn't in my area. We weren't investigating it. Anything I knew about it, I got either from the newspapers or gossip in the canteen, but it always just seemed to me that it was too much of a coincidence for two young people to go missing around the same time within a few miles of each other, and the more I got to know Louise Sloan and heard her talking about her son, the less I thought he would just go off and leave her. Seems I was wrong,' he added.

'You kept in touch with Mrs Sloan?'

'Yes.'

Gawn remembered the cookery book, a Christmas gift complete with personal inscription and asked, 'Did you have an affair with her?'

'My God, Gawn, you don't beat about the bush, do you?'

'I like people to be straight with me and I don't think you have been.'

He didn't respond immediately. He took another slow sip of his drink before looking her in the eye and replying.

'I did not have an affair with Louise Sloan. I admit I found her attractive and there was something appealing about her vulnerability to a young man, as I was then. And we have stayed in touch over the years.'

'And she told you what Scott Alexander had said at the funeral, didn't she? And you knew, if I looked into it, I would have a good chance of finding Jason if he was still alive. And if I found Jason, then he might know something about Karen's murder. And you knew me well enough to know that I would follow it wherever it led.'

He had the good grace to look sheepish.

'I don't like being manipulated.'

'You're a police officer, Gawn. You're told where to go and what to do every day. We all are. You're assigned to some cases and sometimes you're not when you'd like to be. That's manipulation too. We don't get to choose. All I did was interest you in a case. This time you could have said no.'

'And what about Sebastian? Was that another way to ensure I would go along with your plan?'

'What about Sebastian?' He seemed genuinely bemused.

'You didn't know he was the Jacob York on the list of people interviewed?' She didn't mention what she had found out about him driving the boys that night.

He looked surprised. 'I had no idea. Believe me.'

Gawn wasn't sure whether she could believe him at all now. She was beginning to wonder just whom she could believe.

'Did you know anything about this sex ring?'

'There were whispers at the time.'

'What sort of whispers?'

He ran his finger around the collar of his shirt as if it was too tight for him. He was uncomfortable answering her questions now. He had expected this meeting to be about encouraging her to keep going, not for him to get a grilling.

'Just that. Just whispers. Nothing definite. Just suggestions that sometimes cops looked the other way when certain things were reported, discouraged people from pursuing a complaint, but no one wanted to ask any awkward questions.'

'Did *you* look the other way?'

She saw not the indignation she had expected but sadness in his eyes as he answered her.

'Never.'

Gawn lifted her glass and took a sip of the wine.

'Do you want to drop the case?' he asked.

Did she? She had probably lost Seb forever. Her work was all she had left. Did she want to drop the case?

'Hell no.'

* * *

From the darkness of an alleyway directly across the road and down the side of a busy fast-food restaurant, a man with his hoodie pulled up hiding his face was making a call on his mobile. His view of the bar window was obscured for a minute as a glider bus swished past carrying its passengers into central Belfast. His voice was low as he spoke although there was no one about to overhear what he was saying.

'Yes. They seem to be very deep in conversation. He looks very serious. So does she. Do you want me to follow Smyth or should I keep following Girvin?'

Chapter 26

She had still been in a deep sleep when her alarm went off the next morning. Most unusual for her. She had been feeling so tired recently. The previous evening after her meeting with Smyth she had driven home almost on auto-pilot with so many thoughts about the case and her private life swirling around in her brain. She had stopped at an Asian fusion takeaway near her apartment and the roast duck in honey chilli sauce and a small glass of wine along with the one she had drunk earlier with Smyth had done the trick.

She showered and dressed but when she put on her favourite grey trouser suit, she noted the waistband was just a little tighter than she would have liked. It was all the comfort junk food and takeaways she had been living on recently. She needed to be more careful in her diet now Seb wasn't cooking the good wholesome food he always raved about. Just another thing she missed about him.

She was surprised but pleased to find Jo Hill already at her desk focused on her computer screen when she pushed open the office door. Hill was turning out to be more of a workaholic than she was.

'Good morning, boss.'

'Good morning. You're here early – not that I'm complaining.'

'Couldn't sleep. I never can when I'm in the house on my own. My "whatever"' – she looked up and smiled at Gawn as she referred back to what had been said the previous evening – 'is away on business this week.'

'Oh, I see.'

Gawn was almost into her cupboard when she was stopped by the younger woman's next words.

'How do you do it, ma'am? Balance doing what you do with a relationship?' She saw the frown that came to Gawn's face and quickly added, 'Sorry. Too personal. Not my business.'

'I don't think I'm the best person to be asking that. My success rate with relationships isn't great.'

The door opened and Pepper walked in carrying a box of donuts.

'Fighting food for the troops,' he announced. 'Give us all a wee sugar rush at tea break.'

Gawn was immediately reminded of her last sergeant, who had brought donuts for her team.

Pepper saw the look that crossed her face and, immediately misinterpreting it, added, 'Sorry. Did I do something wrong? You're not against treats, are you?'

'I'm not but my waistline is already complaining.' She smiled to ease the slight embarrassment of the moment.

'Sarge,' Hill asked, 'you're married, aren't you? How do you do it?'

'Do what? You two weren't having a girlie talk, were you? I've already had to do the birds and the bees talk with my son. Bloody awful it was too. I made sure my wife did the rest.'

'It's just, Mike, my partner, wants us to settle down, as he calls it, and start a family and I don't think I could go on with my career if I had kids. I just think it would be too hard.'

'Well, I would never presume to offer advice about someone else's marriage. All I would say is what you already know. It's hard enough being a cop. All the baggage that goes along with it. The unsocial hours. The emotional rollercoaster you sometimes find yourself on and taking it out on the ones at home. We've all done it. You need someone at home whom you can depend on. I got lucky. I found my soulmate at a Young Farmers' Club dance of all places before I joined the force.' He laughed.

No matter what. That was what Seb had said to her. He would love her no matter what. He would be there for her no matter what. She had never made the same commitment to him. He had said he was no hero, but he had rescued her and not just from drowning. She had found her soulmate and she had pushed him away.

'Well, what about it, ma'am?' Gawn was brought back to the present as Pepper held out the box of donuts to her.

'I'll have a plain one, please. And I'll put the kettle on, shall I?'

She was just about to lift the kettle when Hill let out a call.

'Bingo! Got him!'

They gathered around and looked at the frozen picture on the younger woman's screen.

'I had to go back nearly two hours before the funeral to find him. He was obviously being really careful, getting into place long before anyone else would have been there.'

The image was indistinct, but their tech boys would be able to clean it up, Gawn was sure. It was definitely a swarthy-skinned man of around the right age but only seen in profile out of the side window of a car. Possibly, but not definitely Jason Sloan.

'Are there any cameras inside the cemetery?'

'No. Only the one at the gate.'

'If you could find him walking or driving out, then we could get a full-face image.'

'On it.'

It took another twenty minutes of watching for her to find what she was looking for. They saw a man who looked like a twenty-year-older but still recognisable Jason Sloan seated at the wheel of a car waiting to exit onto the main Upper Newtownards Road into the traffic.

'Can you read the number plate?'

Hill reeled off the letters and numbers which Pepper put into the database he had called up on his screen.

'It's a black VW Golf.'

'That looks right.'

'Who's it registered to?' Gawn asked.

'Airport Rentals.'

'Get on to them and find who rented the car on that date. This might be easier than we thought.'

The two women sat in silence listening to Pepper's half of the conversation as he spoke to the rental company. He scribbled something down on his notepad.

'Thank you. That's great. Really helpful.'

'Well?' Gawn asked.

'The car was rented by Jason Simpson.'

'Kept the same first name. OK. Where does Mr Simpson live?'

'The address on the driving licence he used was Edinburgh. I'll just do a check now and get some more details.'

The phone rang in Gawn's office. Three strides and she was able to pick it up.

'Girvin.'

'Is that the policewoman who was here yesterday?'

'It depends where here is?'

'Sorry. It's the hospice here. I just wanted to let you know Mr Alexander passed away during the night. Just in case you were intending to visit him again.'

Gawn's upbeat mood dropped a little. She didn't think Scott would have been able to tell them much more, if anything. But she was sorry that they had not been able to tell him that they had found Jason and by the look of things he was doing alright. She just hoped he had found the peace he was looking for. She thanked the nurse and turned back to the outer room.

'Bad news, ma'am?' Pepper said.

'Scott Alexander's dead.'

'Ah.'

'But life and our inquiry goes on. What have you found?' She thought her words sounded a little harsh but she was excited to be making progress on the case at last.

'Jason Simpson lives in the centre of Edinburgh just off Princes Street. I did a wee search for images of his house.' He swung his monitor around. The picture on the screen was of a large Georgian-style townhouse.

'Worth a bob or two in the middle of Edinburgh. He must have done well for himself,' Gawn reacted. 'What else have you found out about him?'

'He's a car dealer.'

'That makes sense. He was working as a mechanic in Belfast when he went missing.'

He turned the screen around again and they saw a website for Simpson Motors. One click and the smiling face of Jason Sloan appeared. In a strong Scottish accent he extolled the virtues of his motor dealership. Their motto was 'Honesty, Value and Service'.

'Not very honest to be living under an assumed name,' Hill commented.

'Or to be keeping his mother in the dark about what happened to him,' Gawn added. 'Right, we'll need to speak to him and make one hundred percent sure it is our Jason Sloan. I'm not inclined to phone. Too easy for him to lie or to do a runner afterwards. I'll book flights. Jo, seeing you're on your own this week, do you fancy a trip to Edinburgh? We mightn't be back until late.'

The young officer beamed from ear to ear.

'Absolutely.'

Chapter 27

They left Pepper manning the office. He was going to check up on Paul Esdale, to see if the judge was still alive. He was still waiting to hear back from his contacts about Jock Irvine who had retired from the police service in the early 2000s. He would chase them up. Pepper had assured Gawn he would have plenty to do until they came back.

They booked seats on the 2pm flight to Edinburgh. They checked in at City Airport where Gawn's last big case had begun. Today there were no disgruntled crowds held up by a dead body found on an incoming plane. They had passed through check-in and security quickly and easily. Both had only hand luggage. Gawn wondered what they would do if they couldn't get back in the evening. She had booked them on the 8pm flight but she knew that sometimes the evening flights got cancelled and hoped that wouldn't happen to them. Their flight took off on time and was smooth and uneventful. Gawn had flicked through the pages of the onboard magazine to pass the time while Hill had snoozed.

Just before the rush-hour traffic started to build up, they found themselves exiting a taxi outside the premises of Simpson Motors. A forecourt of shiny brand-new models suggested a successful business. Inside the glass-fronted offices, between the latest top-of-the-range models parked around the open space of the showroom, they spotted a salesman, not Simpson or Sloan or whatever he called himself now, but a younger man dressed in a snappy three-piece suit.

In a friendly Scottish lilt he asked, 'Can I help you, ladies?' He walked forward, beaming, anticipating a sale, probably already calculating his commission, Gawn thought to herself. 'Have you anything specific in mind? A nippy wee town car for shopping?'

Gawn delved into her pocket and withdrew her warrant card. She had not informed the local police that she was investigating on their patch. Quick in-and-out and, if they needed to speak to Jason again or bring him over to Belfast for questioning, then she could do it through official channels.

'DCI Girvin and this is DC Hill.' She didn't mention PSNI and thought he wouldn't be able to identify the insignia from the distance between them. 'We'd like to speak to Mr Simpson, please.'

The young man's eyes flicked across the room to a line of inner offices with windows looking out over the sales area. All of them seemed to be empty.

'I'll see if he's about. He doesn't seem to be in his office. Maybe he had to nip out. Please, have a seat in here, ladies.' He led them across to a door marked "Manager" and opened it for them. Inside was a desk and some comfortable chairs. 'Have a seat and I'll get him.'

The women sat and waited. It was only a couple of minutes before he returned. He popped his head round the door and said, 'Mr Simpson will be with you in a minute.' He smiled and closed the door again.

'Do you think he's doing a runner, ma'am?'

'No. Not unless he's up to no good here. He wouldn't know why we want to talk to him. How could he?'

The minutes ticked by. Just when Gawn was beginning to think Simpson had somehow sussed them out, the door opened and a smiling Jason Sloan/Simpson, as she thought of him, stood in front of them in the flesh.

'Good afternoon. Sorry to keep you waiting. My assistant was saying you're police officers. How can I help you? I'm always happy to help the police. It's not Charity Benefit tickets again, already?' He had only a slight Scottish accent, less pronounced than it had been in the advertisement. His Belfast roots still sounded through but he seemed super confident and super relaxed. He obviously had no inkling why they were there.

'Mr Sloan,' Gawn began.

He had been making his way across the room to his desk when she spoke. He froze for an instant. 'Simpson. My name's Simpson.' But the colour had drained from his face. The smile had quickly faded and he looked at them warily.

'Jason Sloan, I'm DCI Girvin and this is DC Hill from the PSNI.'

He continued making his way across the room past them, only more slowly, giving himself time to think, and sat down behind the desk before he spoke again. He looked just like the successful businessman from the advertisement they'd watched. His suit was expensive, probably Italian, Gawn thought. His tie was silk and his shoes, stylish two-tone leather. There was obviously no shortage of money. How did a runaway boy from Belfast with little in the way of qualifications end up with all this?

Albert and Scott had been paid off. Was Jason still benefiting from that night in the Craigantlet Hills?

He ran his fingers through his neatly trimmed hair and licked his lips. Gawn could see he was coming to some sort of decision and when he spoke she knew he was not going to try to keep up his pretence.

'How did you find me?'

'Scott Alexander spotted you at your uncle John's funeral.'

'I knew I shouldn't have gone.' He slammed his fist down hard on the desk. The noise and its unexpectedness made the two women jump. He shook his head. 'I just couldn't stay away.'

'But you managed to stay away from your mother all these years.' Gawn recognised the implied criticism in her statement.

'It was for her own good.' He looked up and saw the look of scepticism on the policewoman's face.

'In the beginning, anyway. I knew they'd be after me.'

'Who?'

'Don't you know?'

When an answer was not immediately forthcoming Sloan began to gain in confidence.

'Why exactly are you here? What do you know?'

'We're here because the PSNI re-opened your missing persons case. To try to find closure for your mother,' Gawn said flatly, trying not to antagonise him or give too much away.

'Oh, I see.'

Gawn realized immediately he thought they didn't know why he had disappeared; didn't know about Karen Houston's murder and his part in it. He was starting to relax. No doubt he'd had some plausible cover story worked out for some occasion just like today if it ever came.

'Scott Alexander is dead.' Gawn watched his face closely as he took in the news.

'How? I mean was he killed?'

'Why would you think that?'

'I don't know. Scott was always a bit outside the law. I just thought maybe he'd crossed somebody or something.'

'When we tell someone that a friend is dead they don't usually jump to the conclusion that they've been murdered, especially when they haven't seen them for years. Did you have a special reason for thinking he might be likely to have crossed someone?'

Silence. Sloan didn't respond.

'Like being an accessory to a murder?'

His head went down. He covered his face with his hands and began to cry. This was not what the two women had expected. They looked at each other and then simply waited until he had composed himself a little. It was Gawn who spoke first.

'You obviously feel bad about what happened, Jason. It really helped Scott to get it all off his chest.'

'And look how he ended up – dead.'

'But he wasn't killed, Jason. Scott had been ill. He died of natural causes but he spoke to us before he died. He wanted people to know what had happened to Karen Houston.'

Sloan's head came up slowly and his eyes met Gawn's.

'I didn't even know her name until weeks later. I came across an old newspaper, wrapped round my fish and chips of all things, with an article about her in it. I recognised her picture. Just. She hadn't looked exactly like that when I saw her.'

'Before we go any further, I must warn you that we are investigating the murder of Karen Houston.' As Gawn spoke she was aware of Hill glancing across at her in surprise. 'You do not have to say anything, but it may harm your defence if you do not mention, when questioned, something which you later rely on in court. Do you understand, Jason?'

He only nodded, didn't speak. Hill had taken a mini recorder from her bag. It wasn't ideal. They hadn't really anticipated that Jason would crack so easily. They had expected he might deny everything, bluster a bit and then agree to come back for questioning. Instead, he seemed to just cave in completely. He was like Scott, thought Gawn, he wanted to get this off his conscience.

'Do you want a solicitor present? We can arrange it, if you can't afford one.' There was little chance of that, she thought to herself.

'No. Let's get it all out in the open. I've been living with this secret long enough.' He settled back in his seat. He had a lot to say.

Chapter 28

'Why don't you tell us what happened that night, in your own words?'

All the fight seemed to have gone out of the man. He had shrunk down into his seat and when he started talking it seemed, like Scott, that he was relieved to be able to admit what had happened.

'It started out just an ordinary night. Like any other Saturday. Then Sam came round and told us there was going to be another party and we were being invited again.' He paused and looked up. 'You know about Sam?'

'Big Sam, yes.'

'OK, we decided to go down to the Starlit just to pass the time before the party. We knew we'd be picked up about midnight.'

'Sam arranged that too?'

'Yes.'

'Always the same driver?' Hill asked.

Gawn held her breath until Jason had answered.

'No. Mostly Sam drove us himself but if he had some other business on hand he'd arrange for someone else to do it.'

'And that night it was…?' Gawn waited for him to finish the sentence. She knew what his answer was going to be, of course.

'That night it was Jake the Geek. He lived across the street from me. Square eyes. Studied all the time. I don't know how Sam thought of him. I suppose he had a driving licence so that was all he needed in case we were stopped on the way there by the polis.'

Gawn let out her breath slowly.

'How did he know where to take you?'

'He didn't. Albert directed him. Jake was dead slow, trying to find the right turning. He was so bloody nervous. But he got us there in one piece.'

'He didn't go in?' For Gawn, this was the crucial question. She saw Hill glance across at her surprised, no doubt wondering why the DCI seemed so focused on the driver.

'To the party?'

'Yes.'

'No. He… actually I don't know where he went. Home, I suppose. He didn't come into the party, anyway. That would have blown his mind. I remember Scotty inviting him in for a laugh. We told him we could get him in. He was almost pissing his pants at the thought. The wee geek didn't even smoke, never mind do drugs, and he wouldn't have known what to do with a girl.' He laughed at the thought.

Well, he certainly does now, Gawn thought to herself.

'So what happened at the party, Jason?' she asked, keen now to hear no more about Seb. It seemed he was as innocent as he had claimed and hearing this had only made her feel guilty for how she'd treated him.

'Just the usual at first. Do you want all the graphic details?'

'Eventually, yes, but maybe not all just now. That can come later. Cut to when you saw Karen Houston,' Gawn suggested.

'I didn't see her at all at first. We'd probably been there a couple of hours. My stomach was a bit gippy. I'd ended up spending a lot of the night in the bog. It meant I wasn't as off my face as the others were. About three o'clock there was a bit of a panic. There were loud voices upstairs. Some of the big men, "the jury" they called themselves, were arguing. Then one of them came running down and grabbed me and Albert and told us to help carry something out to a car. It was heavy. I don't think we realised right away it was a body. Well, I didn't anyway. It was wrapped up. We were told to put it in the boot of the car and then to get in the back. We drove–'

Gawn interrupted him, 'Who drove?'

'The judge. I don't know his real name. I didn't know it then either. I didn't want to. You didn't want to be called to his room. He liked boys as well as girls and he liked to be rough too. He drove us out into the countryside. I've no idea where. I didn't know that area and it was pitch black. He stopped and told us to take the thing out of the boot.' Jason hesitated and the two women just waited. Eventually he continued. 'It was only then I realised it was a body. Her arm came out of the wrapping. I saw it and I let go and she dropped on the ground. I'd been taking most of the weight because Albert was bloody useless. When she hit the ground more of the curtain she'd been wrapped up in came loose. The moon had come out and you could see her face in the moonlight. Christ, I'll never forget it.'

'This is very important, Jason, was she still alive?'

He didn't answer straightaway. She was sure he must have thought of this over the years and also about the implications of admitting she was still alive and she could have been saved if he'd done something.

'I don't think so. I mean I don't really know. But there was no sign of life. Nothing obvious. She wasn't moving or making any noise. She didn't cry out when we dropped her.'

'Then what, Jason?' asked Hill.

'The judge got back into the car. The engine was still running. Albert jumped in the back. I was just about to get in when he drove the car over her. Then he reversed and did it again. I was still standing outside, and he looked at me and yelled at me to get in. I was frozen to the spot. I couldn't move. Then I saw his eyes. I'll never forget them either.' He looked up at Gawn and Hill and they could see the fear on his face. 'He was crazy, mad, scary. No way was I getting into the car with him. I ran away into the woods and I kept running until I couldn't run anymore.'

'How did you get away?'

'I walked all night. Miles and miles. I didn't have a clue where I was going. I ended up somewhere near Lisburn, I think. I was shattered. I slept in a ditch during that day and then the next evening I hitched with a French lorry driver heading over the border to catch the ferry to Roscoff. He took me as far as Dublin. I stayed there for a couple of weeks sleeping rough and doing odd jobs until I could get a bit of money together and then I got the boat over to Wales.'

The original investigation had failed to get any sightings of Jason and it was clear now why. The driver would have been back in France before Jason was reported missing. He would never even have realised he had picked up a missing person. By the time he might have been back in Ireland, if he ever was, it would have been old news.

'And you ended up in Scotland?'

'Eventually, yes. I changed my name and got a job with Riverside Motors. I married the boss's daughter and now it's all mine.' He smiled, a weak smile, and waved his hand around the room in a proprietorial gesture.

'And you never contacted your mother?'

'I wanted her left well out of it. I contacted Sam and told him as long as my mother was OK I would keep quiet about what had happened. If she got any grief, if she had a sudden accident or whatever, I'd spill the beans. And I got him to arrange a wee bit of regular money for her to help her out. He went round and spun her some sob story about the boys having a whip-round for her and then Jock told her he'd arranged some kind of benefit payment for her. Mum never had much of a business head. She wouldn't have questioned it. Just been glad of the help.'

So Jock Irvine had been in it up to his neck.

'It's twenty years ago now, Jason. Surely you could have gone back. Most of the men must be dead.'

'Most of them. But not all. Some of them weren't that much older than us. The old boys would be gone but there's still some of the jury out there and they're still powerful people. I'm sure.'

'And you can identify them?' Gawn asked.

'I think I need a lawyer now.'

Chapter 29

They had contacted the local police then. The Chief Superintendent was outraged at first that they had been investigating without having the courtesy to let their Scottish counterparts know. Gawn had apologised and done quite a lot of grovelling and eventually he had sent two of his officers to bring Jason in. She wasn't sure what he would be charged with yet, if anything. It wasn't a crime to run away and make a new life for yourself. Whether he would repeat what he had told them about his part in Karen Houston's murder or if their recording would be permissible as evidence she didn't know. That would be someone else's problem. She presumed he would be brought over to Belfast so at least his mother would get to see him again.

By the time they had finished with Jason at the dealership and he had been taken away to a local police station, to be held until a request to get him back to Belfast for further questioning could be processed, they had missed their flight home. They managed to get two rooms in a budget hotel near the city centre and had a late meal together in a noisy pizza restaurant round the corner. More calories, Gawn thought to herself ruefully. Once they had parted and Gawn was sitting on her bed, shoes cast aside, massaging her toes, she phoned Norman Smyth. It rang twice before he answered.

'Smyth.'

'It's Gawn, sir.'

'Good to hear from you. Do you have some news for me?'

'Yes.' She launched into a recital of what they had learned from Jason so far. Although he didn't stop her or ask any questions, at several points she heard him sucking in his breath sharply.

'That poor girl and her family.'

'Yes, sir. We'll be able to close the misper case and Mrs Sloan will know what happened to her son. But I take it you'll be re-opening Karen Houston's murder investigation now.'

'I think you've already managed to do that all by yourself, my dear, don't you? And, that being so, I think you should see it through. This all seems to point to very serious criminal activity, sexual assaults, drugs, murder, perverting the course of justice. And it's all about people at the highest echelons of our society. This PC, Irvine, was it? He seems to have been in it up to his neck. That could suggest some police collusion too. You have opened one almighty can of worms, Gawn, my dear. How would you feel about moving back to Serious Crimes and your old team and seeing it through?'

Talk about poisoned chalices, she thought to herself. She hesitated, but only for a moment. She realised this had probably been Smyth's plan all along. He had had his suspicions about Karen Houston's murder right from the start. But the truth was, she had enjoyed the last few days. She felt she was getting back at least part of the way to her old self. And she was angry. Angry at what had happened to an innocent young woman and, although she had no reason to suspect other deaths, there were obviously a lot of other young women and some men too traumatised by their experiences at the hands of this judge and jury.

A fleeting thought crossed her mind and it was on the tip of her tongue to tell Smyth about the details of Seb's involvement. She should probably recuse herself from the investigation. But she couldn't. Not when she had come so far. Not when she had looked Valerie Houston in the eye and promised she would follow up anything she found. She was sure now Seb had been telling her the truth. He had had no part in any of it other than innocently driving the others to the house. She said nothing. She would keep Seb out of it.

'Only if I can take DC Hill and Sergeant Pepper with me.' She waited for his response. It came right away.

'If you want them, you've got them. But tread lightly, Gawn. Sloan is probably right. There could well be some of these people still about in very high places.'

'Will do, sir.'

'Come to my office in the morning and we'll discuss it.'

'I'm still in Edinburgh at the minute.'

'Then let's say, noon tomorrow. That should give you time to get back. There's someone I want you to meet.'

With that cryptic comment he was gone. It was late, after eleven, but she didn't feel particularly tired. In fact she could feel the adrenaline pumping through her like the old days when she was in the thick of the chase. What she would give just to be able to lift the phone again and speak to Seb now. Just for a few minutes.

Chapter 30

They got seats on the 8am flight to Belfast so it had been an early start, a greasy breakfast at the airport and a rush home to shower and change before heading to Police HQ opposite the hospice. Gawn glanced across at that building with its fundraising sign outside as she waited at the barrier to drive into the police compound. It was really Scott who had started all this by spotting his old friend and making a casual comment to Louise Sloan. They had him to thank for finding Jason. Gawn speculated if the woman would be happy to see her son when she found out what he had done. She imagined that a mother could forgive her child most things. She thought of Angela York and how she protected her son. But would Louise Sloan forgive Jason for leaving her in limbo for twenty years not knowing if he were dead or alive? He might say it was to protect her but would she see it that way? Would she have preferred to take her chances and know that Jason was alive and well? He had built a new life in Scotland with a wife and two sons of his own. He had his business, a beautiful home and a position of respectability among the Edinburgh business community. Meanwhile she had lived with the nagging doubt always at the back of her mind that he had died that night, becoming one of 'the disappeared'.

Gawn made her way to Smyth's office with some trepidation. She had spent some of the time on the flight thinking who he might want her to meet. She wondered if he intended to introduce a superintendent into the team to work alongside her but really to oversee it and her. Might he still have a nagging doubt, as she knew some of the other senior officers did, about her ability to run an investigation, her willingness to follow orders and her tendency to rush in to get things done? The Houston murder would require patience and diplomacy as well as tenacity, skill and luck.

She knocked.

'Come in.'

Gawn walked into the room and was immediately aware that there was someone else there as well as Smyth. The man had his back to her. As she turned back from closing the door behind her, he rose and turned to face her. It was Paul Maxwell.

'Obviously no introductions are required.' Smyth smiled.

'Ma'am.' Paul nodded his head in greeting.

'Inspector, I didn't expect to see you here.' She wasn't quite sure what his presence meant.

'Sit down, Chief Inspector,' Smyth said.

Gawn sat and then Paul sat back down too.

'Paul here has been brought to my attention. His superiors are very impressed with his work. What I want to suggest is that if you come back to Serious Crimes, if you feel you're sufficiently recovered, then Paul moves across as your number two. How would you feel about that?'

She took a moment before replying.

'Paul has the experience and we've worked together before of course. I think it would be a good idea.' She didn't want to come across as too enthusiastic. Secretly she was delighted. She knew him, she knew his work and she trusted him. Whether he still trusted her and her judgement after what had happened during her last case was another question.

'We've already spoken about the possibility and he's keen to make the move. Aren't you, Paul?'

'Yes, sir.'

'Now all that remains is for you to decide if you're ready.'

Then Smyth sat back in his chair, steepled his fingers and waited for her answer. Seconds passed. Was she ready? If she wasn't ready now, then she feared she never would be. If she didn't come back to Serious Crimes now, she might as well resign for she wouldn't be accepting some desk job making up the numbers until she could take early retirement.

'I'm ready, sir.'

'Good. Then I suggest the pair of you go out to lunch. You get Paul caught up on all that's happened so far. Then take a day to get yourself sorted and for the folk here to set up your office and get the paperwork done for your return to duty and then you can meet up with your team on Friday and take it from there. But, Gawn, I want regular updates. I don't want any charging in half-cocked at any of these people.'

'Understood, sir.'

Chapter 31

Lunch was a strange affair. She'd only spoken to Maxwell briefly when she got back to the office on Thursday morning, less than a week ago. He had seemed happy enough to see her. Before then it had been at the very start of her last case when a body had been found on a plane at City Airport. That seemed like a lifetime ago now. So much had happened since then.

They had travelled in separate cars to a popular brasserie on the corner of North Road, a busy intersection not too far away from HQ. The lunchtime rush was nearly over and getting a table was easy even without a booking.

'Like old times, ma'am.' Maxwell smiled at her.

'I think we can dispense with the ma'am, don't you? At least when we're alone.'

He looked at her directly, maintaining eye contact as he asked, 'What do you really think of Smyth bringing me in, Gawn?'

'I'm delighted of course. Why wouldn't I be? You're a good detective. I trained you myself.' She laughed and he joined in.

'How are you? It must have been pretty rough with Harris and everything. He seemed like a good bloke that time I met him.'

She took a moment before she answered.

'He was. I'm doing alright. Now. But it was tough there for a while.'

'And how's Seb? Still dating?' He smiled as he asked, a little private joke where Seb had claimed to be dating the Chief Inspector to get Maxwell to help him look for her.

'No. We've split up.' It was the first time she had said it out loud. Not that she discussed her private life very often and very few of her colleagues would even be aware of any man in her life. But to vocalise it was to make it real and she didn't want it to be real. She had realized that now, when it was too late.

'I'm really sorry to hear that, Gawn. He seemed like…' He paused to think of how he would describe the man they had once suspected of being a serial killer. 'He was good for you.'

'He was. We were good together. Very good. But I've come to realise I'm high-maintenance, Paul. I can't expect any man to put up with me.' Changing the subject abruptly, she asked, 'How will Kerri feel about you coming on to the team again?' His wife had always railed against the hours he had to work and the demands Gawn made on him.

'We've already discussed it. The ACC spoke to me last week about the possible move, asked me to consider it.'

Gawn was stunned at this revelation. This had all been part of Smyth's plan to get her back to work.

'Kerri and I talked it through. She knows my heart has never been in uniform. When it comes down to it, if I'm happy, she's happy and vice versa of course. She's happy with the extra money I'm earning now. We've moved house. We've got a nice detached one with four bedrooms so room for the in-laws to come and stay.' He laughed at the thought and pulled a face. 'She'll complain but we'll be OK. We always are.'

Gawn felt they had both done enough soul baring and sharing, more than in all the time he had been her sergeant. Time to bring him up to speed on what they knew so far. Keeping her voice low, she told him the bare outline of how they had tracked down Jason Sloan and what they had found out about the parties and Karen Houston's death. It didn't seem to be a surprise to him and she realised Smyth must have already spoken to him about it.

'God. You don't know what's going on behind closed doors, do you? Sometimes, when I'm tucking Molly in at night, I think about all the things she'll have to face growing up. I don't know how I'll cope when she's old enough to want to go out clubbing.'

By the time she had got to the end of her update, they had finished their meal. They paid the bill, Gawn insisting on paying as a celebration of their working together again, and were just leaving when the door to the street opened and an attractive blonde walked in followed by Sebastian York. He didn't notice them at first, too intent on helping the woman out of her coat. When he looked round and spotted first Maxwell and then Gawn standing behind him, a shadow fell across his face for an instant.

'Maxwell, how are you? Gawn.' He smiled at her. She could feel her face flushing and hoped he wasn't going to introduce them to the latest bimbo he had taken up with. Then she corrected herself. The woman looked perfectly respectable, an attractive woman of about her own age, not a fawnish student type he might be out to impress. But he didn't say anything else. He merely nodded and placing his hand on the woman's arm guided her past them to a table near the back of the restaurant. Gawn caught a whiff of his aftershave as he passed. Such a familiar aroma to her.

'Shall we?' Maxwell asked, nodding towards the door. They left.

It was only with the greatest of difficulty she didn't turn back to get another look at Seb where he sat in a corner with his estate agent. If she had, she would have seen his eyes follow her sadly as she walked away.

Chapter 32

They parted and drove back separately to the station, Maxwell back to his desk to start clearing it out for the move and Gawn to break the news to Hill and Pepper. She wondered how they would take the offer to join her at Serious Crimes. She suspected the young woman would be excited; up for the challenge. Gawn knew she was ambitious, and her career had been on an upward trajectory until it got derailed by her complaint about sexual harassment. It might well be upheld, Gawn thought it probably would be, but it would leave a mark and some would not be keen to work with her again. Pepper she was not so sure about. His injury didn't impinge on his work in the office, his mind was still sharp, and he had good investigative instincts in the interview room but there would be things he couldn't do, times when he was prevented from taking a full active part. That didn't worry her. In a team you needed all kinds of skills and not everyone had to be the one rushing into the burning building or confronting thugs head on. But she worried that he would feel a lesser part of the team and measure himself against some of the others. It might be the easier option for him to turn the offer down. She hoped not.

She had deliberately driven more slowly than usual so that Maxwell would be safely back in his own office before she arrived. She didn't want them seen walking in together. She was surprised when she opened the door to see Hill and Pepper sitting over cups of tea with a blank whiteboard behind them and their desks cleared of all paper. What was going on?

'Cup of coffee, ma'am.'

'Yes. Thanks, Jo. What's happening?'

'We tidied everything away for the move. We've found Jason so we reckoned you'd be moving back to Serious Crimes to re-open the Houston murder.'

Either they were very good detectives, almost psychic, or something had leaked.

'What have you heard?'

'Some of the PCs were talking in the canteen. They mentioned that they'd be able to get their store cupboards back again tomorrow so we put two and two together.'

'I see. And where do you think you're going?'

'I would imagine back from whence we came,' Pepper said in his more pedantic way, 'back to shuffling paper.'

'Like hell you are. You're both much too good to be wasting your time doing work a sixteen-year-old straight out of school could do.' She paused a moment. She thought she had detected a glimmer of excitement in Hill's eye. 'How would you feel about coming to Serious Crimes?'

She had been looking directly at Jo Hill as she spoke and the young woman responded instantly.

'Seriously, ma'am?'

'I don't joke about things like that.'

'Yes. Yes, please.'

It was like Christmas morning round the tree, thought Gawn. Then she turned to Pepper. 'And what about you, Walter? What do you think? Would that be something you'd be interested in doing?'

From his expression she could see that he had thought the offer only extended to Hill.

'I, eh, I'd need to think about it. I'd need to discuss it with my wife, Mags. She's been quite happy for me to be a desk jockey and keep out of harm's way.' He looked embarrassed that he was having to respond in this way.

'I understand, Walter. Talk it over with her. I'll be at Serious Crimes from Friday. I hope you'll be there too but if you feel you can't then I understand. It's been a pleasure to work with you. You've both done excellent work.' She reached out her hand and shook his.

'Now, where's this coffee?'

Chapter 33

She was drinking too much and she knew it. She had never had a problem with alcohol. Until now. The nights were just too long and too lonely. She'd been alone for so long and that had been alright. That was just her life and she'd accepted it. When Max was killed, she had literally worked her way through her grief, filling her days and nights with work and nothing else until she had collapsed from exhaustion. It was then she'd decided on the move back to Northern Ireland. She had cut herself off from other people, focused only on her work. She didn't even try to make new friends. She didn't want the burden of relationships and caring about another human being and then Sebastian York had walked into her life in the most unexpected way.

That call-out to the body found in the Botanic Gardens and that first meeting in front of the university were etched on her memory. It hadn't made any sense at the time. It still didn't. The spark between them, which she hadn't understood then and didn't completely now, had rocked her world. She had never found equilibrium again. The times together were wonderful. He made her feel alive but it was all too messy, too difficult, too emotionally demanding of her. With him she had to make compromises, she couldn't be the detective she wanted to be, commit herself to the work that had been the centre of her life for so long.

So what now? Was this really what she wanted for herself? To work each day, come home to an empty apartment and drink herself to sleep? All the time wondering what he was doing; who he was with? Maudlin. That's what she was becoming. She'd seen middle-aged burnt-out detectives in the Met like that. Full of regrets. Then she remembered the words of the minister at her father's funeral. 'A life well lived'. That's what he'd said. She didn't think anyone would say that of her.

This morning she woke up, on the sofa. She hadn't made it as far as the bed. But this morning she didn't even have a hangover. She was becoming inured to the wine. That was the scariest part of all.

'What do you look like?' It was Martha. No words of greeting. She chevied her into the bedroom, told her to get herself together and she would make breakfast. It was only as she was standing under the shower, the water playing over her skin, that she suddenly realised it was Thursday. What was Martha even doing here? She didn't come on Thursday, only on Tuesdays and Fridays unless Gawn asked her especially.

When she'd dressed, in her oldest pair of jeans, last season's offering, she skulked back into the lounge. There was no other word for it. She didn't want to face the older woman. Either Martha would be critical of Gawn's life as she had let it deteriorate or she would be overly sympathetic and she didn't want that either.

'You need to get out. Get a bit of fresh air around you,' Martha said, handing her a cup of tea. 'And you drink far too much coffee.'

No one had spoken to her like this since her mother had died.

'Martha, what are you doing here?'

The woman looked a little sheepish. It didn't take any great detecting skills to know she was hiding something.

'I was talking to Sebastian last night...' she started. Gawn had suspected that they kept in touch. He had always been her favourite. 'And he said he might pop down today to collect his things. I offered to box anything up for him but he said he'd do it himself. So I thought you'd either like to be out when he comes or else you'd like the place looking neat and tidy and…' She hesitated before adding, 'And looking a bit better yourself.'

The cheek of the woman and the cheek of the man. Just going to pop down, was he? She remembered he still had his key. So he had been hoping to slip in when she was out and clear all traces of their life together away? He'd prefer to come during the week, during the daytime when he thought she'd be at work and avoid a confrontation.

With a coldness in her voice, Gawn looked Martha in the eye and spoke. 'I will deal with Sebastian, thank you, Martha. I don't need you trying to organise my life. If he pops down, I'll be here and I will see he gets what he needs. You don't need to stay.'

She saw the hurt in the woman's eyes. She knew Martha cared. But the way Gawn felt, she wasn't looking for sympathy or support. Without another word, Martha gathered up her coat and bag and turned to leave. As she was walking out the door, she turned and looked back at Gawn but didn't say anything.

Gawn looked around the room. It was tidy enough. It would do. All it needed was to get the empty wine bottles into the recycling bin and it would be alright. She, herself, was a different matter. She walked quickly into the bedroom and changed into her latest jeans and a new shirt she had bought online just last week. Then she spent the next fifteen minutes applying make-up carefully. She noticed the dark marks under her eyes. Some concealer should deal with that. A splash of lipstick to bring some colour to her face which was looking a bit pasty. Now she could face him. She thought she could pull it off. No way did she want him to realise how much their split was affecting her.

She sat and waited. And waited. She cursed that she had no window overlooking the roadway where she could watch out for his car. Her view was only over the marina. So she continued waiting. He mightn't come at all if Martha had phoned him. Then she heard a gentle knock on her door. It had to be him. He knew the code to gain entry from the street but he hadn't used his key to get in.

She stood facing her front door and watched her own hand reach out to open it as if it belonged to someone else. Then he was there. Right in front of her. Only not alone. A small boy stood clinging tightly to his hand and looking shyly at her.

'Hi Gawn. This is Murphy. His school has an exceptional closure day today, his dad's working and Helen had to take Charley to a ballet competition so I drew the short straw and have to babysit.'

'Uncle Seb!' The boy's high-pitched voice rebuked him.

'Sorry. You don't need a babysitter, do you, buddy? You are my right-hand man today.' He gave the boy a high five and mouthed 'sorry' to Gawn. 'May we come in?' She had been so surprised at his appearance, with a child in tow, that they were all still standing in the doorway.

'Of course. Sorry. Come in. Pleased to meet you, Murphy.'

The boy just smiled shyly at her, his big brown eyes, pools of excitement.

'Look, Gawn has a view of all the boats. You can see them in the harbour.'

The boy skipped across the room and stepped out onto the balcony.

'Watch you don't fall. No climbing. Do you want a drink, McMurphy, my man?' Seb asked.

'I don't think I have any suitable drinks,' Gawn mumbled.

'No problem.' He withdrew a purple plastic bottle from his pocket. 'Juice, Murph? Do you want your game thingy?'

'It's not a thingy.'

'Well, whatever, do you want to play one of your games?'

'Yes, please, Uncle Seb.'

Seb handed it over and the boy rushed to the sofa, threw himself down on it and began playing. They were left facing each other. There was an awkward silence. Seb broke it.

'I hope you don't mind me coming. It's just it made sense when I was packing everything up to get my stuff from here too so it could all go into storage together.'

Was he finally going to tell her he was selling his house?

'Of course, go ahead. I'll make some coffee.'

It only took him a few minutes to gather everything together into two M&S plastic carrier bags he had brought with him. Not much to show for the months they had spent together. But he stayed in the bedroom just looking around, lifting her hairbrush and setting it down again, running his hand along the dark wood of the dressing table and sitting on her side of the bed. He lifted her pillow and held it to his face to smell her perfume, then hastily set it down again. He was taking too long and she might walk in at any minute. He didn't want her to think he had turned into some kind of perv or stalker. He picked up the bags and walked out of the room. Gawn and Murphy were sitting side by side, heads close together, giggling on the sofa. The boy let out a yell of triumph.

'Gawn's shot a real gun, in the army, Uncle Seb. She got the highest score on my game.' His voice was full of excitement and his eyes were sparkling.

'Don't go telling your mother that,' Seb said, half seriously.

Gawn stood up, it seemed reluctantly.

'The coffee's ready.' She walked past him and poured two cups handing one to him.

He sat down on one of the high stools at the countertop facing her.

'How are you really?'

What was she supposed to say? Falling apart? A wreck? 'I'm fine. Busy as usual.'

'Did you ever find out what Jason and the others were doing at that house?' he asked but she felt it was more to make conversation than any real interest in the case.

'I can't discuss an on-going case.'

'Of course not. Sorry.'

He took a deep drink of the coffee and set the cup down.

'Well, I guess we'd better go.'

'Do we have to, Uncle Seb? Can't Gawn play another game?' Murphy pleaded.

'Gawn's much too busy to be playing games. At least not the type you play.'

She had noticed the look of disappointment on the boy's face and heard the note of bitterness in Seb's voice. She wondered what he'd meant.

'I think I could manage one more. Why not let Uncle Seb try first and then we'll see if I can beat him?'

'Please, Uncle Seb? Please?'

He couldn't resist the challenge. Of course, he was rubbish at it, deliberately so, not even matching Murphy's score. He watched Gawn's face closely as she concentrated on the screen. He knew every line on that face, the little crinkle creases at the sides of her eyes, the way she held her mouth when she was concentrating on something. At one point her tongue had peeked out from the corner of her mouth as she had focused on hitting the targets and his heart had done a somersault.

'Wow!' Murphy jumped up and down with excitement then threw his arms around Gawn's neck. 'Brilliant. You're the best! Top Gun! Wait till I tell my friends at school. Can we go for ice cream now, Uncle Seb? There's a fantastic ice cream shop just along the road, Gawn. You could come with us. Couldn't she, Uncle Seb?'

'If she likes.'

Gawn wondered how Murphy knew about the ice cream parlour in the Scotch Quarter. When had he been there before?

Chapter 34

They walked in line abreast, Murphy in the middle, along the Marine Highway. Gawn felt she was caught in some sort of video game of happy families especially when the little boy took her hand and then Seb's so the three were linked. Traffic whizzed past heading to Belfast. The car park in front of the library was nearly full with vehicles and food stalls from the Thursday market, and groups of tourists were making their way up the slope to the heavy wooden gates which guarded entry to the castle, stopping for the obligatory photo opportunity at the portcullis. Everything was so normal and yet so surreal for her.

Soon they approached the noisy playground. It was busy today. Kids, mostly younger, the older ones in school, swarmed over a large wooden replica pirate ship. Happy screams and shouts echoed across the open space.

'Want to go to the Pirate Ship Park?'

'Ice cream first, then park. You know how we do it, Uncle Seb.'

'You've been here before?' Gawn asked turning a quizzical look at Seb.

'A few times.' He was giving nothing away.

They joined a queue of mostly women with prams and excited children, which snaked its way out of the door of the ice cream café and onto the pavement outside. Murphy was hopping from foot to foot as he waited impatiently for his turn. He kept glancing at the glass-fronted counters with their enticing colourful ice creams laid out in rows. Before too long, they reached the top of the queue and he chose a cone of honeycomb ice cream covered in pink and white marshmallow pieces.

'What are you having, Gawn?' he asked as he licked the ice cream leaving a trail of white across his upper lip like a creamy moustache.

'I'm fine, thank you, Murphy. I don't need any.'

'Murphy doesn't need any either,' Seb said. 'But sometimes there's a difference between what you want and what you need.'

It was a strange thing to say and Gawn was uncertain what Seb was trying to tell her.

They sat in silence on a low stone wall outside the shop and watched the sea as Murphy licked his way through the ice cream savouring the sweetness, blissfully unaware that some of it was escaping down the front of his jumper.

'Your mother will have my life,' Seb mock-scolded as he wiped the boy's jumper.

One of the ferry boats to Scotland was making its way down the lough as they sat waiting for him to finish.

'Uncle Seb's gonna take me on a big boat to Scotland someday. Aren't you?' the boy declared to Gawn before seeking agreement from his uncle.

'You bet, buddy. Ready for the park now?'

Seb took a paper hankie out of his pocket and wiped Murphy's mouth. Then the little boy ran ahead while the two adults followed along behind him. They found an empty bench near the swings and sat down keeping a distance between them. From here they could see the whole park and keep an eye on Murphy as he moved from swings to slides and finally to the pirate ship. He climbed up to the deck and stood waving to them from the very top.

'The innocence of youth, eh? His biggest worry is whether his mother will let him stay up to watch his favourite cartoon tonight.'

'You're in a very strange frame of mind,' she remarked.

'Am I? I suppose I am. You never get that simplicity back. Life just gets more and more bloody complicated. If Murphy wants something he asks until he gets it. If he likes something, he'll say so. Not hide behind subterfuge and play games to convince himself he doesn't really like it at all.'

Gawn was about to challenge him to explain what he meant when their conversation was interrupted by a wailing Murphy propelling himself across to where they were sitting and flinging himself into Gawn's arms. The tears were streaming down his face. She looked down and saw his knees were cut and bleeding, a little rivulet of red trickling down to meet the top of his sock.

'Hey, wee man. You're OK. We'll make it better. It'll be alright, Murphy. You have to be a brave soldier. We'll patch you up. OK?' She held him tightly and rocked him gently back and forth stroking his hair until his sobs had subsided. It reminded her of how Seb had held her so many nights when she had been racked with sobs too.

Seb's face had first shown concern but when he realised the boy's injuries were not too bad he had relaxed and marvelled as Gawn comforted his nephew.

'I have antiseptic and plasters back at the apartment,' she said.

Seb picked the little figure up out of her arms and carried him back, Gawn striding along beside him.

Ten minutes later, Murphy was lying on the sofa. Gawn had cleaned his cuts. He had been very brave. It had stung but she had talked to him and told him of some of her adventures in the army like having to jump out of a plane in the desert and he had been so enthralled he had hardly noticed. Now he had his game and a biscuit from a packet Martha had left.

'Thanks,' Seb said.

'Just returning the compliment for what you did for me.' She smiled.

'I'll never forget that night.'

'Me neither.'

'That was the first time I realised I loved you.' He spoke softly, no drama, no bitterness. Gawn was very aware of the little boy sitting just a few feet away. She was stunned into silence. She didn't know what he expected her to say.

The silence grew between them like a barrier until she almost felt she could have reached out and touched it. She looked up and straightened her back. He had said Murphy would ask for what he wanted. She wanted to know where Seb was going.

'When were you going to tell me you're moving?'

'It's not a secret. I've had the house up for sale for a while. But I only accepted an offer yesterday. I'll be signing the final contract in a couple of weeks.'

'And then what?'

'They want me in LA.' He must have recognised the shock his answer had given her even though she had tried to disguise it. She had never thought of him moving out of the country, moving to the other side of the world. 'You know, I've sold the rights to my book to a production company. They'd like me to be involved in the development of the script.'

'And that would mean living there?'

'It would be a full-time job until the series was made. And then who knows what happens if one of the major networks picks it up? It gets renewed and so it goes.'

'I see. That's a great opportunity for you.'

'Yes.' He didn't sound exactly like someone who had had marvellous news and was excited about it. Quite the opposite. 'I better get this wee man home to his mother. Come on, buddy. Time to go.'

Murphy stood up reluctantly. 'Can we come back... next time we're in Carrick?'

'Maybe, buddy. We'll see.'

'Bye, Gawn. Thank you for the biscuit.'

'You're very welcome, Murphy–'

Before she could finish her sentence, he had reached out and flung his arms around her and given her a hug. 'Bye. Aren't you going to give Gawn a hug too, Uncle Seb?'

Seb allowed a slight smile to play on his lips. Gawn wasn't sure how to interpret it. He stepped forward and gave her a quick kiss on the cheek.

'Bye, Gawn.'

'Goodbye.'

Seb took Murphy's hand and the two bags and walked out of the door and out of her life.

Chapter 35

As she walked up the so-familiar corridor, she felt butterflies in her stomach. The last time she had done this, she would have opened the door and seen Michael Harris sitting at his desk or standing chatting with Jamie Grant or Erin McKeown or one of the others over a cuppa. Not today. Today the old team would be there minus Harris.

Maxwell would be there organizing everything for her arrival. She expected Hill to have found herself a niche already but she wasn't sure if Pepper would have convinced his wife that he should work for her. She felt her hands sweaty and for one second a bit lightheaded. She paused and practised the deep breathing exercises she had been taught years ago in rehabilitation. They seemed to work, well enough anyway for her to move off again and walk up to the door. Head up, she walked in.

Every face seemed to be turned in her direction. Then just as quickly they looked away.

'Morning, ma'am.' It was Grant, a beaming smile on his face.

They were all glad to see her back. Of course, they would never say so. Her temporary replacement had had his own way of doing things. Better the devil you know.

'Morning.'

She spotted Maxwell in her inner office and walked across.

'Morning. I'm just wondering how you want to work this,' he said. 'They've allocated you an office next door. I'm supposed to be in here but I didn't know how you would feel about that.'

He knew her well. He knew she wouldn't want that disconnect. She would want to be where she could see them, and they could see her; to be part of the team.

'I think we could just about fit two desks in here at a pinch or I could work in the outer office.'

It was a generous offer. He was an inspector now. He was entitled to the benefits his rank brought with it.

'Let's not rock any boats changing things around. I don't spend that much time in my office and, when I do, it might be nice to have a quiet little hidey-hole and not see all the shenanigans that that lot can get up to.'

'Are you sure?'

'Absolutely.'

Truth was, she was not sure about a lot of things, but she would give it a go and see how it went. Everything was changing in her life. She walked out and made it as far as the door before she almost collided with Pepper. He looked at her sheepishly.

'Good morning, ma'am. I had a bit of bother with my pass.'

'Don't worry. Just glad to see you, Walter. Paul, you've met Walter Pepper. I think he should be somewhere near Erin. They'll work well together.' Erin McKeown was their research and computer specialist who liked nothing better than collating and organising all their information.

'OK. I'll sort it.'

Gawn was about to hurry on when Pepper spoke.

'I forgot to tell you, ma'am, but I tracked down Paul Esdale.'

'Where is he? Can we question him?'

'I'm afraid not. He's a resident of Roselawn.' Gawn recognized where he meant, a place which held such sad memories for her. It was at Roselawn Cemetery she had stood and watched Michael Harris' coffin placed into the ground. 'He died three years ago.'

'Thanks anyway, Walter.'

Another dead end.

She left Pepper and Maxwell to get seats and desks organised and walked along the corridor to a door marked with her name. She opened it and was pleasantly surprised to see a large office space with not only a desk and comfortable-looking revolving chair, but a seating area with two armchairs and a coffee table. She could picture Maxwell and herself sitting here discussing cases, plotting actions to be taken, going over information learned. Better still, there was a view. Not much, just out over the main road but she could see the passing traffic and in the far distance the hills heading towards Newtownards and Comber. That made her think of Karen Houston. She better get everyone together and bring them up to date on the case. They needed to get started. They were facing a deadline, even if the others didn't know that.

Before she could even set her bag down or hang her coat up, the phone on her new desk rang.

'Girvin.'

'There's a Sebastian York on the phone asking to speak with you, ma'am. He says it's very important and urgent.'

She hadn't expected that. She thought she would never hear from him again and what could be so important and urgent about anything he would have to say to her that he would phone her at work at this time of the day? She could have made an excuse, asked them to take a message, but something made her say, 'Put him through, please.'

'Gawn?' From one word she could hear the anxiety and urgency in his voice.

'Seb, what's wrong?'

'Murphy's missing.'

Chapter 36

First she had to try to calm him down. His words were coming in a rush, jumbled together as he tried to tell her what had happened. She could hear the tremble in his voice. Eventually she managed to make out that his sister, Helen, had called in to see him briefly first thing, on her way to take Murphy to school and that the little boy had been playing in the front garden while they talked. When they had come out of the house, only a few minutes later he assured her, there was no sign of the boy. They had run the length of the street calling his name and out onto the main road but he was nowhere to be seen. Then they had rung 999 and begun calling on Seb's neighbours to find out if they had seen anything; noticed anyone suspicious hanging around. Seb repeated over and over that Murphy wouldn't just wander away. It was his turn to do 'show-and-tell' in school today and he'd been so looking forward to it.

'Are you sure he wasn't worried about having to stand up in front of the whole class and talk?'

'No. No way,' he assured her. 'He'd been practising all last night. He was going to tell them about his new video game and about you playing it. He was really excited about it.'

She couldn't tell him not to worry, that trite advice. It was obvious he was frantic.

'I'll be there as soon as I can.'

'Thank you, Gawn.' She could hear the relief in his voice.

It was easy to say she'd be there but not so easy to see what she could do to help and she wasn't sure how the officers on the scene would react to her rushing to the rescue. When she told Maxwell, he insisted on going with her.

'It'll be my old station dealing with this. It's their district. They'll talk to me; let me know what's going on; what they're thinking.'

'Have you had other child abduction cases like this?'

'There's always the odd report of people in white vans inviting children to get in, enticing them with sweets, but most of them are apocryphal. You know what it's like. Rumours start and mothers are seeing strange cars and strange men all over the place for a day or two and then it dies down again. There are a few on the sex register in the area but we keep a close eye on them, as far as we can with the resources we have.' He paused for a beat and then asked, 'Are they sure it's an abduction?'

'Murphy's a sensible wee boy. I don't think he'd just wander off but Seb didn't say anything about anyone being seen with him.'

'The local guys will be taking it seriously, you can be sure. They always do when there's a kid involved.'

She'd been driving as they talked and now Gawn pulled into Seb's driveway behind a car she didn't recognise but presumed must be Helen's. A PC stood guard at the front of the house but he recognised Maxwell and nodded them past. The front door opened before she was barely halfway out of the car. Seb must have been watching out for her. He was ashen-faced and she could see he was holding himself together. Barely. Trying to be strong for his sister.

'Paul's gone to get me an update on what they have so far.'

He offered a weak smile. He seemed about to reach out to her and then withdrew his hand. 'Thank you. Thank you for coming.' He moved aside to let her pass.

When she walked into the main room Helen was standing there in the centre of the floor with Seb's mother beside her, her arm around her daughter's shoulder. She had met Helen once before when she had mistakenly identified her as Seb's one-night stand. Helen was obviously in bits. Her eyes were red and swollen from crying. Angela York looked at Gawn belligerently. She imagined the woman would somehow blame her for Murphy's disappearance as if any involvement of Gawn with her family could only mean trouble.

'Any word? Have they found him?' Helen asked, distraught.

Gawn walked across to her and placed her hand on the woman's arm in a gesture of support. 'Not yet, I'm afraid, Helen. My inspector's just checking now. Why don't we all sit down and you can tell me exactly what happened this morning?'

'We've already been over everything with the others,' Seb said.

'I know, Seb, but sometimes when you go over it again you remember something, some tiny little detail that didn't mean anything at the time but suddenly you realise it could be significant.'

Just as they were about to sit down, an anxious-looking man, who Gawn realized must be Helen's husband and Murphy's father, burst into the room. Helen took one look at him and flung herself into his arms. Before Seb could introduce his brother-in-law Gawn heard the crackle of a police radio from the hallway. She wondered if they were getting an update for Maxwell and, sure enough, within seconds he had appeared and bent down to whisper in her ear.

'What is it, for God's sake?' asked Seb as his eyes moved from Gawn to Maxwell and back again trying to guess what she was being told.

'Is it bad news?' Helen broke in, her voice cracking.

Gawn saw her body tense waiting to hear the feared news and saw her husband tighten his grip on her hand.

Instead Gawn's face broke into a smile and they all knew then. The fraught atmosphere in the room evaporated instantly as she spoke.

'He's been found… at the fast-food restaurant opposite the hospital. Safe and sound.'

'Thank God. Thank God.' Helen turned and hid her face in her husband's shoulder. Her body shook as she shed tears of joy and relief.

Seb's mother turned her head away hiding the tears she now felt free to shed; now that she no longer needed to be strong for her children.

'When can we see him?' Helen's husband asked, his arm around both his wife and his mother-in-law now.

'It's not really my call. It's not my case but I would imagine you should be able to see him straightaway. Do you know where they've taken him, Paul?'

Maxwell glanced at the quartet of anxious adults and then bent down to whisper in her ear. Gawn was surprised that he had not just spoken aloud but when she heard what he had to say she realised why.

'Where?' Seb asked.

'He's at the special suite of rooms we have for sexual offences and offences involving children.' She saw the look of horror on the faces of all four and quickly added, 'It doesn't mean that he was assaulted. It's just that it's a more child-friendly environment for an interview and they have specially trained officers there who'll deal with him. Please don't assume the worst.'

'I want to be with him,' Helen stood up and announced firmly.

'Of course you do. Paul, can you arrange to get them over?'

'Of course. Come with me.' Maxwell turned to lead the way out of the room.

The relieved parents smiled at Gawn as they left.

'Thank you,' Angela York said softly as she passed her.

Seb began, 'Thank you. I don't know—'

She broke into what he was saying, not allowing him to finish. 'Go on. Go to Murphy. He'll want to see his uncle Seb.' She had wanted to hug him as David and Helen had drawn comfort and support from each other but she knew if she did she would end up crying too and that wouldn't help anyone.

It was only when they had all exited the room and she was alone that she allowed herself to suck in a deep breath and slump down on the arm of the sofa. She knew they had been very lucky. Incredibly lucky. Cases of missing children, abductions, didn't always end so quickly or so happily. She thought of Louise Sloan who had waited twenty years to find out what had happened to her son, and thanked a loving God she remembered vaguely from her childhood days at Sunday school for bringing Murphy back safely to his family. But she couldn't help wondering why the boy had been snatched and then abandoned again so quickly. Had the kidnappers been scared off in some way? It was strange. She filed these thoughts away at the back of her mind.

Chapter 37

She had gone straight back to her office and was trying to get her paperwork into some kind of order for the briefing when her phone rang again. She sighed. Was she never going to get speaking to the team so they could start on Karen Houston's murder investigation? The girl had been killed twenty years ago so another few hours wouldn't matter but she didn't want any more interruptions.

'Gawn, it's Paul. They want you to come down and interview Murphy.'

'Why me?'

'Apparently he likes you. They think he might talk to you. They're not having much luck.' She heard the chuckle in his voice. 'Who knew you were a hit with kids? If I'd known that I'd have asked you to babysit years ago.'

'Don't push your luck, Inspector.'

She had never had to interview a child before and had little experience of cases involving children or of child abduction. She felt woefully ill-prepared to deal with this little boy and she didn't want to let him or his family down.

She made her way to the interview suite to be greeted by a young woman.

'DS Gates, ma'am. We've tried to question Murphy but he's not very forthcoming. We can hardly get a word out of him and his mother won't consent to a doctor examining him. She says she doesn't want him traumatized any more than he already is. Inspector Maxwell suggested maybe you would have a better chance of getting him to speak.'

So she had Maxwell to thank for this. She pushed open the double swing doors and saw Seb, his mother and Murphy's father all sitting in silence on a row of hard plastic chairs outside the interview room. They had been staring straight ahead into space each with their own private thoughts and fears. Seb stood up as soon as he saw her and turned expectantly towards her.

'Has something happened? Is there news?'

'I've been asked to talk to Murphy.' She included everyone in what she was saying. 'I'll be as gentle as I can. Helen will be there all the time. We don't want it to be any more traumatic for him than it has to be. Hopefully, you'll be able to take him home very soon.'

She didn't wait for a response but walked past them. When she entered the room she saw Helen and her son, looking tinier and more vulnerable than she remembered, sitting on a sofa facing the door. The boy was on his mother's knee and from the way she was holding his hand and arm it looked like Helen never intended to let him go again. A young policewoman was in the room too.

'It's OK. You can leave us to it.' She waited until the PC had left and then said, 'Hi, Murphy. I didn't think I was going to be seeing you again so soon. How are you doing, buddy?' She smiled and moved closer. She had hunkered down in front of him as she spoke so she was at his eye level. 'Would it be OK if I sat down beside you?' He didn't say anything but nodded. 'Great.' She slipped in gently beside him, careful not to get too close. 'I hear you were going to tell all your classmates about my adventures today. Were you going to tell them about me parachuting into the desert?' He nodded and smiled. 'Now I'll have to tell all my friends about how brave you are.' She watched his face as he wondered what she meant. 'You're going to help me catch a criminal, aren't you?'

'Can I really?' He sat up straighter. His face brightened. He had been snuggled into his mother but now he turned to face Gawn.

'Of course. Can you tell me what happened this morning when you were playing in Uncle Seb's garden?'

He glanced at his mother before he started speaking. 'Mummy always told me not to talk to strangers.' He looked over at his mother again. 'I didn't forget. You always told me if I was in trouble I could go to a policeman.' He sought her reassurance. And she nodded and smiled at him encouragingly.

'What do you mean, Murphy?'

'It was the policeman. He asked me to come and help him. He said there was a kitten stuck under a car up the street and he was too big to get down to get it out. He said I would fit and I could rescue the poor wee kitten.'

'How did you know he was a policeman, Murphy?' Gawn asked, but she knew what his answer was going to be before he said anything.

'His uniform. And he knew my name.'

Gawn's eyes met Helen's. This had been planned. It was not a spur of the moment decision to grab any child who just happened to be out by himself. Murphy had been targeted.

'Then what happened?'

'The kitten was gone. He said it must have got out by itself and he said I should get a reward for being a good boy. He said he was going to take me for ice cream. I said Mummy wouldn't like me to go away.' He glanced across to his mother again to see if she was displeased.

'It's alright, Murphy. You weren't naughty,' Helen reassured him.

'He said he knew I liked honeycomb ice cream with marshmallow pieces.'

Gawn's blood ran cold. Maybe it was coincidence or a fluke that they had said honeycomb was his favourite ice cream but there could be no question that adding the marshmallow pieces was a lucky guess. Someone had been watching them yesterday when Seb had bought him ice cream in Carrickfergus. They had been near enough to see and hear what he had chosen.

'Then what happened, Murphy?'

'The lady was driving.'

'A lady?'

'Well, I think it was a lady. She had long hair but she had a deep voice like Daddy's.' He spoke in a deep voice to show what he meant. 'I didn't see her face, just her back.'

'Great. This is brilliant, Murphy. You are so clever and very brave.'

He beamed and got off his mother's knee to sit down between the two women.

'They took me and gave me money to get an ice cream and they told me to tell the man in the café my name and to phone the police.'

'Fantastic. Now, here's the really hard bit. Can you tell me what the car was like that you went in? Was it a police car?'

'No. It wasn't a car. It was a van.'

'What colour was it? Do you remember?'

'Blue, I think.'

'Was it a big van?'

'It was quite big.' He sounded uncertain.

'As big as the bus you go to swimming class in?' Helen prompted. She mouthed 'minibus' to Gawn.

'No. There was only room for me and some boxes in the back and there were no windows to look out of.'

'Brilliant, Murphy. That's fantastic. Now let's see just how observant you are. Do you know what that means?'

The little boy shook his head.

'It means you see things and you remember them and you can describe them afterwards, like what the policeman looked like. I think you're really, really observant and I'm going to get one of my friends to come and he's going to draw the policeman and we'll see if you can help him draw the picture. What do you think? Could you do that?'

He nodded. 'But what about the note?'

'What note, Murphy?'

'The one the policeman gave me for Uncle Seb?'

'He gave you a note?'

He nodded.

'Where is it now?'

He reached into his blazer pocket and drew out a folded sheet of paper holding it out for her to take.

'I'm not going to touch it, Murphy. I want you to set it down on the table there and I'll get someone to come and get it checked for fingerprints. You know about fingerprints, don't you?'

'Yes. They have them in *Marvin the Mouse Detective*.'

'It's a cartoon he watches,' Helen explained.

'I'm going to go away now and send my friend to get the note and someone to come and draw the picture with you, but Mummy will stay here with you all the time. You've been so very brave. I'm really, really proud of you, buddy.'

He reached across and hugged her. Her eyes welled up as she felt his tiny arms around her neck and his baby soft skin against her cheek.

'Thank you, Gawn,' said Helen.

Gawn touched Helen's arm in encouragement.

'And you've done really well too, Mummy.' She smiled.

When she walked out into the corridor, Seb immediately jumped up.

'You can go in and see him now. There'll be an artist along to try to build a photofit with him of his abductor.'

A policewoman had passed behind them and now re-emerged from the room carrying an evidence bag.

'Is that the note? May I see it?' Gawn read it aloud. 'Stay out of it. You will not be warned again.'

Seb was looking over her shoulder. She heard him gasp.

'That's like the one on my car.'

'I know, DI Cairns told me about it.'

'The printing looks the same. Do you think Murphy was taken because of me?'

'I don't know. What have you been up to? Have you annoyed someone?'

'No. I've been trying to write. I did some cooking. I went to a farm shop one afternoon for coffee. But that's the only place I've been.'

'And nothing happened there?'

'No. What would happen? It's some sort of commune. All peace and love and pseudo hippies.'

Gawn remembered what Cairns had told her. 'Stay away from it, Seb.'

'You think it's someone from that farm who did this?'

'It could be. They might know you write about crime and you've been nosing around the commune.'

'But I was only there doing a bit of shopping and having a cup of coffee.'

'They don't know that. If someone there is covering up a murder, they could see you as a threat.'

Angela York had been listening silently to their conversation.

'Just get the bastards, whoever they are.'

Chapter 38

Gawn went straight back to her office and phoned Cairns.

'Chief Inspector, this is a surprise. I didn't expect to hear from you.' His voice was friendly but wary.

'Yes, well, normally I wouldn't interfere in someone else's case but as a courtesy I was hoping you'd bring me up to speed on Magda Gorecki's murder investigation.'

'Is there any particular reason for that, ma'am? I'm sure you're busy with your own work.' The implication that it was none of her concern and he had it in hand was obvious.

'There's been an incident here which could be connected. Dr York's nephew was abducted from outside his house this morning.' It was easy enough to say this now. Now that Murphy was safely back with his mother unharmed.

Cairns took a moment to react.

'And you think it has something to do with the murder up here?'

'The boy was given a note – another warning like the one left on Dr York's car.'

'Aye, well that seems like a link right enough. If the first one related to Magda's death then that could too. Unfortunately, we haven't been able to establish that the first note up here had anything to do with Magda. It's still possible it was just some local yobs drunk and having a laugh. There can sometimes be a bit of anti-tourist feeling and Dr York's fancy car would have got him noticed and maybe annoyed some of the lads.'

'Or what about the commune?'

'Why do you ask about the commune?'

'Because Seb, Dr York' – she corrected herself – 'visited it just a couple of days ago. He says nothing happened when he was there, but someone could have seen him and put two and two together and maybe thought he was snooping around.'

'I see. We're looking into the commune and especially the three men who live there as a matter of priority.'

'No one stands out of the three of them?'

'If I say yes, it's only that old chestnut "the gut feeling" with very little evidence at all.'

'Who is it?'

'The commune leader. Moon Happiness or to give him his real name Arthur Dellman.'

'What have you discovered about him so far?'

'He's an American. He was born in San Francisco. He's fifty-two. He showed up in England about fifteen years ago and seems to have been involved in various schemes and scams but nothing has ever been proved. Nothing's stuck. One of those Teflon characters or just lucky. He's a charmer with the old ladies. There was an investigation a couple of years back when a family complained because their wealthy grandmother had changed her will and left Moon all her money – a considerable amount. The Met looked at it but couldn't prove undue influence or coercion, so nothing happened, and they think he came to some arrangement with the family to drop everything and he kept some of the money. From the family's point of view it was probably a sensible compromise. They could have been fighting through the courts for years with the lawyers getting the most money out of it in the end. It was after that he moved over here and used some of the money to set up his commune.'

'Any violence in his background?'

'None that we've traced so far but America's such a big place and he's lived all over. We haven't found any convictions but that doesn't mean he mightn't have come up in someone's investigation somewhere. We'd really need to access the FBI database and I don't see that happening anytime soon.'

'Do you have any other lines of inquiry?'

'Not really. She didn't mix much with the locals. She doesn't seem to have had a local boyfriend or anything. The other three girls in the commune seem to have got on well with her but they say she was homesick. They weren't surprised when she left but they were a wee bit surprised that she didn't say goodbye to anyone.'

'Did she have any money?'

'No. Her family couldn't even afford for both parents to come over to identify her body. Just her father came. Nobody killed her for her money,' he finished sadly.

'Not money. Sex then?'

'I think that's more likely, yes. The pathologist says she was sexually active and had had sexual intercourse shortly before her death which would chime with the romantic scene you described seeing. He also says she'd had an abortion within the last few weeks. She was Catholic and her father was shattered when we told him that. We're trying to find where she might have had that done. Her doctor in Coleraine hadn't seen her for anything other than a throat infection last winter. He knew nothing about a pregnancy so he didn't refer her anywhere. That means she had it done privately and we might have a paper trail back to whoever paid for it, or more likely she had it done on the QT and it'll be virtually impossible to trace. We're looking into it anyway.'

'Did you question the other three girls about Magda with the men in the commune?'

'They all expressed surprise. One even told me Magda had told them she was a virgin. As for Moon, they practically worship the ground he walks on, which means he can probably manipulate them whatever way he likes. They could be covering for him or one of the other two men. Or it could have been a secret relationship outside the commune. To be frank, ma'am, we're not making a lot of progress at the minute. If I say I hope you have more luck with the notes now they might be part of a kidnapping case in Belfast, please understand I'm not happy that Dr York's nephew was abducted.'

'Thank you for your frankness, Thomas. Can you email a copy of the note from Dr York's car and I'll get them to run a comparison on the handwriting? Meanwhile I'll let you know what we turn up here if it affects your investigation and I would appreciate it if you would do the same.'

'Of course, ma'am.'

'And, Thomas, please keep an eye out for Dr York. He's still down in Belfast at the minute but when he goes back up to the coast he'll be there by himself. I would appreciate it if you could just–'

He cut across her and said, 'Of course, ma'am, we'll keep an eye on him.'

'Thank you.'

Chapter 39

It was early afternoon before Gawn was able to get the whole team together. She introduced Hill and Pepper and explained how they had been working with her on the Jason Sloan missing persons case and would now be joining them to investigate Karen Houston's murder. Then she let Hill take over. The young woman had organised photographs of Karen Houston, the three young men who had been taken to the party and several other faces Gawn didn't recognise. One face, however, jumped out at her – Seb's, a very young-looking Jacob York. She wondered where the policewoman had got it. It hadn't been in any file she'd seen. Hill didn't know of their relationship and, as far as she was concerned, he was involved in the case. Gawn caught Maxwell's eye and raised an eyebrow at him in warning to say nothing.

'This is Big Sam. His real name is or rather was Samuel Legget. He died in 2018. He had a record for receiving stolen property, burglary, demanding money with menaces and he did seven years for his part in a bank robbery. By all accounts he was a fixer. If you wanted someone roughed up, he could arrange it. It seems his reputation was enough for people to do what they were told, for he was only ever charged once for any offence involving violence – the one case of demanding money with menaces which came very early in his career.'

'What about the bank robbery?'

'They think he had helped plan the job and was the lookout but they only got him for handling the stolen money.'

'Was he married? Do we have a wife or partner we could question whom he might have talked to? Who might be able to give us some info?' asked Maxwell.

'He did have a partner. Gemma Loughlin. She lives in North Belfast now.'

'What else, Jo?'

'This is Jock Irvine or Scott Irvine to give him his proper name, former constable. He retired from the force in 2005 and moved to Spain. He's been living near Malaga ever since.'

'A wee trip to the sunshine for someone, ma'am?' asked Grant. 'I'm volunteering.' He grinned.

'I'll bear that in mind, thank you, Jamie,' Gawn said. 'We'll definitely need to talk to him but we'll leave him for now. We don't have anything like enough evidence for a European Arrest Warrant to get him extradited and I don't see him rushing back out of the goodness of his heart to help our investigation so let's get as much as we can before we turn to him.'

'There are a couple of other photographs I haven't put up yet, ma'am.' Hill's intonation suggested she was asking if she now should.

'No, we'll leave them for now. Paul, I think you should have a crack at Jason. See if he's more forthcoming with you. Maybe he's remembered something more, or spending time in the cells will have loosened his tongue a bit. He might be able to give us some more names of people at the parties. He must surely have heard the men talking to each other.'

'Who's the other guy?' asked DC Billy Logan.

Maxwell stepped in quickly. 'He's just the driver. Jacob. He's already been questioned. We can leave him for now.'

Gawn hurried on before there were any follow-up questions about Seb's involvement or Hill could add his second name. She didn't think any of the rest except Maxwell knew of her relationship but she caught McKeown looking at her strangely and wondered if she had recognized Seb. She had been at the harbour when he had rescued Gawn and would have seen him.

'Walter, you and I will go to see Gemma Loughlin tomorrow. I know it's Saturday,' she added as a light groan had passed around the room, 'but you're all on overtime at least until the end of next week. We have a deadline.' She didn't mention Smyth's retirement although it was now common knowledge, but once he went, if they hadn't made significant progress, she feared the investigation would be stepped down so they were running against the clock. 'Erin, can you dig into Karen's life, please? We know of one boyfriend but I'm sure there were more. She was a very pretty girl. You know better than me what a twenty-something would get up to. The rest of you, I want a full background dive on Jock Irvine. Some of you' – she looked directly at Logan – 'may have friends who were on the force with him. Have a chat. Someone needs to be going through reports of disturbances, attempted sexual assaults and driving offences in the area of Cultra, Craigavad and Helen's Bay for – let's say – six months either side of the murder. We've already made a start on it but go over it again, widen the search area and check every report. Divide it up between you. Scope them out and see if we can establish any patterns. Jo, can I speak to you for a minute please?'

She led Hill into her private office. Having a separate space was already proving an advantage.

'Jo, I don't want Esdale's or Patterson's photographs on the board yet. Esdale's dead. Walter confirmed that but the man still has a lot of powerful friends, and Patterson is very much alive and his involvement with the family is sensitive to say the very least. Keep it to yourself but check into them. Put together a file for me. If you need help, use Walter once he comes back tomorrow from the interview.'

'Yes, ma'am.'

She turned on her heel and walked out purposefully.

Chapter 40

She was tired. It seemed like it had been a very long day, starting with the panic over Murphy's disappearance. That had been stressful for her, God knows what it had done to his mother and father. She was reminded of what Norman Smyth had remarked to her about how long anyone could keep doing this type of work. Seeing what one human being could do to another wore you down after a while.

She poured herself a glass of wine. She had made a conscious decision to cut down on her wine drinking. She had just taken her first sip when the intercom buzzed.

'Yes?'

'Delivery for Girvin.'

'Can't you leave it in the pigeonhole?'

'Won't fit,' came the terse reply.

She hadn't ordered anything. She wasn't expecting anything.

'I'll be right down.'

She found her shoes where she had slung them when she slipped her feet out of them and hastily put them back on and headed down in the elevator. She wondered what on earth it could be. With all that was going on, she hoped it wasn't some kind of nasty surprise, another warning, like Seb's. The delivery man was standing at the door but she couldn't see his face. He was totally concealed by a huge bouquet of yellow roses. There must be at least three dozen. She buzzed the door to unlock it and he thrust the flowers into her arms.

'Is there a message with them?'

'There's a card,' he replied brusquely as he walked away eager to get his shift over.

She carried the flowers up to her apartment. The glorious floral aroma filled the cramped space in the elevator for the short trip up. As soon as she had set the flowers down on the countertop she searched through them for a card. It read, "Thank you, Gawn, from all of us. Seb x". No love but an x. Then she caught sight of writing on the back of the card too. It said, "Mother says have you caught the bastards yet?" and a smiley face drawn beside it.

She remembered, for one of his books, he had researched the meaning of flowers and plants because Agatha Christie had used it in one of her stories and he had considered doing the same. He had told her then that yellow roses symbolize friendship. Was that what they were now? Just friends? He could hardly send her red roses, as he had once done. But maybe he was trying to recall their better days with the yellow roses. She allowed herself to hope that. She had lots of wonderful memories of her time with him. Better to think of them rather than where they had ended up.

Chapter 41

It had seemed like a good idea at the time. The mapping exercise of complaints and assaults had produced a less than satisfactory result. The area had essentially a low crime rate. The main issue was burglaries with many of the houses and their contents worth in the high six and seven figures. Not for nothing did it have the nickname of The

Gold Coast. They had not been able to identify a sufficiently clear pattern to point them definitively to one property. If they could have a witness identify the house that would give them probable cause to search it and interview the people associated with it. With Scott Alexander dead, Jason Sloan was their best hope. Of course, Gawn didn't realistically expect to find any physical evidence after twenty years but you could never be sure. Advances in crime scene technology, new bits of kit and new tests were being developed all the time. Even she was sometimes amazed at what the CSU team could come up with.

Pepper by her side, she had made the trip to the outskirts of Belfast to interview Gemma Loughlin. Even from a perfunctory meeting Gawn could tell Gemma attracted a certain type of man. Having been abused and used by Big Sam until his death, she was now living with a man who didn't seem much better from Gawn's quick scan of his police record. He had made it plain they were not helping any police investigation and had told them to clear off, slamming the scuffed front door in their faces.

Maxwell had done his very best to get more information from Jason. The man had sworn he didn't know any names of either the men who ran the parties or any of the other young people who were there. Then the inspector had tried to get him to agree to identify the house. He had been there on at least two occasions that he was admitting to. He should be able to lead them there but he was still insisting that he had just sat in the back of the car, not paying attention, and it had been Scott Alexander who had done the directing. So that left Seb. Gawn was reluctant to ask for his help. She had pondered long and hard before ringing him. She had even discussed it with Maxwell. He knew they had split up so he could take a pragmatic objective approach. He suggested she ask him to help. She had nothing to lose. But she knew she had. Somehow she still hoped they might be able to get past this some day. If they never mentioned it, if he went to LA for a while and they had time to miss each other – or, if she was being honest with herself, she hoped he might come to miss her as much as she already missed him. Bringing him out on a hunt for a house that featured in one of the worst nights of his life wouldn't help.

She had rung. He had agreed. Their conversation was terse. She arranged to pick him up at his house just before midnight so that they could replicate the journey. Of course road improvements and improvements in road lighting were going to make a significant difference, not to mention new housing and additions to properties. It was a long shot. He stressed he would do his best but he couldn't guarantee he would be able to find the house.

She was outside his home at 11.45 but she didn't need to get out of the car. He had been watching out for her and emerged as soon as she drove up. He was wearing a long heavy dark overcoat against the cold night air and his beloved fedora. He looked just as he had the very first time she had set eyes on him. She felt a flutter in her stomach just looking at him.

The night air came into the car with him as he sat down and adjusted the seat belt. Only when he was settled did he look across at her and speak.

'Right, Chief Inspector. Off on our adventure then.'

The look on his face didn't match his words. His eyes were wary, his face strained, his smile forced. It felt surreal to be so close to him physically within the tight confines of her car and yet so far from him in every other way. She was acutely aware of his aftershave and the closeness of their bodies.

She set off towards Belfast city centre so they could start their quest from the same spot where he had picked up the trio of young men. It was not as busy as she had expected for a Saturday night.

'Queen's Bridge or Albert?' she asked, naming two of the main routes across the River Lagan to get to the east side of the city.

'Albert,' he replied without hesitation.

Traffic was light, mostly taxis. The deserted streets to left and right could be hiding who knew what? They were searching for a house which held all kinds of terrible secrets. Who knew what other secrets lurked behind the closed front doors of these little terraced houses? They passed a drive-thru fast-food restaurant, its blazing lights a standout in the dark. The illuminated sign was working its magic for trade seemed brisk. A few stragglers and groups of young people were walking up the road clutching their takeaways. At a set of traffic lights at a fork in the road, Seb's monosyllabic direction, 'Left,' was all that was spoken.

There was no chat, no playful banter. He looked deadly serious every time she stole a glance at him. They passed a cinema where Gawn remembered nights spent with schoolfriends. Then a particularly dark stretch of road. An open recreational space shrouded in darkness lay to their left, and in the distance she knew were the airport runways, invisible to them, darkened now with no flights in or out at this time of night. Opposite, a school lurked behind a set of high railings, its dark bulk and shadowy spaces a lair for who knew what. No houses. No pedestrians and only a few cars passing.

Soon they reached the main road to Bangor. The dual carriageway was well lit but still surprisingly empty. She glanced in her rearview mirror and noticed a dark SUV some distance behind. She had noticed one sitting in the street outside Seb's house. The thought of being followed entered her mind but she quickly shook it off. The commune people wouldn't chance coming back here again after the episode with Murphy. It was just a coincidence. SUVs were everywhere these days.

An army barracks stretched along one side of the road now while an empty rail track, the trains having stopped running earlier in the evening, filled the other. Gawn knew MI5 worked out of this army base. She had always tried to stay well out of their way but had come under their scrutiny while she was investigating the death of a Dutch businessman. She thought of spooks. Businessmen, judges, politicians, policemen, men with money, positions of power and influence could all have attended these parties. Was it possible some spooks had been involved too? That would go a long way to explaining how the investigation had made such little progress. She shook her head to clear any thoughts of being followed and any fanciful idea that the Security Service had been involved in Karen's death. Too much imagination, she chided herself. Her attention was caught by a slight movement in the seat beside her. Seb was sitting up a little bit straighter now. His focus was heightened. He was concentrating on the road ahead obviously trying to bring that night to mind.

They passed the turn into Holywood and continued towards Bangor. He made no sign of recognition.

'Do you remember that petrol station?' she asked as they drove past a brightly lit forecourt.

'I've driven this road thousands of times. I know it's there. I've seen it but I don't remember seeing it that night. Scott had told me we would be making a left turn so that was what I was looking out for.'

'What about here?' She indicated a road off to the left.

'No. He would have said turn left at that billboard and he didn't. That would have been easy to see.'

Gawn wondered if the billboard had been there then. She realised Seb was beginning to sound agitated.

Now the houses were detached, larger, set back from the road. Some had high fences but most were separated from the roadway by hedges which enclosed their neatly manicured lawns and mature trees.

'Surely you remember whether you passed this or not?' Gawn indicated the illuminated sign for a hotel and its gatehouse. The stone pillars and baronial-style building were almost lost in the blanket of the night but the sign shone brightly doing its job of identifying the prestigious venue for passers-by.

'Yes. Yes I did.' He sounded excited. Then he sat up and pointed. 'There, that's what I told your man. We passed under the bridge for the museum.'

The grey concrete bridge spanned the road allowing access to both parts of the Folk and Transport Museum. Both sides of the road were in total darkness, the museum buildings buried deep in the undergrowth.

'Was it far now?'

'No. I don't think so, but I wasn't driving as fast as you. Slow down a bit. Give me a chance.'

She hadn't realised she had speeded up slightly. She was aware that this section of road was covered by average speed cameras. She didn't want to attract anyone's attention by speeding nor by driving too slowly, raising suspicions that they might be casing somewhere. Being stopped by a police patrol was not part of her plan.

'Might be this one. I think. Maybe.' He sounded anything but confident.

She drove slowly down the narrowing road.

'No. It doesn't look familiar. Maybe it was a little further along. She did a three-point turn back out to the main road and drove straight ahead but not for long.

'Try this one.'

They turned off again. The road narrowed quickly and round a sharp bend a stone railway bridge crossed over it.

'Yes,' he shouted and slapped his hand on the dashboard. 'That's why I thought I might be able to get a train back to Belfast because I'd noticed the railway bridge. How could I have forgotten that?'

'The mind can play funny tricks, Seb. You probably tried very hard to forget all about that night.'

He looked across at her, surprised at the understanding he could hear in her voice.

The road had narrowed even further so that in places it was nearly single track now and dense shrubbery lined both sides so that it was hard to see what was there, just feet away. There could be houses. They kept going.

'Anything?' she asked hopefully.

He shook his head.

'Was the house on the left or the right?'

'It was on my left and I remember the turn in was difficult. The road wasn't very wide, and I had to swing over to the right-hand side to make the entry past the gate pillar. I was scared I was going to hit it and worried what Sam would do to me if I scraped his precious car.'

And then, there it was. A high stone wall replaced the hedgerow. Iron gates hung on pillars but no house was visible from the road. But it was there. They both knew it.

'How sure are you, Seb?'

'As sure as I can be.'

All she had to do now was find out the address and then who had been living here twenty years ago.

Chapter 42

'Would you mind if we take a slightly different route back?'

Seb looked puzzled. He wondered what she had in mind.

'No. Of course not. Is this for your case too?'

'Yes.'

'Oh, I see. I thought you were maybe going to whisk me over the Craigantlet Hills for a quick snog.' He noticed her consternation. 'Not a joking matter? Sorry. That was, probably still is for all I know, a favourite spot for couples to hook up,' he explained, a mischievous grin on his face. He had done what he had promised. Now he could enjoy being with her in close proximity for a little while; tease her a little.

'Do you mean the car park at the forestry walk?'

'Yes.'

'Have you ever been there?'

'Of course. Many years ago. Any red-blooded young man in East Belfast who had access to a car has been there. Don't tell me no one ever took you.'

This was where Karen Houston's body had been dumped.

'Were you going there twenty years ago?'

'No. I didn't have a car, remember? I think once a school friend and I double-dated and we might have stopped there on our way back from a gig in Bangor but it's a bit of a passion-killer to be trying to have your wicked way with a young lady alongside someone else doing the same.'

He had been smiling but, as he noticed the look on her face, his smile disappeared.

'What is it, Gawn?'

'That was where they dumped Karen Houston's body.'

'God. I didn't know. Sorry.'

He reached across to take her hand to apologise but she was driving and pulled her hand away from him.

They had been travelling along the hill climbing up out of Holywood and now turned until the twinkling lights of Belfast came into view, laid out before them like a blanket lying spread out on the ground. Rows of lights marked out the roads. They could pick out the yellow sodium lights of the dual carriageway snaking away from them. To their right, brightly illuminated as befitted its importance, was the wide lamp-edged road leading up to Stormont, the home of the local assembly, and the impressive building itself floodlit, standing grandly on its site, its physical prominence dominating the Belfast skyline.

'Can we stop for a minute? I've always loved this view,' Seb explained.

She pulled over but kept the engine running.

'My city.'

'Soon Los Angeles will be your city.'

'If I go.'

'Is there any doubt?'

'It depends. Does it matter to you whether I go or stay?'

It had been on the tip of her tongue to say it was none of her business what he did but then she remembered what he had said when they were with Murphy about the kind of games people played and how, when Murphy wanted something, he just asked for it.

She turned in her seat and faced him. Then she leant across and kissed him. Just for a moment, not too passionately, just enough to give him her answer. She went to move back but he stopped her. He took her face in both his hands and kissed her. The kiss went on for a long time and, when he moved away from her, she was breathless.

'Let's go home,' he said.

'Your home or mine?'

'Who the hell cares?'

She put the car into gear and they set off down the hill.

Chapter 43

Seb woke first. Gawn was lying, her back towards him, her knees drawn up. He kissed the nape of her neck and then her shoulder and ran his hand down her arm until he was able to rest it lightly on her hip. She stirred and turned to face him. He didn't say anything, just traced the contours of her face with his finger, the scar on her forehead, her eyebrows and then he smothered her in little kisses until he reached her mouth. He kissed her then for a long time, her lips parted, his tongue probing gently.

When he moved back and looked at her, she joked, 'Better than any alarm clock.'

'Good morning, my darling.' He moved her hair back from her face so that he could look into her eyes.

'Talking about alarm clocks, what time is it?'

He reached round for his watch on the bedside table.

'Seven thirty.'

She threw the duvet aside and sat on the edge of the bed, her back turned to him.

'I need to get ready for work.'

He reached out and moved his finger down the line of her spine, sending a tingle through her body. 'It's Sunday, Gawn. Surely you're not working today. I thought we could spend the day together.'

She looked round at him. He was pouting but she knew he wasn't really annoyed. He knew her too well; knew what she was like whenever she was engrossed in a case.

'Do you think anyone will notice that I'll be wearing the same clothes as yesterday?'

'Who cares?' he responded. He jumped out of bed. 'You shower and I'll make breakfast.'

He slipped on his boxers and when he turned to walk out of the room she noticed the red trail her nails had made down his back. He made his way downstairs collecting a large brown envelope sticking through his letterbox as he passed. He didn't look at it, just picked it up and carried it into the kitchen with him, throwing it down casually on the countertop. More unwanted junk mail, some local business inviting him to an opening or some special offer he couldn't miss. He got them all the time.

Looking slightly harassed, Gawn appeared barely ten minutes later, her hair still wet.

'God, you look hot when your hair's wet like that.' He eyed her up and down.

She looked at him sternly but not too sternly. Life was good. She was back doing the job she loved and she was back with the man she loved. The way ahead for them was still uncertain. They hadn't spoken of the future. Would he go to LA? Would he ask her to go with him? And what would she do if he did? But for now, she would live in the minute and just enjoy being with him again.

She lifted the mug of coffee he had already poured for her.

'Toast's ready.'

He handed her a plate with a slice of toast on it and she took it across to the countertop to butter it. Her eyes fell on the envelope sitting there, her name on the front.

'When did this come, Seb? Have you been keeping it for me?'

'Is it for you? I didn't even look at the name on it. I just assumed it was some junk mail for me. It was delivered this morning.'

'Who would be writing to me here? And delivering it on a Sunday morning.'

She picked the envelope up and turned it over. There was no return address. Her name and his address had been printed on the front. It had been hand-delivered. Her senses heightened.

'Here.' Seb handed her a letter opener.

She slit it open and drew out a single A4 sheet of paper. It seemed to be blank until she turned it over. It contained three images. They were printouts of photographs and there was no mistaking when and where they had been taken. The first was of them sitting together side by side in the car. The second showed them kissing when she had leaned over and kissed him on their way back to Belfast. The final picture showed them at the front door of his house. Seb had his hand on her butt pressing her body into him while he nuzzled her neck. There could be no doubt about the identity of the two figures in the sequence of pictures. Underneath the photos in large black printed letters was a message: "Police chief inspector seduces witness at murder scene. New PSNI interview technique? Keep out of it or else."

'Shit!'

She let the page drop back onto the countertop. Seb picked it up. He looked at it and surprise registered on his face.

'Someone was watching us last night? Who would want to watch us? Why? What do they want?'

'I think that's pretty obvious, Seb. They want me to stop investigating.'

'Is it the commune people again?'

'I don't think it was ever the commune people. I think it's all been about the Houston murder. All the time. The car, Murphy and now this. Someone's worried I'm getting close and they want it shut down.'

'But they must know you won't stop just because of a few pictures. We're adults. We're both single. We're not committing any crime. If these photos appear in the paper, so what? I don't care who knows about us. The more the merrier.'

'It's not quite that simple, Seb. I'm SIO on the case. You were helping to identify the house where the crime took place so we could connect individuals to it and have probable cause for a search. If I'm compromised or you're compromised that's no good. Can you imagine the fallout if these photos appeared on the front page of the paper if you were testifying at a trial? The defence would argue I seduced you to get you to identify the house I wanted you to pick out; that you really hadn't known which house it was. Any evidence we obtained from any subsequent searches would be disallowed.'

He looked thoughtful, then asked, 'So what happens now?'

'I don't know. We're screwed as far as your identification evidence goes. I know I can't involve you at all. Any barrister who got hold of this would tear your credibility to shreds if you were giving evidence. And unfortunately that includes your identification of Patterson from that night.'

'But it was him. I was with him in the car as close to him as I am to you now. I'm certain it was him.'

'I know. I'll just have to find some other way to get an identification.' She was already planning how they could go about it. Knowing which house they were looking to have identified should make it easier and quicker but, even if it didn't, she was glad she had asked Seb to help. If she hadn't, then last night would never have happened.

'I'm so sorry, darling. If only we hadn't kissed.'

'I kissed you, remember? And I don't regret it.' She looked into his eyes. 'Not for one second.'

He drew her in and hugged her.

'Whatever you need to do, I'll support you. Whatever you need me to do, I'll do it.'

'One thing I do know, we can't see each other again until this is over. I want to keep you and your family safe.'

* * *

She had a lot to think about as she made the journey from his house to her office. She needed to find another way to identify the house and at least one of the people who had attended the parties, if they couldn't get Jason to help – but she was still hopeful about that. Maybe putting him together with his mother might loosen his tongue? There was so much she didn't know but one thing she did. No way was she stopping. If they thought they could blackmail her or scare her off, they had the wrong woman.

Chapter 44

Gawn headed straight for the main office and spoke to Logan. He was tucking into his morning bacon and egg roll from the canteen and soon they were poring over an Ordnance Survey map of the North Down area, heads together. She noticed he was wearing slacks and a polo shirt this morning, a nod to the fact it was not a normal working day. The others were similarly more casually dressed and she sensed a slight holiday atmosphere. She hoped that didn't extend to their work. Eventually she was able to show him on the map the house Seb had picked out.

'Find out the exact address, Billy, and then get the records. I know you won't get anyone in the Land Registry today but do what you can today and then get on to them first thing in the morning. We need to know who was living there when Karen was murdered. And, Billy.'

'Yes, boss?'

'No more boiled eggs in the office.'

'OK, boss.' She had never worried about him eating in the office before. Lack of progress on this case was making her crabbit. 'Is this the house where she was killed?'

'It could be. It's one possibility.'

She didn't tell him anything more but left him to get on with it. If it turned out to be the locus of the crime they would have to find another way of linking it to Karen.

Maxwell was in his office and had merely watched as she talked to Logan. Now she walked across to his door.

'We need to try to put some pressure on Jason. Seb was able to identify the house last night.'

He smiled broadly at the good news.

'But we need corroboration. Talk to Jason again, Paul. Threaten to bring his mother in to speak to him or see if you can get him to agree to a wee trip round Cultra with Jack and Jamie. They can watch how he reacts when they come to the house. He may give himself away. In the meantime I'll get Erin to pull together some photographs of all the men involved in the case including Karen's father and Philip Patterson and see how Jason reacts to them. We'll just have to keep our fingers crossed. He's not a criminal. He'll give himself away.'

Maxwell wasn't sure but he knew they needed to come up with something.

Gawn then spent the rest of the morning in her office sequestered with all the files from the case. She didn't expect to make any startling new discoveries but she read through everything carefully again even though she practically knew it all word for word by now. Eventually she felt that she needed to talk in person to the young woman, her fellow medical student, who Karen had been visiting on the night of her murder. The girl was called Sarah-Anne Wakely and there were details of two interviews the investigating team had undertaken with her. The first had been almost as soon as Karen's body had been discovered. She had been re-interviewed about a week later when no progress was being made and they were going over everything again but she wasn't able to add anything to her first statement. Neither interview seemed to have been very probing, almost as if they had already given up and were just keeping up the appearance of trying to find the killer. That was how it seemed to Gawn as she read the notes.

Karen had arrived at Sarah-Anne's house shortly after 7.30. They had a couple of glasses of wine, listened to music and chatted. No one else had been there. Nothing had happened. Nothing out of the ordinary had been said and Karen had left just before 10.30 to catch a bus home.

Sarah-Anne had seen her to the front door and waved to her as she walked down the street towards the main Upper Newtownards Road.

Gawn was struck by how quickly the original investigation had seemed to stall. Nowadays with social media she imagined there would be all kinds of appeals and support groups championing the case of the beautiful young student and demands for more resources to be put into the hunt. She couldn't pinpoint anything specific they had missed and yet it seemed the killer or killers had been able to cover their tracks very successfully or they had been very lucky. As Seb had said, that car park at the forestry walk was a favourite spot for couples, yet none had come forward to admit being there that Saturday night or seeing anything or anyone in spite of several appeals. Had they been warned off? Or had their evidence, if there ever was any, been conveniently misplaced? She realised with everything that was happening around her she was beginning to suspect that someone had been hampering the original investigation and was trying to do the same to theirs. A lowly PC like Scott Irvine wouldn't have been capable of doing that. Someone further up the chain of command had to have been involved. MI5 came into her mind again.

She shared that thought with Maxwell when he came back from talking to Jason. He had already told her that the man was still refusing to help them. In fact he was getting a bit cocky with it and demanding to be charged or released. When Maxwell heard her suggestion now that the Security Service could be mixed up in the case he looked shocked at first but he didn't contradict her. Tentatively he suggested she might be reading too much into things. The times had been different then. The PSNI had been under all kinds of pressures. OK, they still were. The Belfast Agreement might have been signed but there were still dangers and while the Houston case would have attracted media interest, the chances were some other event would quickly have overtaken it. The papers had been full of punishment shootings, nightly rioting and police coming under attack from petrol bombs. So it didn't have to be anything sinister, any sort of conspiracy, he argued.

Gawn decided her best hope of finding something useful was Karen's fellow medical student. She asked Pepper to trace where Sarah-Anne was now. She could be anywhere in the world. But they were lucky. A few phone calls and a check of the medical register and he was able to tell her that Sarah-Anne had married and stayed in Northern Ireland and was now a GP in East Belfast. She tasked him with phoning the doctor's surgery first thing next morning and she would head straight there from home.

By mid-afternoon she realised they all needed a break. They had been working hard and if things turned out as she hoped, they would be working even harder next week. She could practically hear the countdown clock ticking in her ear. They needed a breakthrough. She had hoped Seb could provide it and in a way he had but she knew if they couldn't link Karen and the house some other way Smyth would probably pull the plug before his leaving party on Friday. Five days.

Chapter 45

Pepper let Gawn know the doctor had agreed to fit her in after her early morning surgery. Once again Gawn drove the so-familiar road past Dundonald Cemetery and on to one of the sprawling modern housing estates which had sprung up all around the city to meet the demand of an upwardly mobile and cash-rich generation who wanted the convenience of city life with the proximity of the countryside. The health centre building was modern and purpose-built in a block of shops and restaurants and a leisure complex. Everything at the residents' fingertips.

'I'm here to see Dr Wakely,' Gawn said, holding up her warrant card to the smiling receptionist.

'The doctor's just finishing off morning surgery. If you would just take a seat, I'll let you know as soon as she's free.'

The waiting area was empty. Gawn sat down on one of the hard plastic chairs. She chose a red one but there were blue and grey ones too and even a corner filled with miniature matching pale blue and pink chairs and a selection of toys to keep children happy when they were waiting to see the doctor. Gawn read a metal sign on the wall and was surprised to see the toys had been donated by Houston and Patterson's Charity Team. She wondered if the doctor was still in touch with the Houston family. She scanned a row of posters extolling the virtues of certain products. There were notices about special clinics and a rather grim poster warning of the dangers of smoking when pregnant.

'Dr Wakely's free now.' The receptionist's friendly voice broke into her thoughts.

'Thank you.' Gawn smiled at the woman and followed the arrows on the wall down a corridor with a row of identical doors. Eventually, four doors down, there was Dr Wakely's name.

Gawn knocked.

'Come in.' The friendly voice from within sounded upbeat. The doctor was probably delighted to have her morning surgery over. She would be looking forward to a break before her next patients.

As soon as Gawn opened the door she came face to face with a tall serene-looking woman who exuded professional friendliness. She could imagine Dr Wakely was a popular doctor.

'Sorry to have kept you waiting but when someone needs to talk, it's my job to listen.'

Gawn saw compassion in the other woman's eyes. She was the kind of doctor she would have liked for herself.

'No problem. I understand. I really appreciate you taking the time to talk to me at all.'

'Your officer said on the phone it was about Karen Houston. Has something new happened?' The woman was interested but not anxious. She seemed open and happy to talk.

'We're looking over the case. We've had some new information and we're following it up. I'd really just like to go over your meeting with Karen that night.'

Dr Wakely had listened while Gawn was explaining the reason for her visit but her face had become more perplexed.

'I don't see how I can be of any help. It's twenty years ago. I can barely remember it. It was one night.'

'Of course, but please bear with me. I'll try not to keep you too long. I know you're very busy.' It might have been only one night, but surely the woman remembered a night when her friend had been murdered?

Dr Wakely walked to her desk and sat down, directing Gawn to sit too.

'Had Karen visited you often? Was this a regular thing?'

'No. Never. This was the first time. The idea came out of nowhere.'

'Didn't you think it was strange when she suddenly wanted to visit you?' No one had asked this at the time, at least as far as any reports Gawn had read. It had been assumed the two girls were close friends and the fact that the chairs in the waiting area had been provided by Houston and Patterson seemed to suggest a continuing friendship.

'Not strange. No. Why should I? We had classes together. We'd had coffee or lunch in the Students' Union a few times, usually with others from our group but when

174

she suggested getting together I never thought that much about it. Her parents were away for the week somewhere or other and I'd mentioned that my parents had a golf club dinner that night so then she suggested we get together.'

'She didn't suggest you go to her house?'

The doctor's reply came quickly. 'I didn't drive then. I hadn't passed my test.'

'But she wasn't driving either.'

'I was surprised about that.' The doctor's brow wrinkled a little. 'I expected her to have driven over. She'd been using the car all week to get to classes as far as I knew.'

'What did the two of you do that evening? What did you talk about?' Gawn asked, making a mental note to get Logan to check when Karen had left her mother's car at the garage to be repaired.

'All the usual stuff. Our lecturers – the good, the bad and the absolutely diabolical.' She laughed. 'We played some music. Had a few glasses of wine – one bottle between us,' she quickly added.

'What about boyfriends? Did you discuss any of your fellow students?'

'What do you think, Chief Inspector? We were normal young women. Of course we discussed men. There were one or two good-looking guys on the course but unfortunately they tended to think they were God's gift to women.'

'Did Karen mention her ex whom she'd split up with?'

'I think she did say something about not looking for anything too serious because her last boyfriend had been a bit intense.'

'But she didn't mention anyone she was dating?'

There was a pause before the doctor answered.

'She didn't *say* anything but I got the impression she was keen on someone.' When she noticed Gawn's reaction, she added, 'Look, since your officer phoned and said you'd be here this morning, I've been thinking over that night. It was just an impression I remember having and I couldn't honestly say why I thought it. Maybe the way she was so dismissive of any of the men our own age we were discussing, as if she knew someone a bit older, more experienced. But maybe I was reading more into it than was there.'

'I know the original investigators did talk to some of the other students in your year group but not all. Did Karen have any other close friends on the course?'

'If you're classing me as a close friend, you're making a mistake. I knew her. I liked her well enough. But I wouldn't say we were close friends. She was a friendly enough girl but I don't think she was particular friends with anyone on the course.'

Gawn was struck by Karen's sudden desire to be in Belfast that night. Did she have an ulterior motive? As an afterthought, she commented, mostly to herself, 'It's a pity Karen wasn't one of those young women who write copious diary entries with all their thoughts and angst so we could know what she was thinking.'

'I don't know about keeping a diary but I know she did have a habit of scribbling and doodling down the sides of her lecture notes. The pages used to be crammed with the usual girly things. I remember seeing an arrowed heart once and a name.'

'Do you remember the name?'

'Twenty years ago for a split second? No way!'

Gawn stood up.

'I won't take up any more of your time. You've been really helpful. Thank you, doctor.'

'I hope you have more success than your predecessors.'

Gawn came away thoughtful. This woman hadn't been as forthcoming with the original investigation. She would probably argue that she had answered all their questions truthfully but hadn't been asked anything else. Just as Seb had argued. So why was she happy enough to give the doctor a bye when she had treated Seb as if he was a major criminal because he hadn't come forward to volunteer information? She felt so guilty about him now.

They needed to check the car angle. When exactly had Karen known she wouldn't have a car? A sudden thought struck her. What was the name of the garage the Houstons used? She couldn't remember that or the name of the garage where Jason had been apprenticed. They couldn't be one and the same, could they? That needed to be checked right away. Jason might be more involved in all this than they had thought. If he knew Karen, that could mean he was the mystery boyfriend. She couldn't imagine the Houstons with all their money and prestige and a daughter aiming for a career as a doctor would be exactly delighted to have her hook up with a boy with his prospects. He certainly wouldn't have been capable of keeping her in the style she was used to, that was for sure. But Gawn had seen plenty of cases of girls attracted by 'bad boys', the thrill of defying their parents. She didn't exactly see Karen in that light but perhaps he had been her secret lover and he had taken her to the party. That would mean Seb would have seen her and he hadn't, she was sure. But why had Karen gone ahead with her visit to Belfast without a car? Gawn felt that was an important question for their investigation. She knew she wouldn't fancy that walk down the laneway late at night by herself, no matter what Karen's mother had said. Did the girl actually have other plans that meant she wanted to be in East Belfast but not for a girly night with Sarah-Anne? And those plans had somehow ended up with her being taken to the house at Cultra? But by whom? And she wondered if Valerie Houston, in homage to her daughter, had kept her old university notes. If so, they could be worth a look. Clutching at straws maybe but you had to get lucky sometime.

Chapter 46

As soon as Gawn got back to her car, she called Julie Patterson to ask if Karen's notes had been destroyed or if, by any chance, her mother had retained them. Julie told her their mother had kept absolutely everything. Karen's room was like a shrine. Did Gawn detect a note of resignation in the woman's voice? She thought she did. Could they borrow the notes, Gawn asked, if they were there? Julie was sure her mother wouldn't mind if it was going to help catch Karen's killer. As an afterthought, Gawn asked if they still used the same garage for repair work on their cars and where was it. The woman responded straightaway. Wilson's, on the Cregagh Road. Gawn was surprised that they had used a small garage in East Belfast rather than one of the big main dealers. Bobby Wilson had worked for her in the firm before starting up his own garage and Dad had wanted to give him their business to help him get started, Julie explained.

When she had disconnected the call Gawn had taken her iPad and started scrolling through her notes. It took a minute to find where Jason had been working. When she found what she was looking for, she had to read the name twice to make sure she wasn't imagining it. He had worked at Wilson's Garage.

Her hands were shaking with excitement as she lifted her phone again and rang the office. McKeown answered. She ordered her to take Hill and pick up Karen's notes. She thought it would be a good idea if the two young women who were closer to Karen in age than she was, had the opportunity to have a look around the girl's room to get a sense of what she had been like.

Then she asked to speak to Maxwell. Without preamble she barked, 'Get Jason Sloan into an interview room. Now! I'm on my way.' She didn't explain and before he could ask anything she had already hung up.

Chapter 47

Jason Sloan was sitting on one side of the battered desk while Maxwell was sitting in silence on the other staring at him. Grant was standing in the corner of the room glaring at Sloan too in what he hoped was a menacing way. Maxwell had told him the boss wanted to interview Sloan herself and they both knew she was tired of playing games with him and would want to come down hard.

They all reacted when the door was suddenly flung open and Gawn swept in. Maxwell thought she looked like the drawing of Boadicea in his daughter's school textbook or maybe one of the avenging Furies of mythology. He would have been intimidated by her himself if he didn't know she always played by the book in an interview and wasn't really going to lose her cool with Sloan.

She started talking before she had even reached the desk.

'No more wasting our bloody time, Jason. Just how well did you know Karen Houston?'

Maxwell was surprised at the question. She hadn't told him of her discovery of the garage connection between them. But Sloan reacted as if she had slapped him across the face. His eyes widened, his mouth hung open and he started to shake. He seemed to try to speak a few times but no words would come. He was like a fish floundering out of water. Eventually he started to cry.

'No, Jason. I fell for your tears back in Edinburgh. I'm not going to fall for them again. You weren't just some innocent wee boy who got pulled in by some psycho sex monster to help him get rid of a stranger's body. You were Karen's boyfriend, weren't you?'

Maxwell tried very hard not to display his surprise at Gawn's words. Sloan was sobbing now. Between gulps of air, he spoke.

'That's why I didn't tell anybody I recognized her. I wasn't Karen's boyfriend.' He looked up and saw she didn't believe him. 'I knew her. Yes. OK. I did. She'd been into the garage a few times. She'd been in the day before the party about damage to the back of her mother's car but I wasn't her boyfriend.' His voice had risen to emphasise what he was saying. 'I didn't even see her at the party. She must have already been upstairs when we arrived. And then she was all wrapped up when we were called upstairs. Honestly.' He looked from Gawn to Maxwell and back to the chief inspector again. 'I swear. When the wrapping came off and I saw her face, I recognized her. I threw my guts up there and then.'

Gawn glanced across at Maxwell. There had been nothing in the forensics evidence about vomit found at the scene. She couldn't think that it had been overlooked. She knew how fastidious all the forensics team were and even though it would have been different personnel then, they would have done a thorough job – if they'd been allowed to; if everything hadn't been sanitized before they got to the scene. To her mind this was more evidence of some kind of cover-up.

'Everything else happened exactly as I told you. I ran because I thought I would get the blame. If your lot found out I knew Karen, I would be a suspect and I didn't fancy my chances if it came to pinning it on me or some of those men from the party. So I ran and I've been looking over my shoulder ever since. That's the truth. I swear.'

'If you're telling the truth, then the best way to prove that to us and help yourself is to help us find the house.'

This time Jason didn't hesitate.

'OK.' He wiped his eyes with the back of his sleeve. 'But I want police protection.'

Chapter 48

They got lucky with the notebooks. The two detectives came back to the office burdened with a pile of lever arch files and other textbooks too. Karen's mother had kept her room exactly as the girl had left it. Her files and textbooks were mostly in a bookcase with one or two books strewn over her desk where she'd been working earlier in the day before she went out for the evening.

'We brought back her textbooks too, ma'am. I know I used to write things inside the covers of my books at school so we thought Karen might have too,' Hill had explained.

'Good thinking. Now I want the pair of you to go through them. You may not find anything – you probably won't – but we won't know until you look.' Gawn smiled at Hill, pleased she seemed to be fitting in so well.

'Coffee?' Maxwell queried.

'Tea I think,' Gawn replied. She saw his surprise and added, 'I'm trying to cut down on the caffeine. I think I might have an ulcer. It wouldn't be surprising if I had.'

'Have you seen a doctor?'

'You know I try to keep out of their clutches as much as I can. I've had more than enough of them. We'll see if a change to my diet helps. Bring the tea into my office. I want to go over the case with you,' she added.

Her separate office was proving very useful. She didn't feel too cut off from the team as Maxwell was her eyes and ears but it meant she had somewhere to think in peace and somewhere to discuss things in private with him. She was aware, and becoming more so, of the need to keep information to a bare minimum of people. It was too easy for things to slip out and so much of this was so delicate. And now she knew someone was watching. Very closely.

Maxwell followed her into the room, carrying two cups of tea. He set them down on the table and then made himself comfortable in one of the easy chairs. With a leisurely movement he crossed his legs. Gawn thought he looked so at home, so confident, and thought back just a couple of years to when he had been her rookie sergeant all embarrassment and anxiety to do well. Taking a careful sip of the very hot tea, Gawn spoke. She filled him in on what Dr Wakely had told her of the Saturday night spent with Karen.

'I'm beginning to form a slightly different opinion of our victim.'

'You think she had a reason for wanting to meet other than a girly get-together?' Maxwell asked.

'Doesn't it sound like that to you? She suggested it out of the blue. The two weren't particularly friends. She went ahead with it even though she had no car and supposedly was going to have to get home in the dark up a lane. The premise from the very start of the original investigation was that she was picked up probably by someone she knew while she was waiting for a bus, just a chance encounter. The bus driver insisted he didn't see anybody waiting and no one got on his bus there. I think she was picked up alright by someone she knew, but not by chance. I think it was arranged.'

'A boyfriend?'

Gawn nodded. 'Yes, but a boyfriend who for some reason she wanted to keep secret.'

'What about her ex? Could it have been him? Could he have been two-timing her sister?'

'Her sister was already dating him by then so it would certainly be a reason to hide it if she was hooking up with him but Julie Patterson says he was with her in New York.'

'But she's his wife and even then she must have been his girlfriend. She might be covering for him. It should be easy enough to check. I'll put Jamie on to it,' Paul suggested. 'Let's hope Jo and Erin have turned something up, some name we can identify,' he added.

'There is something else, Paul.' Unintentionally she found she had dropped the volume of her voice. 'Seb and I went over his route on Saturday night as I told you and he was able to point out the house to me but we won't be able to use his identification. If Jason comes up with the same house, we should have enough for a search warrant, I hope, but…' She hesitated and then explained about spending the night with Seb, the photographs and their link to the vandalism of the car and to Murphy's abduction.

At first Maxwell didn't say anything. She watched his face closely but couldn't discern what he was thinking. Eventually she could wait no longer. 'OK. Tell me I was stupid to spend the night with him.'

He paused before speaking. 'Maybe a bit unwise, Gawn, but someone was watching you? Seriously? This isn't just a cold case anymore, is it? Someone who's still very much alive is trying to influence our investigation and pervert the course of justice. They're still out there and they intend to stop us.'

Chapter 49

Monday was proving a bit of a frustrating day. Logan had contacted the Land Registry first thing about the house in Cultra but he was still waiting impatiently until they got back to him with the information he had asked for. He had stressed how urgent it was. He wondered what part of urgent they didn't understand. Meanwhile he had managed to track down Wilson's Garage but the business had changed hands and the current owner didn't think there were any records from that time still left. He wasn't able to give Logan any information about when the car had been booked in for repair although they knew now from Jason that it had been the day before Karen's murder.

Grant had begun trying to check Andrew Patterson's alibi as Maxwell had ordered but had had no luck yet getting independent corroboration of him being in New York on that night. So it was only Julie's say-so and Gawn and Maxwell had discussed the possibility of her lying to cover for him. The two females on the team had spent hours looking through notes and files trying to decipher doodles and squiggles, many of which just seemed random gobbledegook, sign of a wandering attention span during lectures.

'Time to call it a day, I think, ma'am?' Maxwell queried, aware that the others would be keen to get away, to have at least some sort of home life after missing out on their weekend. Maxwell's wife had her Weight Watchers class on a Monday night and she wouldn't be pleased if she had to miss it because he was working late but he couldn't tell Gawn that. Grant would no doubt have a hot date. He always did – at least that was what he claimed.

'Yes, I suppose so. But we're running out of time, Paul.' She felt she had pushed them as far as she could. 'Briefing at ten sharp tomorrow morning and everyone can report whatever they've got.'

There was general movement, packing up, coats being donned. Soon it was just Gawn and Maxwell left.

'Fancy a drink?' He felt he should offer. He realised she would be on her own and no doubt mulling over the case all night.

'No. I don't think so and neither do you, really. Go home to Kerri and the kids. You'll be in time to read the bedtime stories.' She smiled benignly at him. There was a time when she would have expected them all to stay on working for as long as it took; when she would have pushed Maxwell not to go home rather than encouraging him to head home to his family. Times change and she knew she was changing too. Just what that meant for her career, she wasn't sure yet.

Gawn made her way back into her own office and was sorting through papers on her desk when her phone rang. It was Norman Smyth. She was disappointed not to hear Seb's voice even though they had decided not to see each other again until the case was over. Above all she wanted to keep him and his family safe.

'Gawn, I got a tip off from a friend this afternoon that you were looking at a particular house in Cultra over the weekend.'

So the secret photographer had contacted Smyth too. She hadn't wanted him to know anything about Seb's involvement in case he pulled her off the investigation. She couldn't deny it. He obviously knew. 'Yes I was.'

'Can you tell me the address?'

'We're keeping it on a need-to-know basis but I don't suppose it would hurt to tell you, sir. It was 5 Seacrest Road. Why would someone be tipping you off about that?'

There was a beat before he answered.

'Because that's my house.' He said the words without intonation or inflection. It was a statement. It took no account of the waves of shock it had sent through Gawn's mind.

Eventually she managed to find her voice.

'Who told you about me looking?'

'I have no idea. I didn't recognise the voice.'

'You say *the* voice. Does that mean you don't even know if it was a man or a woman?'

'Exactly. They were using one of those voice distorters you can buy on the internet.'

'What about tracing the call?'

'I thought of that. I got someone onto it but it was a mobile phone. Pay as you go. No contract.'

'And what exactly did they say?'

'Just that it was all coming very close to home and I'd better call you off.'

'So they know you're involved in the investigation?'

'I think they know a hell of a lot more than that, don't you?'

She didn't reply. She was furiously thinking. Why would they warn him? He hadn't been living in the house twenty years ago. Who was trying to pull their strings, mess with the investigation?

'One of my men is actually trying to trace who owned the house and who lived there at the time of the murder. How long have you lived there, sir?' she asked.

'Just under two years. I certainly couldn't have afforded a place like this twenty years ago on my salary.'

'And what about before you? Who did you buy it from?'

'Not a judge anyway. It was a businessman. Philip Patterson.'

Gawn gasped.

'Sir *Philip* Patterson?'

'Yes.'

'But he was Karen's father's business partner. They started their business together. His son is married to Karen's sister.'

Had Smyth not known this? She couldn't believe he hadn't. Northern Ireland was a very small place. Houston and Patterson had been, still was, a major employer and Smyth had followed the case at the time of Karen's murder. He must have been aware of the link to Patterson.

'I didn't realise at first when I was dealing with the purchase. It was all handled through estate agents and solicitors. It was only when we got to the final haggling about me buying some of the fixtures and fittings that I found out who the owner was. And I never actually met the man. By that time, he was already in a nursing home so I was getting it for a good price.'

'It didn't put you off, sir?'

'No. Why should it have? It's a lovely house, Gawn. I didn't realise it might have anything to do with Karen's murder, just that there was a link to the Houstons. Anyway, I wasn't even thinking about the case then. I hadn't thought about it for years until I was chatting one day about old times with a colleague. There was nothing to suggest a link between the girl and the house. It hadn't been identified as the site of the whole sex party business and even the sex parties were more a rumour than anything definite. I went ahead with the purchase. If you ask me now would I, should I have, then I'd say probably not but at the time it didn't seem like an issue.'

He sounded plausible. Until Saturday night she hadn't known it was his house so how could he know of its connections?

'We've been trying to work out how to get access to the house for a CSU search, trying to think of probable cause, but you could give us permission now, sir, and let us get started.' She didn't tell him Jason Sloan had agreed to identify the house for them.

She waited for his answer and waited. Finally he responded.

'Can you imagine the front-page headlines if anyone got wind of a forensics search of my home? They'd be putting two and two together and accusing me of everything under the sun from being Jack the Ripper to the head of some paramilitary group. My reputation would be in tatters. Even if you didn't find anything that wouldn't matter. And if you did find something, my God, they'd have a field day speculating even though I bought it years after the event.'

His voice had risen as he spoke. He was agitated. Gawn realised the terrible situation he was in. If he said yes, then he was right. She'd do her best to keep it all under wraps but it would inevitably leak. Someone would talk to someone. Someone might even sell the story to the press or their secret watcher would do it. If he said no, he must know, she would work away at the case until she linked it all together and then he would come out of it worse because he had known and refused to help. It would make him seem complicit.

'I will do my very best to keep it under wraps, sir. I'll only use a very small team; people I know and trust but I guess you would have to prepare yourself for the worst.' She was speaking to him as she would to a small child trying to convince them that the injection they were facing was all for the best.

'And if I stand the investigation down? I started it and it was supposed to be about Jason Sloan. You've found him. We could simply reunite him with his mother and any admissions he might have made about why he ran off could simply disappear. I'm sure he'd be happy to agree to that.'

She couldn't believe she was hearing this. Not from him, a man she trusted, a man she had always admired.

'Apart from what Scott Alexander told you – and he's dead – and Jason Sloan's story, what else do you have?

Nothing. Nothing to link my house to anything. Nothing to link Karen to any parties. Or Patterson to any involvement in anything.'

Oh yes she did. She had Seb and now she had Jason prepared to help them too but she wasn't going to tell him that.

'I can't believe you're saying this, sir.'

'I'm less than a week off my retirement, Gawn, after a long and pretty successful career that I'm rather proud of. I don't want my reputation sullied by any connection with Karen Houston's murder. Is that so hard to understand?'

'Oh, I understand it, sir. I just don't believe it of you.'

'I'm not some superman, Gawn. I don't have your unflinching sense of right and wrong; good and evil. And I don't have your courage either, my dear.' His voice had dropped down to almost a whisper as he spoke the last words.

'So what happens now, sir?'

'I'm going to sleep on it. I'll speak to you in the morning.' And he rang off before she had the chance to say anything more.

Chapter 50

Gawn sat looking at the phone in her hand for a stunned second. She couldn't even begin to take in the conversation she had just had. Then she replaced the receiver and before she even realised it, she had started to cry. It began with a few tears running silently down her cheeks but soon she was crying, trying valiantly not to make a sound. She was grateful then for her separate office and solid wooden door with no glass for a passer-by to see in. She allowed herself the luxury of crying for a few minutes and then gave herself a stern talking to. What was she crying for? Recently she seemed to be on the verge of tears more and more often. She was a grown woman. All men and women had feet of clay. Norman Smyth was no different to anyone else. He wanted a peaceful retirement, not for his reputation to be stained by association with a scandal and murder. Did she want to risk her reputation by the publishing of those photographs with Seb? No? Would she tell them to publish and be damned? Yes. But that was her. She couldn't live her life differently.

If there was one thing she wanted more than anything else it was to talk to Seb. She mightn't be able to be with him but she could phone him. She selected her contacts and heard his number start to ring. There was a gap before he spoke and she had started to worry that something had happened to him.

'Hi, beautiful.' He sounded just the same as normal as if the whole world hadn't just turned upside down as it had for her.

'Hi.' Then she stopped. She realised she couldn't share with him what had happened. Not only would it be unprofessional but it could be dangerous for him and he would probably want to come back to Belfast to be with her and insist on giving evidence no matter what.

'Still at work or safely curled up on the sofa with a glass of wine and a good book?'

'I'm just getting ready to leave the office.'

'Right. Just as long as you're not curled up on the sofa with a glass of wine and a good man.' He laughed. When she didn't laugh in return he added, 'That was a joke. You sound a bit funny. Is everything alright?'

'Yes. Yes. It's just been a long day,' she lied.

'Things going well with the case? Oh, sorry, shouldn't ask. Don't tell me about your day. Tell me how much you're missing me,' he joked again.

'Like a sore head,' she joked back. He would never know how much she was missing him. 'I love you. And I'm missing you. Happy now?'

'No and I won't be until we can be together again.'

'Hopefully not long.'

'Hey, you'll never guess what happened today.' His voice sounded chirpy. It was obviously something good. 'I got invited to become a member of a private gentlemen's club in Belfast. Some of my old school chums are members and my mate, Jonah – you know, the editor – put me up for membership ages ago. I'd forgotten all about it. I think he had too. But they contacted him today and told him to bring me along to the next meeting. I didn't think I'd any chance of being allowed to join. It's very exclusive but I've been accepted. Isn't that brilliant? They're all real movers and shakers. Top businessmen, media people, lawyers. I think maybe even the Chief Constable so I might be able to put in a good word for you.'

Something made Gawn feel uneasy. She couldn't have said what. She knew of at least one gentlemen's club in Belfast but there could be others. They provided opportunities for business networking, private dinners and charitable events. She had never heard anything negative about it but something about the timing of Seb's invitation to join rang just the tiniest alarm bell with her.

'Well, aren't you going to congratulate me? It's a big deal to be invited to become a member of the Raffles Club.' He sounded just a little bit disappointed that she wasn't suitably impressed.

'Of course, that's brilliant. So what happens now?'

'I'm not sure yet. I mean, I don't think there's any sort of initiation ceremony or anything. I won't be rolling my trouser legs up or drinking pig's blood or any of that malarkey.' He laughed. 'At least I don't think so. No, Jonah's taking me there for dinner next Saturday night to introduce me to some of the others. It'll be all big cigars and boasting about the size of your yacht I would imagine.'

'I'll have to buy you a new one for the bath then, Seb,' she joked back.

She heard an alarm going off in the background.

'Ah that's my oven timer. My dinner's ready,' he explained.

'Go and eat. Enjoy it and think of me with my leftover lasagne from the fridge.'

'I always think of you. Goodnight, my love.'

'Love you, Seb.'

'Love you more.'

And he rang off.

It had been good to hear his voice but there was still that niggle about the gentlemen's club. She had had enough experience of old boys' networks from her army days. She was innately suspicious of them though she knew most were benign and many provided really useful support for their members and undertook excellent charity work. It was just the timing that seemed so suspicious to her. Seb had never mentioned wanting to be a member of this club. They had never spoken of it at all. She knew he had a bit of an inferiority complex about his working class background but he had made good all through his own hard work and intelligence. She could see how being accepted as one of the boys by this type of group would appeal to him. She hoped it was nothing more than a coincidence but still she wished there was some way she could check it out, perhaps see who the other members were.

As soon as she got home and ate some of the lasagne Martha had left for her, she sat with a glass of wine and googled "gentlemen's clubs". She could find very little about the Raffles Club and no information about its members.

Chapter 51

Eventually, when she could think of nothing else to do but couldn't settle either, she went back to the office. The corridors were strangely silent. Only a skeleton staff were on duty in the building for a Monday night. She spent her time reading and re-reading every scrap of evidence, statements, reports, everything to see if there was anything she had missed, any other line of enquiry they could follow. She fell asleep over yet another computer search. When she woke it was late, so rather than driving home, she moved across and curled up in one of the easy chairs, and that was where she was when Maxwell knocked on her door early on Tuesday morning.

'Have you been here all night?' he asked, surprised as he walked into her office.

'Yes. I fell asleep at my desk and then it was just easier to sleep here. It wasn't too uncomfortable.' She said it as much to convince herself as Maxwell as she unwound herself slowly from the chair and stretched.

'Was there any reason why you pulled an all-nighter? Did something come up after I left?'

Maybe she was just being paranoid but she decided not to mention anything to him about her telephone conversations with either Smyth or Seb. Not yet. She trusted Maxwell. She knew him well but then she'd thought she knew Norman Smyth well and anyway she wondered if she was seeing conspiracies where there were none.

'No. Just me working too hard as usual.'

'I was going to make some coffee. Do you want to freshen up and I'll have it ready for you?'

'Very diplomatic, Paul. I must look a mess.'

'You look fine, boss.'

Thirty minutes later – and she was pleased to note, well before the set time of 10am – they were all assembled. Gawn was pleased to notice how smart Logan was looking these days. She had heard from Maxwell that he had a new woman in his life, an old friend of his ex-wife. She was obviously being a good influence on him. He had neatened himself up. He was taking a lot more care with his appearance and he seemed to have got a new lease of life, putting a lot more effort into his work.

'OK. Who's going to start?' asked the inspector.

'We will.' It was McKeown. She and Hill were sitting side by side at her desk with a sheaf of papers gathered in front of them.

'Karen was quite the doodler,' McKeown said. 'Most of it was just random shapes and designs but there were some names. Andrew Patterson was there.' Gawn's ears pricked up. 'But he was in her notes from first year when they were together. He didn't feature in the more recent notes from before her death.'

'Who did, Erin?' Maxwell asked.

'There was a Jonathan, sexy Simon and a Dr K.'

'Did you check the list of her fellow students?'

'Yes. There were two Jonathans – a Jonathan Pritchard and a Jonathan McMichael.'

'What about Simon?'

'Only one Simon in her year group – Simon Johnston.'

'But of course the men may not have been in her year group. They could have been the year above or from another faculty, maybe she met them in university clubs or societies,' Maxwell interjected.

'Yes. I think we all realise it's a bit of a needle in a haystack job but we have to try,' Gawn responded.

'Were any of these men questioned in the original investigation?' Logan asked.

'If they were, I saw no record of it. What about the Dr K you mentioned?' Gawn asked.

'We drew a bit of a blank there I'm afraid. There were none of her lecturers who had either a first name or a surname beginning with K.'

'I wonder if it would be worthwhile asking Dr Wakely if she remembers any of these men, especially Dr K?' Gawn asked.

'Worth a try, ma'am.'

'Right. She's a busy woman. Jo, give her a ring. You should be able to ask her over the phone. If she needs time to think about it, you can ring her back. I think she's probably our best hope.'

'The garage where Mrs Houston's car was repaired got in touch this morning, ma'am. They managed to turn up some old records, after all,' Logan announced.

'And?'

'Karen Houston booked the car in for repair on the Friday afternoon.'

Just as Jason had already admitted. So Karen did have time to cancel her evening out if she'd wanted to. But she went ahead with her plans. Gawn nodded thoughtfully.

'Thanks, Billy. That's useful to know.'

When Gawn's mobile rang and she saw Norman Smyth's name on the screen, she excused herself and left Maxwell to finish briefing the team and allocating tasks. She didn't speak until she had closed her office door behind her.

'Sir?'

'Gawn, can you come up to my office, please?'

He didn't wait for a reply, just hung up.

* * *

Her mind was working overtime as she walked along the corridor and approached Smyth's door. Was he going to make good on his threat to end the investigation? She knocked. She had already decided she wasn't going to go quietly. She owed it to Karen and to her mother.

'Come.'

Inside she saw Smyth sitting behind his desk. She'd been expecting that. What she had not been expecting was that ACC Mackie would also be there seated across from him.

'You know Assistant Chief Constable Mackie, of course.'

'Yes, sir. Good morning, ma'am.'

'Sit down, Gawn.' Smyth sounded weary and looked ill. He seemed to have aged in just a few days. She didn't think he'd had much sleep last night. 'I've been explaining to ACC Mackie about my predicament.'

Gawn was surprised. She hadn't expected that. Was there something going on between these two? Smyth was a bachelor. He had never married. If she remembered correctly, Mackie was a widow. Still, sharing information with her about the Houston murder was a surprise. She was duty-bound to follow up on any crime. She couldn't turn a blind eye to what he had started even if they were in some sort of a relationship.

'Deirdre agrees with me that we have to do whatever we can to bring Karen Houston's killer or killers to justice. That being the situation I'm giving you permission for a search of my house. I trust you can deliver on what you said, Gawn, about having trusted officers you could call on.'

'Yes. Of course, sir. I'll get it organised straightaway.' She was surprised after his reaction the previous evening but obviously he'd had time to think about it. She was delighted that her opinion of Smyth's character had not been wrong. His sense of duty and honesty had won out.

'Here's a key. I want you to supervise it personally. I don't want anyone else to know. Obviously if they find something that will change everything and you can do whatever needs doing but for now we keep it tight. Agreed?'

'Of course, sir.' She took the key he was holding out to her.

Once back in her own office, Gawn rang Mark Ferguson. He was the best CSI she had ever worked with. He was meticulous and, more importantly for her now, she trusted his discretion completely. 'Mark, are you busy at the minute?'

'Not really. There's nothing very urgent.'

'I have a very delicate piece of work for you. I don't think it's a one-man job. Do you have someone you can trust?'

'That's a bit of a weird question, ma'am.' He sounded suspicious.

'Yes. It is. But I need a preliminary search done asap and very discreetly.'

'A search of what?'

'A house which may or may not have been a crime scene.' She thought she better be as upfront with him as she could be, so she added, 'Twenty years ago.'

There was a long pause and she could picture the look on his face as he said, 'Are you serious?'

'Yes. Very. I've got access to the property. I just want you to go over it with your experienced eye and see if there's anything that might be worth following up. I've spoken with the current owner. He only moved in two years ago so the crime has nothing to do with him and he hasn't done much work to the house since he moved in.' She wasn't going to tell him who the owner was but the chances were they would spot a photograph somewhere in the house or some memento from his career and be able to identify Smyth. They might be lucky. Norman Smyth had told her he'd had little time to do much to the house since moving in so a lot of it was much as when Patterson had lived there. He had been leaving it all until he retired, planning major renovations and refurbishment then.

'Ma'am, if it's a whole house with that time elapsed, we'd need a team working for days to go over it. It's impossible.'

'I know it's a big ask, Mark.' She waited. Obviously she could order him to do it but what she was asking was very unusual and he'd be within his rights to demand she make it all official and he'd come with a full team, but she needed this done off the books.

'When?'

'Today. As soon as possible.'

'Where?'

'Cultra.'

'Give me an hour to get in touch with someone and I'll meet you there. Text me the address.'

'Use your own vehicles. Not anything marked. No one must know about this, Mark. I mean absolutely no one. I'll owe you big time for this.'

'OK, ma'am. Understood.'

Chapter 52

She met Mark Ferguson and another man she didn't recognise at the tall front gates of Smyth's house.

'I don't think you've ever met my brother, Sean, ma'am.'

She hadn't. She hadn't even known he had a brother and she certainly hadn't known he was a forensic scientist too.

'He's normally locked away in the lab but I thought, seeing as you wanted this done under the radar, so to speak, I could use him to help me.'

'Good idea. Nice to meet you, Sean. Thank you for helping.'

'What are we looking for, ma'am?' the new man asked.

'I wish I knew.' She needed to tell them enough to give them some chance to find something useful but she didn't want to tell them too much. 'We suspect that a murder was committed here twenty years ago.' She caught the two brothers exchanging looks. 'I know. It's a long time. I have no good reason to believe you'll be able to find anything but I'm clutching at straws here, guys. You've seen crime scenes of all shapes and sizes, in all sorts of conditions. You're the experts. I just want your best professional opinion, your gut reaction as to what could maybe offer some chance of finding evidence. I don't expect you to test anything today. But if you could cast your eyes over the house and see where there might be some possible evidence which mightn't have deteriorated over the years that would be great. I know it's asking a lot. I admit this is a Hail Mary call.'

She knew she sounded a bit desperate. Truth was, she was getting a bit desperate. If she could have brought in a whole team, they could have taken the place apart, maybe found blood under floorboards or trace DNA on a wooden handle somewhere. Forensics seemed to be able to work miracles every day. Now she needed them to work one for her. Just the two of them. In an afternoon.

'I'll wait in the car. I've some paperwork to catch up on.' She doubted she would be able to concentrate on any paperwork but she didn't want to be hovering over them, interrupting their method of working. She'd just let them get on with it.

She had settled in the car with a file to read when her phone rang. Seb's name appeared on her screen. She couldn't help smiling. Something good for a change.

'Hi there.'

'Hi, babe. It's so good to hear your voice. It's lonely up here. Even the weather's been awful today.'

'At least you had time to notice. I've been so busy I haven't had time to look out the window.' She didn't want to give him any details of where she was or what she was doing. Better for him not to know anything.

'Oh, yeah. Make me feel guilty, why don't you? I've been working too, you know. I got two chapters written today which I will probably start off tomorrow by deleting. That is if I am in any state to do any work tomorrow.'

'What do you mean?'

'I'm going to my new club tonight. I promise I'll be on my best behaviour but I imagine there'll be a lot of hand-shaking and back-slapping and lots of toasts so I'm taking a taxi there and back. I won't embarrass you by getting caught for DUI.'

Gawn was surprised by his announcement.

'I thought Jonah was taking you next Saturday.'

'That was the original plan but apparently there's some special meeting tonight and he phoned this morning and invited me along. Practically everyone will be there so it'll be the perfect chance to meet lots of the members.' He sounded so pleased with himself. There was a pause and she knew he had something else to say. 'I'll be staying in Belfast tonight obviously after the dinner. Any chance of seeing you? You could sneak in through the hedge from my neighbours' at the back and come in by the back door. No one would see you and we could spend the night together.' He paused and she knew he was waiting for her reply. She could picture his little-boy-lost expression. Then he added as an afterthought, 'It would be a very good way of ensuring I don't drink too much.' He was making a joke of it but she knew he was serious. He wanted to see her and she wanted to see him too.

'I'd love that, Seb, but we mustn't.' She could imagine how it would look if she was caught slinking through back gardens late at night to meet him.

'Is this damn case nearly finished? I'm going to have to kidnap you or something if this goes on much longer.'

'It will end soon, I promise, one way or another.'

Possible endings came into her mind, few of them good.

'Well, I suppose I better go and get ready for the drive to Belfast then if I can't convince you. Wish me luck facing the judge and the jury.'

Gawn's stomach did a somersault.

'What did you just say?'

'I said I'll have to leave soon to drive down.'

'No. No. The other bit.'

'I'll be facing the judge and the jury, is that what you mean?'

'Who are the judge and the jury?' she asked, her voice sounding unnaturally forced to her ears although he didn't seem to notice anything wrong.

'Just one of the quirks of a closed group, a bit like my Alpha Kappa Lambda fraternity at Berkeley. The club committee is called the jury and the chairman is the judge. The club only has thirteen actual members plus associates. It's very exclusive so it's pretty special to be elected to join. I get to meet them all tonight.'

She thought back to their experiences in Donegal when Seb had been injured because of her. She wanted to tell him not to go but she couldn't, not without telling him why. And she wasn't even sure his invitation to the club meant anything, had anything to do with her case. It might point to the judge and jury at the sex parties being linked to this club, but it didn't mean the current members had had anything to do with Karen's murder. She was sure that most of them would be much too young to have been members of the club then. From Scott Alexander's testimony it seemed the men who ran the parties were older. And it didn't mean that now, twenty years later, this group meant Seb any harm. But she didn't like the sound of it. Someone had already tried to scare her off by damaging his car and abducting Murphy. It seemed they would stop at nothing. They had been watching him or her or both of them. What if they hurt him?

'Be careful, Seb.'

'You sound really strange. I'm only going out to do a bit of socialising. I know some of the jurymen. I was at school with them. Jonah's on the committee. You make it sound like I was James Bond going off on a dangerous secret mission or something. OK, M, I'll be careful.' He spoke with a Scottish accent giving a fair impression of Sean Connery. 'Or should that be Miss Moneypenny? Anyway I do have a licence to swill tonight.' He laughed at his own pun.

'I mean it, Seb, take care. I love you.'

'I will. I promise. Love you more. I'll phone tomorrow night and let you know how I get on. Bye.'

She looked down at the phone in her hand. Then she seemed to make a sudden decision. She dialled Maxwell's number. 'I want a surveillance team immediately on the Raffles Club at Belmont and an ARU put on standby for tonight.'

Then she had to tell him… Everything. She had no other choice.

'I nearly got him killed twice, Paul. First Schneider and then in the debacle in Donegal. Both times it was because of me and I'm not going to let it happen again. No matter what.' She hesitated as she used the words. It was their little mantra. It was what Seb had promised her, that he would always be there for her no matter what.

'Do you think these guys intend doing something to him?'

'The timing just seems so coincidental, so convenient for somebody. Maybe I'm just being paranoid but they might want to use him to force me to stop.'

'Surely they must realise you couldn't stop an investigation all by yourself.'

'But I could sabotage it.' Even as she said it, she realised she would consider that just as Smyth had considered burying everything to save his reputation. She was shocked with herself that she would consider sabotaging the inquiry to save Seb. But she would, she realised. He meant so much to her. What did that make her? She had been quick to sit in judgement on Smyth but she was no better herself. Life isn't always black and white, right and wrong. Most times it's a sludgy shade of grey. Maxwell was still taking in what she had suggested when she continued, 'Or maybe they want to get information from him about what we know.'

'Have you told him anything?'

'Of course not. I don't discuss cases with him. But they wouldn't know that.'

'I'll get it organised.'

'I'll be back in the office as soon as I finish here.'

Chapter 53

For nearly two hours she had sat outside Smyth's house while the Fergusons worked inside. The hands on her watch moved round excruciatingly slowly. She could imagine Seb getting ready to drive to Belfast, excited at the prospect of becoming a member of this club. He would wear his best suit to impress and that aftershave she bought him for Christmas. When she was just about ready to scream, the Ferguson brothers came out of the house.

'It's a big house, ma'am.'

She didn't need him to tell her that.

'And? Anything jump out at you?'

'A couple of things.' She hadn't expected him to say that. She hadn't dared to hope. 'There's a cellar which has a stone floor. If anything happened down there, there could be evidence between or under the paving. The rest of the house is carpeted and newly carpeted at that, probably within the last couple of years. Without lifting it up to check the floor underneath it's impossible to say what there might be.'

'What else?'

'We found some marks on the ceiling of one of the bedrooms. It looks like a spare room; not the main bedroom.'

'Scrapes, scratches, what? Not bloodstains?'

'No. It's a mark of where a small hole had been drilled out at one time directly over the bed and then it had been filled in, not particularly well.'

'And what would that suggest to you?' She was puzzled.

'Well, the one time I've seen it before, it was done for secret filming in a sex blackmail scam.'

'Someone could have been filming what was going on in the bedroom?' She couldn't help letting a trace of excitement sound in her voice.

'It's one possibility. Just a possibility and, of course, it doesn't necessarily mean that anything criminal was going on. What people do in their own bedrooms is their own business but usually if it was someone filming themselves and their wife or girlfriend they wouldn't need to have a hidden camera, would they? For this you would have needed some kind of remote control device, something quite sophisticated twenty years ago if you were going to control the filming while you were...' – he hesitated before finishing his thought – 'on the job, so to speak, ma'am. Of course, even if someone was filming, the films were probably destroyed years ago.'

The prospect that somewhere out there was a film shot in that bedroom was just too wonderful to think of.

'Anything else?'

'There's a huge attic which I don't think anyone's been in for years. We took a quick peek – as much as we could in the time we had. There are old rolls of carpet, a big tin trunk, suitcases with God knows what in them. Old cardboard boxes which seemed to be filled with books, the ones we looked at anyway. I'd ideally love to have the time to go through all of it.'

'Leave it with me but keep yourselves free tomorrow. I'm going to try to arrange for you to have the day to take that attic apart, have a closer look at the bedroom and the cellar too. Thank you, both of you. Great work.'

She locked up the house and watched as the two men drove away. Then she dialled Smyth's number.

'Well?' He answered immediately, sounding anxious. He had obviously been waiting for her call.

'When was the last time you were in your attic?'

'My attic? Probably when I was looking around the house to buy it. I think I popped my head through the hatch. That's about it. I don't use it.'

'So, if there's stuff up there, it's not yours? You didn't put it there?'

'No. I thought everything had been cleared. I assumed it had. If there's anything up there, it's nothing to do with me.'

She didn't tell him about Ferguson's idea that some kind of secret filming had been going on in one of the bedrooms. It sounded like something a lot more sophisticated than some innocent home movies. She shivered as if someone had walked over her grave. She wouldn't allow herself to consider that spooks had been involved in this and yet, if they had been, it would explain a lot.

'Then I'd like my men to have a really good go at it tomorrow.'

His response didn't come immediately. Was he going to say no; stop her now?

'I'm trusting you, Gawn. Go ahead.'

Chapter 54

The waiting game had begun. By six o'clock everything was in place. Detectives Grant and Dee would take the first shift. If the dinner went on past midnight Logan and McKeown would take over. Dee had managed to find a good vantage point from which to watch the club. The car was well-hidden close into the hedge, well off the narrow road. The Raffles Club's premises looked to any casual observer like any other ordinary Edwardian family villa on this affluent tree-lined avenue; nothing to make it stand out from its neighbours. It was set back from the roadway but the hedges were not too high and the front aspect of the house was clearly visible from their parking space in the handy laneway diagonally opposite. Grant had walked the area earlier to recce the surroundings. The properties were all expensive, the lawns kept neatly cut and the road was little trafficked. A desirable established area, in estate-agent speak.

At 6.30 Grant radioed in to report that some people had started to arrive. This was earlier than Gawn had anticipated but it seemed they were more likely staff rather than club members. McKeown was waiting at her desk and had arranged with Dee that he would photograph each man as he arrived and send her the pictures. She would print them out to form what she had called her 'rogues' gallery' on the noticeboard. As she pinned them up the others would try to get an identification. The members were supposed to be successful figures so they hoped most of them would be identifiable.

At seven Grant's voice came over the radio again. The first man who looked as if he could be a member had just arrived. The picture on the board was instantly recognised by everybody in the room. No need for any facial recognition software. It was one of the leading figures in local business. He was interviewed regularly on television. A group of three men arrived at the same time just a few moments later and walked in together laughing and chatting. Only one of them was familiar to anyone. Although she had never met him, Gawn recognised Andrew Patterson from a wedding photograph she had noticed of him and Julie when she had visited the Houston home. Shortly after, a large black chauffeur-driven official car pulled up and an older man got out. Even if they had not recognised him, which they couldn't have failed to do given his public office, they would have realized that he was important with a close protection police officer in the background of Dee's photograph.

'You don't think anything's going to happen with a police bodyguard standing outside, do you?' Maxwell asked between mouthfuls of tea.

'How the hell do I know?' Gawn snapped back at him. 'Sorry, Paul. I don't know.' She was so tense she could barely breathe. She was sitting on the edge of McKeown's desk, tapping her foot on the floor constantly making Maxwell nervy too. Her hands were sweating. Her heart was beating so hard in her chest she expected the others could hear it. 'I don't think I can just stay here waiting. I want to be there on the ground.' She was halfway out the door even as she spoke.

'I'll run things from here then, shall I?' Maxwell shouted after her.

By the time Gawn slipped into the back seat of the surveillance car, it seemed that all the members had already arrived. The whole house was illuminated upstairs and down. Light poured from every window. This was obviously not some kind of secret society, hiding behind closed doors. Maxwell had given the two detectives a heads-up so they were not surprised to see her. She had parked her car further down the dark road and walked, keeping tightly into the cover of the garden hedges, to make her way to join them.

'We counted twelve men who seemed to be members going in, ma'am. We couldn't get photos of them all. Some were turned with their back to the road or they blocked each other. Dr York arrived by taxi about five minutes ago,' Grant reported.

From the cars parked outside, all the members were obviously very successful men, even if they were not necessarily well-known public faces. Mercedes, Jaguars, a couple of Porsches, a flashy red Maserati and an even more eye-catching yellow Ferrari were parked in the spacious paved area in front of the house. It was like a rich man's parking lot, Gawn thought to herself. No, it *was* a rich man's parking lot.

'We've been taking pictures of the car number plates, ma'am. We thought if we couldn't identify the men through facial rec we could get them through their car registrations. I've emailed it all to Erin. She's got some hits already.'

'Good thinking, Jack.'

Dee was aiming the telephoto lens on his camera to try to get some pictures of any figures who approached the windows.

'Toffee, ma'am?' Grant offered her a sweet from a crumpled paper bag he had retrieved from his pocket.

'No, thanks.'

She knew she was making them uncomfortable. They weren't able to exchange banter as they normally would on a stake-out. She knew it, but she couldn't have just waited and listened from afar. She wanted to be on hand if anything happened; if she needed to call in the ARU. She didn't know what she expected to happen but she knew what mustn't happen – she couldn't let Seb be hurt again.

The minutes ticked by. So slowly. She was alert to every sound, even an owl hooting in the trees and the sound of an emergency vehicle, its siren cutting through the silence as it passed by on the nearby main road. She was making the two detectives nervous and tense, she knew. At eleven o'clock the close protection officer came out of the house accompanying his VIP and carrying a cardboard box which looked to be quite heavy. The front door was closed behind them and they drove off.

Silence again. This road was not much trafficked. Only five cars other than the ones going to and from the club had been along it as they sat there and waited. The two watching detectives were finding it hard to keep awake without their normal bragging about their football teams or, for Grant, his female conquests, to pass the time. At one point Dee started quietly snoring and Grant had to quickly elbow him awake.

Then at 11.30 it was obvious that a general exodus was beginning. A taxi drew up and Seb came out flanked by two men. They shook hands. He looked slightly unsteady on his feet, and they helped him into the waiting vehicle, then went back into the building as Seb was driven away.

'Right, that's him safely out. Wait until everyone is out in case anything happens. You can fill me in tomorrow unless it is something serious that requires immediate action. Good job.'

False alarm. She told Maxwell to stand down the ARU. She almost felt disappointed. She had wanted to find an excuse to get inside that building and identify and question those men. But they hadn't provided one.

Chapter 55

Gawn was back in the office at eight the next morning. Knowing Seb was safe, she had slept really well. She was determined to make progress on the case today. Time was running out. Smyth's retirement was looming.

'We're ready for the briefing now.' Maxwell put his head round her door. She followed him to the general office. One or two of the assembled team looked a bit bleary-eyed this morning. Not Jo Hill.

'Dr Wakely got back to me first thing this morning, ma'am.'

Gawn had forgotten about asking her to contact the doctor again with the names of the male students.

'Was she able to shed any light on any of the names?'

'Yes.' Hill's eyes were sparkling. She was enjoying being the bearer of news. 'She remembered all three boys, as she called them. The sexy Simon was a, what did she call him, Erin?'

'A Lothario.'

'Yes, a Lothario. We had to look that up. He dated just about every girl in the year group but it never lasted long. She couldn't see him being serious about anybody nor any girl being stupid enough to be serious about him. The two Jonathans were both nice, she said. One was very quiet and had gone on to marry a girl on their course. They'd already been going steady at the time so she didn't think it would have been him. They're missionary doctors in Africa now. And the other one was gay so she didn't think Karen would have been pining after him either.'

That left the mysterious Dr K.

'And Dr K?' Gawn asked.

'She had two suggestions for that. One was one of their substitute clinical teachers who'd been filling in for their regular lecturer for a semester. His name was Kennedy but according to Dr Wakely, he was ancient then so she couldn't see Karen fancying him. I pushed her on that and she admitted by ancient she meant in his late forties to early fifties when they were all in their twenties, so I don't think we can write him off altogether. He might have had a fling with Karen. And the other wasn't a doctor at all.'

The officer noticed the puzzled expression on Gawn's face.

'Dr Wakely was a bit reluctant to say much about him at first, but it seems he was a student but not of medicine. He was a bit older. A mature student. She thought he might have been studying Law but she wasn't sure. Anyway, everybody called him 'the doctor' because he sorted out all their ills by which I took it to mean he supplied anyone with drugs who wanted them, although she didn't come right out and say that. She said she thought his name might have started with a K.'

'Can you check with the university for him? If they won't provide the information, look at the graduation records – they're public – and see if someone whose name began with a K graduated around that time. Start with the School of Law. And you could try the Law Society Solicitor Directory and check for any Ks who graduated around that time.' It would be like looking for a needle in the proverbial haystack, she knew.

'On it, ma'am.'

There would be a lot of graduates whose name began with a K but at least it was something.

'There was something else, ma'am,' McKeown joined in. 'We were having another look over Karen's notebooks and it seemed to us her work had dropped off quite dramatically over the couple of weeks just before her murder. Early on she seemed to be more or less a straight A student, good grades, encouraging comments on her work but the last couple of pieces barely made a C and one of the comments was that she needed to concentrate more on her studies. We wondered if it might be the influence of some man she'd got involved with or maybe she'd been doing drugs supplied by this Dr K. Just a thought, ma'am.'

'And a good one. Well spotted.'

No one else had ever commented about any concerns about Karen herself or any suggestion she was less than perfect. Now Gawn was beginning to wonder. Not that whatever she might have been involved with made it acceptable that she had been murdered. Gawn was not into victim blaming.

'I had a wee word with Jock Irvine, ma'am. I tracked him down eventually,' Logan piped up.

'In Spain?'

'Aye. I thought I remembered he was a cocky wee bastard and I was right. He was quite happy to tell me that he had been on the take then, seeing we can't touch him for it. He was taking backhanders from all kinds of people. He boasted about it to me. He'd put away enough to bankroll his retirement in a villa outside Malaga. He asked me what the weather was like in Belfast and what my pension would be. And had a good laugh.'

'Was he able to tell you anything about Big Sam's arrangement?'

'He was a wee bit less forthcoming about that. I sensed he might be a bit scared of saying too much. He's not scared of us but the people he dealt with are a different matter. They wouldn't be bothered about extradition or any legal niceties, was what he suggested. He told me there are still some around and he wouldn't want to cross them.'

'Anything useful to us at all?'

'He did say there was one particular guy – not the main man but another one – who he said was off his head most of the time. He was a psycho according to Irvine and he'd hurt a few of the girls but they got paid off.'

'If that's the case, there should be hospital records of girls being treated over Saturday night, Sunday morning after parties. If they were seriously hurt enough to need paying off, they would have needed treatment and the chances are they would have gone to the nearest hospital,' Maxwell suggested.

'Good luck trying to get access to the hospital records,' Gawn interjected cynically.

'Wouldn't be any good anyway,' Logan interrupted them. 'Irvine said there was a pet doctor and he sorted the girls out, including organising abortions.'

'Did he give you a name?'

'He said he never knew a full name. Everybody just called him Dr K.'

'We need to find this man. I want everybody on it. Call in favours, talk to whoever you need to talk to. Jack, make some advances to the Drugs Squad. See if they know anything about a pusher round the university at that time. Paul, with me.'

The clock was ticking and time was running out.

Chapter 56

Gawn had brought Maxwell with her. She wanted to keep it business-like and wasn't sure she could manage that if she went alone. On the other hand, she didn't want Seb to feel he was under suspicion; that she didn't trust him. Above all she didn't want him to know she'd had him watched, even if it was for his own protection. Maxwell rang the doorbell and then stood back. After a significant wait, the door was slowly opened and a wan-looking Seb stood in the door jamb.

'Blimey. This is a surprise.' His face lit up into a smile and he made to move forward to hug her and then moved back again when he spotted Maxwell there too. He obviously didn't know how he was expected to behave, what their visit could be about, what the other man knew about their relationship. She saw wariness in his eyes.

'Do I need a solicitor again?' He spoke only half-jokingly.

'No. Of course not. Can we come in?'

He stood aside to let them pass.

'You're looking a bit rough, mate,' Maxwell remarked in passing.

'Just the result of some merry-making. My own fault I'm afraid. Nobody to blame but myself.'

He directed them into the main room and motioned for them to sit down. Gawn noticed the packet of headache tablets opened on the arm of the chair and a mug of coffee sitting on the fireplace.

'To what do I owe the honour?' He looked from one to the other as he waited for an answer.

'We're investigating the Raffles Club,' Maxwell announced.

Seb looked surprised and cast a questioning look at Gawn.

'I've only just become a member. I wouldn't be the best person to ask anything about it.'

'Who would? Who's the chairman, the judge?'

'Andrew Patterson.' He said it in a matter-of-fact voice as if it was common knowledge.

'Sir Philip Patterson's son?'

'The Philip Paterson I met once?' He looked at Gawn, not sure of how much he should say in front of Maxwell. She didn't react, so he continued, 'I guess so. I don't know for sure. They just said Andrew Patterson.'

'Did you meet Andrew Patterson?'

'Yes. I was introduced to him. He seemed like a nice guy. Friendly. We had a chat about my books.'

'And what about the jury? Were they all there?'

'Probably not all. I don't know. I think maybe one guy hadn't turned up. They were a bit surprised and made a joke about it saying he was one of my biggest fans. But they didn't call a roll or anything so I'm not sure. What is this all about?'

'Scott Alexander told us that the judge and the jury as they were called or called themselves were arguing in the house on the night of Karen's death just before her body was removed.'

'The judge and the jury?' He sounded incredulous. 'You think it was the judge and the jury from the Raffles Club? Some of the men on the jury are younger than me. They would have been teenagers, boys even, twenty years ago. You're not suggesting they were involved?'

'Maybe not them, but their predecessors?' Maxwell responded.

'I'm not even sure it was going twenty years ago. Anyway you make it sound like some sort of secret society. But it's not. They're just ordinary men. Successful, yes. Some of them, very rich but not criminals. I was at school with a few of them. They're respectable businessmen, married. They have families.'

'None of which makes them saints, Seb,' Gawn rejoined. 'Were there any older men there?'

'One or two. Oh, and they toasted Andrew's father.'

'Sir Philip?'

'I don't think they mentioned him by name but he used to be the judge and he's old and not very well now.'

'Did you get the names of either of the older men?'

'Sorry. Can't remember. I'm not on what you would call top form this morning,' he apologised and rubbed his eyes wearily.

'Was there anyone there with a name beginning with K?' Gawn asked.

'Are you joking? Is this some kind of test or a new game we're going to play?'

'No game. It's a simple question.'

'I think there was one guy there and he was a bit older now I come to think of it. I was introduced to him as Keith or maybe it was Ken, but I didn't get his second name. There, did I pass?' He was becoming both annoyed and flippant.

'Why is it called the Raffles Club, Seb?' Maxwell asked.

'For God's sake, you must have heard of Raffles, Paul.' He looked from Gawn to Maxwell.

'The gentleman rogue and jewel thief,' Gawn suggested.

'Yes. I think calling the club that was meant as a bit of fun, a sort of joke. They didn't want the stuffy atmosphere of the normal idea of a gentlemen's club. They might be a bit roguish some of them – not criminals, more Del Boy Trotter – I imagine they might sail a bit close to the wind sometimes in business – but they would also consider themselves gentlemen.'

'What did you talk about with them? Did they ask about me?'

'About you? No. Somebody asked me if I was married. Jonah made a joke about me having the hots for a cop last year because he knew about you but no one else said anything. It was just a pleasant evening. I must have had a wee bit too much to drink although I thought I was being careful but I didn't have to take part in any strange rituals or pledge loyalty unto death or any of that stuff. We had a lovely meal. My favourite porterhouse steak. It was just a good evening. You can't seriously think these men, my friends, are involved in your murder case.'

The two detectives exchanged looks.

'They're not your friends, Seb. Some of them you don't even know. Stay away from them until this is over.'

He could see she was deadly serious.

'Sorry to have disturbed you, Seb. You can go back to the strong black coffee now,' Maxwell joked.

Seb raised his eyebrows at Gawn.

'Give us a minute, Paul. I'll meet you back at the car.'

As soon as the other man was out of the room, Seb turned to her and asked, 'What was all that about? Am I under suspicion for something? What's going on?'

'No. You're not under suspicion. But we thought it was just too coincidental that you'd been invited to join the Raffles Club when we'd just started to investigate the judge and the jury.'

'Like it couldn't just be that a prestigious club wanted me as a member?' He was hurt.

'Of course, it could. You're a successful author. I just needed to check.'

'Well, now you've checked. Can we just forget it? When am I going to be able to see you again?'

'Soon. I promise, soon, Seb.'

Then he pulled her close to him and kissed her.

'It better be.'

Chapter 57

The team was working flat out trying to find the mysterious Dr K.

'I talked to my mate in the Drugs Squad, ma'am,' Dee began. 'He said he would ask around but most of the team there are younger than me. They weren't even on the job then, never mind working Drugs.'

'OK, Jack. Thanks.'

'There was something else, ma'am.'

'Yes?'

'We were going over the photos from last night and we noticed something weird.'

She waited for him to continue.

'There was someone else there.'

'Someone else in the house?'

'No. Someone else in the bushes. Watching. Taking pictures.'

'Of the house?'

'Yes and of us.'

He handed her a photograph. It was a blown-up section of one she'd already seen. In the foreground three men could be seen walking into the house together. A figure, dressed all in black including a black balaclava, was visible, fuzzy but visible, crouching in the bushes. He had a camera in his hands pointed in their direction which blocked his face from view.

'Does he appear in any of the other pictures?'

Dee shook his head. 'No, ma'am. We've checked. He was being careful. It was just a fluke we got him on this one.'

'I want door-to-door on that road. There aren't that many houses. I'm sure some of them, probably most of them, must have some home security cameras. See if they'll give us the footage from last night. And, Jack, go to the houses that back on to the club as well in case he made his way there through the back of the property.'

'Right, boss.'

'Any luck with Dr K? What about law graduates beginning with a K?' she asked of the room in general. No one reacted. 'Or *any* graduates?' Again, no response. 'OK. Keep at it. Paul, I think we need to speak to Sir Philip Patterson now. I don't think we can put it off any longer. We have his house as the venue for these parties and we have Seb putting him on the spot that night and now we know he was the judge. Can you ring his son in case he wants to be there when we talk to him?'

* * *

An hour later Maxwell pulled the car into a space at a nursing home in a leafy suburb of South Belfast and he and Gawn walked side by side to the main door of the converted house, now residential accommodation and nursing home. The place looked expensive. The grounds were laid out with neatly clipped lawns and luxuriant shrubbery and benches were dotted around the perimeter under the shade of mature trees. Several people, obviously residents, some in wheelchairs, were sitting out in the weak sunshine. A security system with an intercom guarded the door. Maxwell pressed the bell and in response to a disembodied voice's query informed them that DCI Girvin and DI Maxwell were there to see Sir Philip Patterson. A buzzer sounded and the door unlocked with a click. Once inside, the two detectives were struck by the consciously cultivated impression of a private home with heavy quality carpeting and chintzy curtains. Paintings – originals, not cheap prints or reproductions – adorned the walls, carefully arranged floral displays sat on heavy mahogany tables and the smells of furniture polish and freshly baked bread wafted through the air. Everything was done to aid the pretence of a home from home. No doubt a very expensive home from home, Maxwell thought to himself.

In a cheery professional voice, they were greeted by a small grey-haired woman dressed in a dark blue uniform. She looked like a typical ward sister, efficient and very much in control. 'Good afternoon. I'm Jane Harvey, the matron. Sir Philip knows you're coming. We've told him but whether he'll remember is another thing, I'm afraid. Without divulging any private medical information, his son has allowed me to warn you he has advanced dementia and he's not always very communicative. However, having said that, he's having a fairly good day today so you may be in luck. He's in room forty on the second floor. We can take the lift or the stairs.'

It was obvious they were not going to be permitted to wander about unattended. The woman led them silently up the stairway. As they walked along to room forty both were taking in their surroundings and thinking ahead, not quite sure what to expect of the once astute and, Gawn's researches had suggested, ruthless former businessman. They couldn't be sure what Sir Philip would remember. He might be too ill to remember anything much at all. On the other hand he might remember enough that he wouldn't want to share with the police. Either way, neither were particularly confident that their visit would prove useful.

Jane Harvey pointed to a door with the number 40 on it.

'Here we are.' She smiled at them and then turned and began walking away as Maxwell knocked respectfully. They expected to hear a feeble voice tell them to come in but instead the door was swung open and a man they recognised as Andrew Patterson filled the doorway. As he moved aside to let them enter, they saw that his wife Julie, Karen's sister, was there too, standing between the bed and the window.

'Chief Inspector. My husband phoned me to tell me you were going to visit his father. We thought we should be here.' Julie half-smiled.

Gawn held out her hand to Andrew Patterson. 'Thank you for agreeing to let us speak to your father, sir. We think, we hope he may be able to help us with our investigation into your sister-in-law's murder.'

There was a sort of gasp. 'Not about your missing persons case? It can't be to do with Karen's murder.' Julie's voice sounded incredulous and her face was creased into a frown. She had not been expecting that.

Gawn glanced at Julie's husband and caught an expression on his face which made her wonder if he was quite so surprised.

'Perhaps if we could just have a word and we'll see where it takes us.'

'My father's ill and rather frail. His memory is patchy at the best of times. I would ask that you remember his condition, Chief Inspector.' Andrew Patterson's voice was deep and rich with a slight English accent. He spoke with the confidence of a man who was used to giving orders and having them obeyed.

Gawn nodded to show she understood what was expected of her. Then she turned and looked for the first time at the elderly man lying propped up against a slew of pillows in the bed. He had paid them no attention so far, ignoring everything around him. Instead, his stare was fixed firmly on the window looking out, past his daughter-in-law, to the lawn and tall trees beyond. Gawn was reminded of Scott Alexander, sitting looking out of his window, perhaps remembering the same scenes or looking towards the same future. Patterson's white hair was still thick and swept back from his face but his eyes were dull and he had what Gawn would have described as a mean mouth, thin and pinched, his lips pursed in a permanent look of disapproval.

'Sir Philip? Can I ask you some questions, sir?' She moved closer to the bed. She didn't think he was the kind of old man who would respond to having his hand held comfortingly, as Scott had done, and she wasn't the kind of touchy-feely cop who sought to empathise with everyone she interviewed but she wanted to make sure she had his attention; that he could hear her.

'May.' His voice was surprisingly strong and clear.

'No, sir, my name is Gawn.'

'May you, not can you. Don't they teach grammar anymore?' He laughed at his own cleverness.

Andrew Patterson shifted his feet behind her.

'My father is a stickler for grammar, Chief Inspector,' he apologised.

'Of course, he's quite correct. May I ask you some questions, sir?'

'It depends what they are.'

Sir Philip was sharper than they had expected. She didn't think there was much point in wasting time. She went straight to what they wanted to know.

'Who is Dr K?'

A frown came over his face for a second.

'Ned.' Then he smiled. 'Our joke.'

'Your joke, sir?' asked Maxwell.

'The bushwhacker.'

Maxwell was totally bemused. It seemed the man was talking rubbish, mixing fact with the ravings of a declining mind. But Gawn remembered the story of Ned Kelly, the infamous Australian outlaw who had come from Banbridge in County Down.

'Ned Kelly? Is that who you mean?'

'Yes. Very good. His name was Ned. We called him Ned Kelly. He shortened it to K and then Dr K.' He seemed happy enough to share this information. He smiled. Obviously thinking about Dr K brought back happy memories for him.

Now they had a first name.

'Why was he called doctor, Sir Philip?'

'He could fix anything. I could use some of his medicine now.' He gave a hearty laugh. It sounded incongruous emanating from his frail body.

'His medicine, sir?'

'Anything you needed he could arrange.'

Gawn wondered what anything might have included. It seemed Dr K had been the fixer, the one who arranged the girls perhaps. So Big Sam must have worked for him.

'The pills they give me here are no good. Ned's pills were…' He left the sentence unfinished, his thoughts wandering again. A drool of saliva escaped his mouth and slid down unchecked dripping off his chin.

Gawn caught sight of a movement to her right as Julie took hold of her husband's arm for support.

'Did Ned bring Karen to the party?'

Julie caught her breath. Gawn was guessing but she needed to try to get him to admit what had been going on while he seemed to be in a reasonably alert and cooperative mood.

'Stupid bugger. What did he think he was doing bringing the wee bitch?' The man's face crinkled into an ugly sneer. When the detectives had first entered the room and seen Sir Philip he could have passed for a benign elderly gentleman but now his appearance betrayed him as an evil hedonist who had no conscience about what he had done. The look on his face was one of self-satisfaction and pride, not regret.

Gawn heard a cry behind her and Maxwell moved across to help Andrew Patterson support his wife to a chair.

'Chief Inspector, I think you should stop now,' Patterson suggested.

But before Gawn could respond it was Julie who almost shouted, 'No.' Her voice was high-pitched as she contradicted her husband. 'No. I want to know the truth. I *need* to know the truth. All these years and your father knew about it.' She was speaking through her tears now.

Andrew Patterson was ashen-faced. He looked from his wife to his father, his loyalties pulled between them.

'Just one more question, Mr Patterson,' Gawn said.

He didn't speak but nodded in acquiescence. Then he took his wife's hand. Gawn didn't know if he was trying to comfort her or to receive comfort from her touch for himself. She couldn't tell which of them was more shocked but there was an expression on Patterson's face, a look she had noticed before which made her wonder if he was shocked by the news or shocked by the fact it was out in the open and his wife now knew about it.

'Who killed Karen, Sir Philip?'

'I don't know. I wasn't there.' There was an almost sing-song effect to his words like a pleased child who has got the better of an adult.

Gawn's heart sank. He could be telling the truth. After all, he was the one who had driven Seb back to Belfast. He wasn't there when the body was being taken away but the fact that he did leave his own house, his own party and warned Seb never to come back there again, suggested he had known something had happened. When she was just about to give up, the old man spoke again, more weakly this time but still clearly.

'You'll just have to watch the film to find out.'

Gawn swung round and looked at Andrew Patterson. She could read the signs of struggle and realisation on his face and knew he had something to tell them.

'My father was a keen photographer and filmmaker. He used to develop all his own prints. He had all the equipment up in the attic. But about three or four years ago, just when he was starting to get really bad and we were considering that he'd have to leave the house and move into residential care, I found him one day burning all his cine films and smashing up his equipment in the garden. I asked him why, but he wouldn't tell me, just that no one must ever see any of it.'

'Where was it kept?'

'I doubt there's anything left, and I wouldn't know where to start looking. My father kept it all in the attic but I'm sure that must have been cleared out. He would have seen to that.'

But he hadn't. The Fergusons had already seen the attic. It was still packed full. For some reason Patterson had not got rid of everything. Maybe in the end his memory had let him down and he had just forgotten to finish the job? Could there be some film, some photographs, something incriminating still there? Something filmed through the ceiling where the Fergusons had found the mark?

Sir Philip had been listening to his son and now he laughed. A hearty laugh. He was enjoying his memories.

'You devil.' It was Julie. Andrew had to hold her back as she tried to reach the bed.

'I think you should leave, Chief Inspector. If you want to speak to my father again, you'll need to do it through his solicitor, and I would expect to be informed and be present at any interview.'

'I understand, sir. Of course. Thank you.' She looked across at Julie slumped now in a chair in the corner. She didn't say anything to her. There really wasn't anything to say.

When they had stepped out into the corridor, Maxwell turned to his boss.

'Do you think there really was a film?'

'With sick bastards like these, yes, they would have filmed everything so they could enjoy it all again and again.'

'We need to find that film then.'

'If it still exists, but at least we do know where to start looking.'

'If we find it, we'll have all the evidence we need.'

Chapter 58

As soon as they got back, Gawn reported what she had learned to Norman Smyth.

'The whole team has started to go over your house this morning, sir. Two men could never have done it by themselves. We need a quick result.'

'I agree, Chief Inspector. I'll stay out of their way.' She heard resignation in his voice as she put the phone down.

Next, she phoned Mark Ferguson to get an update on their progress. They had made a start but there was just so much, he told her. The attic extended over the entire floor plan of the house. She told him they could have whatever resources they needed. She wanted them to work through the night.

She was sitting at her desk drawing up a list of what they knew, what they suspected and what they could prove when Maxwell knocked on the door and walked in. As soon as she saw his face, she knew something was terribly wrong.

'What is it, Paul?'

'Jason Sloan's dead.'

'Bloody hell! How?' She wasn't expecting to hear that.

'He was stabbed.'

'The prison authorities will love that. They'll have public inquiries coming out their ears. The press'll be all over it.'

'He wasn't in prison.' When he saw her reaction he continued, 'He was out on his own recognizance, staying with his mother for a couple of days. They hadn't decided on any charges yet.

She stood up and moved round the desk to face him. 'Who have they put on it?'

'The super's given it to Maitland.'

Her eyebrows rose in resignation. Chief Inspector Davy Maitland was a by-the-book, old-school policeman. He had little sympathy with what he regarded as new-fangled ideas like women in the top jobs on the force. She had locked horns with him a few times in the past; told him to his face he was a dinosaur.

'I suppose he'll be in touch to find out what we know. There must be quite a few men out there glad to hear the news about Sloan. They'll be breathing a little easier today. Unfortunately, it's another witness we've lost.' Then she had a sudden thought. 'Did we get his identification of the house?'

'Yes. Jack and Jamie took him out last night before the stakeout and drove him round. He picked out the house so at least we have that.'

When she looked at him she could see he hadn't finished his news yet.

'Something else?'

'Yes. They recovered the murder weapon, a steak knife.'

'Good. That'll make Maitland's job easier. If he can find who killed Jason, it could lead back to our killer. Were there any fingerprints on it?'

'Yes.'

It was like pulling teeth. What wasn't he telling her?

'Have they got a match?'

'Yes.'

'For God's sake, Paul. Who was it?'

He took a deep breath before he spoke. 'Seb.'

She felt the earth move under her feet. Maxwell caught her before she hit the floor. When she came round, she was sitting on one of her armchairs, the top button of her shirt was undone, and he had a glass of water ready for her.

'Here, take this.'

She sipped the ice-cold water.

'Paul, there's no way Seb did anything to Jason. Why on earth would he?'

'Maitland'll say Jason had identified him as the driver. He was the only person linking Seb and that night. He might even try to suggest Seb was the one who killed Karen.'

'God. No. He couldn't think that. Seb didn't. He couldn't. I know him, Paul. You saw him this morning. He was hungover. We had him under surveillance for most of last night. When was Jason killed?'

'His mother says he got a phone call just before midnight. He told her he was going out to meet an old friend. He didn't tell her who it was or where he was going. His body was found behind a little church hall about half a mile from his mother's house by a couple of boys having a crafty smoke on their way to school this morning. Apparently it was a favourite place for all the kids to hang out when Jason was young too. The pathologist puts TOD between twelve and two.'

Seb had left the club at 11.30. They had watched him get into the taxi. They assumed he had gone home but he could have gone straight out again to meet Jason. That was what Maitland would say. This was a nightmare. She couldn't believe it was happening.

'I need to speak to Maitland.' She was halfway out of her seat when Maxwell placed his hand firmly on her shoulder and pushed her back down again.

'That's one thing you definitely mustn't do. On any account. You won't help Seb and you'll compromise yourself. Maitland may or may not know about you and Seb, but you can be sure once he does, he'll only use it against both of you. You need to stay well out of it.'

'I can't do that.'

'Leave it to me, Gawn. I'll speak to Seb.'

He had never seen her like this before. Gone was the Ice Queen image. She was distraught.

'Can you go to him now? Where are they holding him? Do you know?'

'I'll find out and I'll speak to him. If Maitland questions me wanting to talk to Seb, I'll tell him it's for our case. Seb's a material witness. It'll be OK, Gawn.' He put his hand on her arm. He was trying to be reassuring but he was anything but confident that it would be OK. Someone had set Seb up, presumably for the purposes of interfering with their investigation, but it served the dual purpose of putting Seb in the frame for Karen's murder too.

'It was a set-up, wasn't it? I thought they wanted to pump Seb for information but they were really setting him up. They must have got his fingerprints on the knife somehow. Then all they had to do was wait until he didn't have an alibi and then lure Jason out.' She was on the verge of tears. 'How did they have Seb's fingerprints on file to match them anyway? He doesn't have a criminal record.'

Maxwell looked down at his feet. 'It was our fault I'm afraid.'

'What?'

'When Walter and Jo interviewed him under caution, they had him fingerprinted so he was in the system. He agreed to it,' he added, not that that made it any better. Seb had been trying to help. If he had refused, they wouldn't have been able to match him to the weapon.

Maxwell had been afraid she would be livid and blame the two detectives.

'What a bloody mess.' She ran her fingers through her hair. 'Don't say anything to Walter or Jo. It wasn't their fault. When Murphy was abducted Mrs York told me to get the bastards and I told her I would. I'm going to make these sons of bitches sorry they were ever born no matter what.'

Their mantra had a whole other meaning to her now.

Chapter 59

Maxwell had told Maitland he needed to speak to Seb to get some corroboration for the information he had already given them. It didn't need to be official in an interview room, just a quick word. He would just speak to him in the holding cell. The truth was he didn't want to be questioning him in one of the interview rooms with all the recording equipment in place and the possibility that someone would be watching or listening in. This way he could be reasonably sure no one could hear them. Maitland had not been keen to allow him to question his suspect, but he couldn't really interfere with another investigation, especially one personally sanctioned by the ACC so he had sullenly agreed.

When the custody sergeant opened the cell door, Maxwell was aware of a figure, dressed in a paper coverall, sitting on the bed with his legs hunched up in front of him. Seb seemed to have shrunk into the outfit, but his words showed he was sanguine about the experience and hadn't lost his sense of humour. He wasn't distraught as Gawn had been.

'I wish to lodge an official complaint, Inspector. I've been refused painkillers. It's an infringement of my human rights, cruel and unusual punishment or something. My head's still thumping.' He managed a smile at the other man.

'How are you really?'

'How do you think? I'm pissed off. And to add insult to injury they've taken my best clothes, the ones I was wearing from last night and given me this paper monstrosity.' Then his eyes softened and his voice dropped. 'How is she?'

'Beside herself. She's worried about you and feeling guilty. She blames herself.'

'Tell her not to. I'm OK. This will turn up in one of my books in the future. It's all grist to the mill for a writer. I'm not guilty and I have confidence in the Great British justice system but failing that I have total confidence in her and you too of course. Tell her I don't blame her. If I'd done the right thing twenty years ago, I wouldn't be in this situation today. It's down to me, not her.'

'What did you do when you got home last night, Seb?'

'Honestly? I don't know exactly. I can't really remember too much. I do know I was in no fit state to go driving anywhere to meet Jason Sloan and kill him. I didn't even know his number, for God's sake, so how could I phone him? Anyway, why would I want to kill him? I'd nothing against Jason. I woke up this morning in my own bed but still in my clothes from last night. I guess I managed to get myself upstairs and then just passed out. Tell Gawn it's all her fault. If she'd agreed to come and spend the night with me, I'd have had the perfect alibi.' Then he changed his mind. 'No. Don't tell her that. I'm only joking but she'd take it to heart.'

Maxwell nodded.

'Do you remember handling a knife at the club?'

'Only the steak knives for the meal. No one else handed me a knife or anything. I don't think.' His brow furrowed as he tried to recall the events of the previous evening.

'Have they taken your mobile to trace the call Jason received?'

'Yes, but I didn't phone him either on my mobile or my landline.'

'Of course, they'll argue you had a burner phone and got rid of it.'

'Great,' Seb responded ironically.

'Have they taken a blood sample from you?' Maxwell asked.

'No.'

'I'll suggest it. You may have been slipped something in your drink to help you not remember.'

Seb nodded slowly as the realisation of his situation began to become clear to him.

'You think someone set me up deliberately?' He sounded and looked disbelieving. 'Some of my friends?'

'How well do you know them really?'

'I don't know all of them well. I only met some of them for the first time last night but some of them are old friends.'

'Look, hang in there, mate. We'll be working on it. You can be sure Gawn won't even let us breathe till we get you out. I practically had to hold her back from coming down and breaking you out single-handedly right away.'

Seb smiled at the thought. 'Tell her she should start learning to bake in case I need a file in a cake to escape.' Then he added, a serious look on his face, 'Look after her, Paul. She's not as tough as everyone thinks and she's been under a lot of strain.'

'Will do.'

Maxwell turned to leave.

'And I wasn't joking about the headache. If you could get them to give me something it'd be great. Thanks. And, Paul...' – Maxwell turned round at the cell door and looked at him – 'tell her I love her.'

'Will do, Seb.'

Chapter 60

Gawn was surprised that once again ACC Mackie was with Smyth in his office when she walked in. She had been surprised to be called to his office at all and was hoping he was not going to pull her off the investigation because of Seb's arrest. Her whole team was working every angle they could think of, calling in favours, contacting informers and meanwhile the search was continuing at Smyth's house, but they hadn't found anything useful yet. She'd had to explain to them all who Seb was and she had seen their sympathetic reactions.

'Sit down, Chief Inspector.'

'I'd prefer to stand. I'm very busy at the minute, sir.'

'With your boyfriend being arrested?' It was Mackie who commented.

So word had got up to the top floor. Not surprising. As soon as Maitland had found out, he would have passed it on.

'With the investigation, ma'am. We're making progress. We mounted a surveillance operation last night at the Raffles Club and we've got a picture of a figure who was also there watching and taking photographs.'

'Who?' Smyth asked.

'We don't know who he is yet or how he fits into any of this but we're looking for him. If he followed Dr York home, he could provide an alibi for him. But he might also be able to fill in other details. He might know who's behind all this.'

'He doesn't.' It was ACC Mackie who spoke again in a dull monotone voice. 'I've already spoken to him. He confirmed that Dr York returned home and remained there until at least 3am when he went off duty. I'm just off the phone with Chief Inspector Maitland. Your friend will be released. They have some official paperwork to complete so it'll probably take until the morning. He's already been sent to Maghaberry anyway so they'll release him from there tomorrow.'

Gawn grabbed the edge of Smyth's desk to steady herself.

'Are you alright, my dear? Sit down for goodness' sake.' Smyth walked round the desk and towered over her as she slumped in the straight-back chair.

'Off duty? I don't understand. How did you find this man so quickly? How did you even know about him? We only spotted him this morning when we were going over the surveillance photos.' Gawn looked from Smyth to Mackie, not sure who she should ask, or what was going on.

'He was reporting to me. He works for me,' the woman responded.

Gawn was stunned. She couldn't find words to express what she was feeling. ACC Mackie continued her explanation. 'He's been watching you and sometimes Dr York as well.'

'Why?'

'To keep tabs on what you were doing. To see how close you were to finding out who was responsible for Karen Houston's death. To encourage you to keep going; to make sure no one got to you as they did the original inquiry.' The woman smiled then and Gawn, in that instant, knew exactly what she was admitting to and that she felt pleased with herself for what she had done.

With a dawning realisation of the implication of what Mackie had said, Gawn almost whispered disbelievingly, 'He scraped Seb's car and left the note, didn't he?' They must have thought she was still there then to see it. 'He grabbed Murphy? And took the photographs at Craigantlet to threaten me?'

The woman didn't respond directly but the self-satisfied smile still lingered around her mouth. Smyth placed his hand on Gawn's shoulder. 'Deirdre believed, if you felt someone was trying to stop you, prevent you investigating, you'd keep going even harder and time was running out. We retire on Friday.'

Gawn wasn't listening. She had barely heard what Smyth had said.

'Murphy. You had Murphy abducted? You put his family, his mother through hell?' Without thinking through any implications for herself and before Smyth or Mackie could react, Gawn was out of her seat and had slapped the woman across the face, hard. ACC Mackie staggered back against Smyth's desk with the force of the blow. Smyth grabbed Gawn's arms and pinioned them behind her back before she could do any more damage to the senior officer.

'No, Norman, she has a perfect right to be angry. The boy was never in any danger, Chief Inspector. I would never have had a child hurt. He was missing for only a few minutes. We watched until he was picked up to make sure he was safe.' She was rubbing her cheek as she spoke but Gawn could see a red welt was already forming across it.

'You watched? You were there? I don't understand. What has any of this to do with you?'

Smyth released Gawn's arms and held out a chair for Mackie to sit down, pointed Gawn to a seat, waited until she had sat down too and then sat himself. He took a deep breath and looked at the two women across from him. 'It was Deirdre who got me thinking about Karen Houston's murder again. It was her idea to get someone to look into it. And she suggested you.'

'I was impressed with your work on the Bako gang. I thought if you really got your teeth into this, you wouldn't let anything or anyone stop you but I was worried about you. I realized you were under a lot of pressure because of what had happened with your sergeant and because of your relationship with York. We didn't realise at first that he was the Jacob York from the inquiry and when we did I suspected you might not want to find out too much if he could be involved. And I was concerned the security forces might have had a hand in this originally and they could try to stop you.' So Gawn wasn't the only one who had considered MI5 might have been involved. 'At one point I even thought Norman might pull you off the case and I had to encourage him to keep going. But I was right about you the first time, wasn't I?'

'So, was it your man who framed Seb?'

'No. We can only assume it is our original killer who is now trying to cover his tracks whatever way he can, muddying the water, offering up your friend as a suspect,' Smyth answered, although the question had been directed at Mackie.

'But why does it matter so much to you?' Gawn asked of the woman.

It was Smyth who answered again.

'Deirdre uses her maiden name for work but if I say her husband, Jack Forbes, was the officer in charge of the original inquiry, you'll know why.'

Mackie was still holding her cheek and she worked her jaw from side to side gingerly as if she suspected it might be broken. 'It changed Jack. He was never the same again. They got to him. Somehow. I don't know if they paid him off or threatened him or what they did but he was never the same. He would never talk to me about it. But he couldn't live with himself after it and eventually he lost himself in a bottle of pills washed down with a bottle of vodka. And I was left with two small children. I got an envelope through my door with money and a note warning me to keep quiet or my children would suffer without a mother as well as a father. I still have the envelope and the money. I never used it; never touched it but I never did anything about it until now. They might as well have killed my husband too. They stole my children's father from them.'

'But why now? Why after all this time?' Gawn couldn't help feeling some pity for the woman even after what she had done.

'My boys are both grown up now. They're married with their own families and don't live here anymore. They're out of harm's way. Norman and I are both retiring and when he told me what Louise Sloan had told him I realized there was a chance, my last chance to get the bastards responsible for it all.'

'And the ends justify the means for you?'

'Probably not from where you're sitting, Chief Inspector. But to me, yes. If it had been your Dr York taken from you, wouldn't you have wanted justice?'

'Justice, yes, but not by making innocent people suffer, not by manipulating people to get them to do your dirty work. I would have gone through hell to find these men. I still will but I didn't need my loved ones to be traumatised to make sure I'd do my job.' She looked from Mackie to Smyth. 'May I go now, sir? I have a killer to find.' And she stood up and walked out without waiting for an answer.

Chapter 61

Gawn headed straight from Smyth's office to his house. A policeman was on guard at the gate and waved her through. She was pleased there was no sign of any press or cameras. Yet. She hoped they could keep it that way. At least for a while. The driveway was full of cars and two CSU vans were lined up one behind the other. A tent was set up on the lawn in front of the doorway and white-clad figures were walking in and out carrying articles taken from inside the house. Gawn donned full forensics garb before entering.

'Ferguson?' she asked the first man she met.

'Up in the attic, ma'am.'

She passed two men carrying cardboard boxes as she walked up the wide carpeted stairway hardly noticing the elegant mahogany handrails, product of an age gone by. At the top a pull-down ladder gave access to the attic space. She could see that they had their powerful arc lighting rigged up there from the intensity of the beam which flooded down onto the square beneath the opening. Tentatively she climbed the ladder and poked her head through the gap. She was temporarily blinded by the intense brightness. When her eyes had become accustomed to it, she was surprised at the size of the space before her. Ferguson had been right. There were a lot of boxes and miscellaneous items of different shapes and sizes. It would take a long time just to catalogue it all.

She climbed through the hatch and looked around trying to identify Ferguson among the team of white-clad figures. Camera flashes caught her attention and she turned around and spotted him behind her. She called him over.

'Anything of interest?'

'Not really. We've started here closest to the opening and then we'll work backwards. That's our best chance of finding something from twenty years ago. It would probably be right at the very back. We just need to go about it methodically. Any idea what we might be looking for?'

'Photographs and movie films would be great. Or a weapon. Probably made of wood and preferably with fingerprints on it, please.' He nodded. 'I'll leave you to it. Obviously, if you find anything, I want to know right away – night or day, any time. You have my personal number.'

'Understood, ma'am.'

'Any time. Night or day,' she repeated.

Chapter 62

It was Thursday. Only one day until Smyth retired and she didn't know what would happen then. She was already in her office at her desk before Ferguson called.

'I think we have something you might like.' She waited but she didn't have to wait long. He sounded pleased and excited. 'We found a police baton. One of the old wooden types, a truncheon,' he explained.

'Is it Smyth's?'

'No. He called by this morning checking up on us – he didn't come inside the building, he didn't want any suggestion of compromising the site but he was able to tell us he never kept one. He says he doesn't know who it belongs to.'

'Any chance of fingerprints?'

'Already done and dusted if you'll excuse the CSU joke. Yes, we lifted prints. They're being run through AFIS as we speak. If we get a match, we'll let you know. We've been dusting everything as we find it. There's a year's work here, ma'am.'

'I know, Mark. Great job. Anything else on the baton?'

'Yes. Traces of what could be blood. It's already on its way to the lab. They'll cross-check it with the samples from your victim.'

'Keep me up to date, Mark. Thank you.' She rang off.

There was a knock on her door and Maxwell put his head into the room.

'They released Seb at eight o'clock. His sister picked him up.'

'Yes. I know. I phoned the prison and spoke to the governor.'

'Have you spoken to him yet?'

'No. I need to see him to speak to him. I don't want to talk to him over the phone. I need to concentrate on the case now. We're against the clock.' She didn't just mean now that they were racing against the day when Smyth would retire. She hadn't told Paul about hitting ACC Mackie but she knew at any moment the word could come down that she was suspended. She wanted to get as much done as possible before then.

'But you've had other good news. I can see from your face.'

'They've found a possible weapon, an old police baton with traces of blood on it and fingerprints.'

'Wow. Looks like we might have got lucky.'

Another knock sounded on the door but whoever it was waited for Gawn's 'Come in,' before pushing the door open and stepping into the room. It was DCI Maitland and he looked decidedly uncomfortable.

'I've just been up to the top floor.' The other two knew what that meant.

'Have a seat. You look like you could use it.'

'Look, there was nothing personal or malicious in me arresting your... boyfriend,' he began. 'He looked a dead cert for it. We had the murder weapon with his fingerprints all over it. What did you expect me to do?' He was trying to justify himself in a way he wouldn't have been able to do upstairs with Smyth. There, he would just have had to stand and take whatever was said to him.

'I know, Maitland. I don't blame you. Seb was well and truly set up. You just followed the evidence which is all any of us can ever do.'

He looked a little surprised and very relieved at her attitude.

'Well, perhaps I can make up for it a bit.'

Maxwell and Gawn exchanged a glance.

'We have footage of Sloan's real killer.'

Gawn sat forward in her chair.

'Have you identified him?'

'Yes. Some local kid was flying a drone with an infrared camera on it. He was supposed to be in bed so he didn't tell anyone at first but when he heard his parents talking about a murder, it all came out and they brought him in. He got pictures of the two men meeting behind the church hall.'

'And you got an identification from that?'

'No. Not good enough quality or near enough but we were able to see where he went afterwards. We were able to pick up his trail at the traffic cams at the top of the Castlereagh Road. There was practically no other traffic at that time of night. It was the only car that approached that junction from that direction anytime around then. We got a lovely close-up full face of him and facial rec kicked up a Russian gun-for-hire called Anton Vassiliev. He's friends with your Bako people. We're trying to get him before he heads back over the border or out of the country. If we do get him, he'll sing like a bird.'

'You sound very confident, Chief Inspector,' Maxwell said.

'I am, Paul. He's a paid killer. He has no loyalty to whoever paid for the hit. To save his own skin, he'll talk.' He stood up and straightened the already razor-sharp creases in his trousers. 'Anyhow, as soon as we get him, I'll let you know.'

'It would be good if Paul could question him.'

'I'll see what I can do.' And on that conciliatory note, he left.

Gawn and Maxwell smiled at each other.

'Things are moving, Paul.'

'Yes, and I'm here to remind you we have an interview set up with Andrew Patterson.'

She looked at her watch.

'I didn't realise it was that time already. Is he here yet?'

'Yes. He and his solicitor arrived about ten minutes ago.'

'Right. Better not keep him waiting too long. We don't really have anything on him unless he was the one who paid for the hit on Sloan to protect his father, but I don't see it somehow. But he might be able to provide valuable information about the judge and the jury from twenty years ago.'

'If he'll talk.'

'Yes. If he'll talk. We just have to hope his loyalty to his wife is stronger than his loyalty to his father.'

Chapter 63

Andrew Patterson was formally dressed as if he was attending a business meeting. He looked suave. His suit was well cut, not off the peg for sure. He had taken care with his hair. His tie was perfectly knotted, a Windsor knot. His aftershave was a little more floral than Gawn liked in a man. His solicitor was sitting beside him clutching his fountain pen poised over his file. He was an older man whose bald head was shining under the hot lights in the room. Neither was completely at ease. It was clear this was a new experience for both.

'Good morning, Mr Patterson. Thank you for coming in.'

'This is my solicitor, Daniel Mosgrove. I thought I'd better bring him along.'

Gawn had never heard of him. She suspected he was not a criminal lawyer and might be feeling a little out of his depth in a police interview room rather than his normal habitat of the boardroom.

Maxwell explained they would be recording the interview although he was not under caution.

'I don't know what you think I can tell you. I was three thousand miles away when Karen was killed. Julie can vouch for me. I was with her.'

'We've already confirmed your alibi, sir,' agreed Maxwell.

Grant had searched until he had managed to track down a photograph placing Andrew Patterson very definitely in New York on the night of the murder. It had been the partners' ball of the law firm with whom Julie had been interning. The whole staff had been at a swanky New York hotel and Andrew and Julie had featured in more than one of the photographs taken for the in-house magazine which Grant had eventually found on the internet.

'Then why is my client here?'

'You may not have been in the house on the night of the murder, but you weren't a child then. You must have known what was going on, what happened at your father's so-called parties.'

'Are you sure Karen was killed at my father's house?'

'She was certainly attacked there. We know that. The post-mortem suggested she was still alive when she was taken to the forest and then run over. Whether she would have survived her original injuries is a moot point which no doubt the legal fraternity will argue over,' – she nodded to Mosgrove – 'but they certainly contributed significantly to her death. But this wasn't the first party held in the house. We know they were regular events. You must have been aware of them.'

The nervous-looking solicitor leaned across and whispered in Patterson's ear. He shook his head in response.

'Chief Inspector, my solicitor is advising me not to answer any questions but I have nothing to hide. I wasn't involved in anything, and I'm as horrified as my wife at what happened to her sister. Karen was a lovely girl. We dated for over six months. I was very fond of her, but she changed. I was too…' – he paused to think of the right word to use – 'tame for her. She told me she wanted to live a little when we broke up. I didn't know anything about any parties. My mother and father divorced when I was ten years old. My mother got custody of me and brought me up.'

'I know that, sir, but I also know you were at boarding school here in Belfast and that it was common practice for boys to have weekend passes to visit relatives.' She had done her homework. A couple of teachers still at the school who remembered Patterson as a pupil had suggested that he probably went home to his father, most boys did, and they couldn't remember him spending many weekends in the school.

'Well, yes, I did go to my father's sometimes. It was better than staying in school. But not every weekend. Sometimes I went home with some of my friends to their families and I even went to the Houstons' one weekend after I'd met Julie's mother at a school concert. She was very kind to me and invited me for the weekend. I think she felt sorry for me. She knew what my father could be like.'

'And what could he be like, Mr Patterson?' asked Maxwell.

'He was volatile, I suppose is the best way to put it. He had a temper.'

'Was he violent?'

'With me?'

Gawn nodded.

'Once or twice when I was younger. Once I got big enough to stand up to him he backed off. Bullies always do, don't they?'

'Had he been violent with your mother?'

'I was away at school from the age of seven. They put on a pretty good show in public, but I think even then I knew she wasn't happy. Whether he hit her, I don't know.

It's not the kind of thing a teenage boy discusses with his mother, is it?'

'Going back to your weekends staying with your father, did you ever see any parties?' Gawn asked.

'No. Definitely not. I guess he would have been careful not to have a party on any weekend I was there.'

'Mr Patterson, when we were questioning your father at the nursing home, you didn't seem surprised when he was talking about the drugs and other things he had been involved in. You must have known.'

'Not then. Not at the time.'

'Then when, sir?'

'My father's condition has been deteriorating for some time. Sometimes he would say things to me. Sometimes he got confused. He obviously thought I was someone else. He spoke about drugs and about the girls at the parties as if I'd been there too. But I thought that's what they were, just parties. He was a red-blooded man. He was divorced. He partied. I guess I gave him a bye until he spoke to me about Karen.'

Gawn's eyes widened.

'He confessed to being involved with Karen?'

'No. No. He said some fool had brought her to the house. He was afraid she would recognise him and tell her father. He had left as soon as he saw her, but he didn't tell me it was the night she was killed, Chief Inspector.'

'And you didn't put two and two together? Come on, you're an intelligent man. You didn't suspect?'

Some of Patterson's sophisticated veneer slipped and he raised his voice as he responded. 'What do you want me to say? I couldn't believe my father would be involved in killing anyone. And what good would it do to rake all this up? It wouldn't bring Karen back, would it?'

'It might have helped identify her killer.'

'My father doesn't know whether he's coming or going most of the time these days. He's so confused you couldn't depend on anything he might say.'

'You'll never be able to charge him. He wouldn't be fit for trial and his testimony, if he could give it, wouldn't stand up in court,' the solicitor chipped in. 'I am speaking as Sir Philip's solicitor too, Chief Inspector, when I say that.'

Gawn wasn't so convinced Sir Philip was quite as far gone as Andrew and his solicitor were suggesting. She could imagine he might be aware enough to use his condition as an excuse to escape justice.

'What about the current Raffles Club's judge and jury?'

'What about us?'

'You're the judge?'

'Yes. Judges are selected by the members and serve for five years. This is my second year.'

'Your father must have been pleased to see you following in his footsteps,' Maxwell commented cynically. 'Was he the judge twenty years ago when Karen went missing?'

'No. He came later, after Karen was dead. I knew about the club by then but there were no parties by that time. At least I don't think there were.'

'So who was judge when Karen was killed?'

'I don't know off-hand. I'd have to look it up.'

'Look it up?' Maxwell looked across at Gawn.

'We keep records of all the members and minutes of all the official meetings. Not dinner parties or charity events or anything like that. Only the business meetings.'

'And you have these?'

'Not personally. They're held in the safe at the club.'

'Can we see them?' Gawn worked very hard to keep any trace of excitement from her voice.

'If it was just down to me, I'd say yes straightaway, but I'm afraid I'll have to make a few calls and get my fellow jurors' permission.'

'Can you do that please, sir?'

'I'll make the calls and get back to you.'

Patterson was making to stand up when Gawn asked another question.

'At your dinner on Tuesday, were all the current members there?'

'Not all. Most.'

'Can we have their names?'

'Again, members expect a degree of privacy. I can't just go around giving out that sort of information, but I will ask for permission to let you know.'

Gawn considered threatening to charge him with impeding an investigation but she knew Patterson would have the money and the influence to make it difficult to stick and meanwhile the guilty ones would be getting away. She thought it was better to try to keep his willing cooperation and depend on his wife to pressure him to help. She thought for a minute and then asked, 'Most of the current members are younger men like yourself?'

'Yes.'

'Are there any who would also have been members twenty years ago?'

'Only one I think.'

'What about the sons of members from that time, like yourself?'

'Only two others that I can think of.'

'I would appreciate you getting the names of those three men for us as quickly as possible, Mr Patterson. A man has already died this week, and another was framed for his murder. We're not just talking ancient history here. Much as I want to catch Karen's killer, there is more at stake. Someone is still out there and is prepared to kill to keep his secret.'

Patterson's face displayed shock at the news of a death.

'I'll do what I can.'

Chapter 64

Gawn and Maxwell sat opposite each other at her desk. The atmosphere in the room was electric.

'We're gonna get this bastard. I can feel it, Gawn.'

'I hope you're right.'

'We've got the baton–'

'Which may or may not have been used on Karen. We haven't proved that yet and we haven't got a match for the fingerprints on it yet either,' Gawn interrupted him.

'OK, Maitland seems pretty confident he'll be able to get Vassiliev to talk.'

'If he finds him.'

'God, Gawn, try to be a bit more positive, will you?'

'OK. I think Patterson wants to help. That's a positive. I'm sure his wife will be putting him under all kinds of pressure to help us. If we get the names of the other men that will definitely give us something to work with.'

'You asked him about sons of previous members. Why?'

'I reckon whoever took the steak knife to give to Vassiliev to kill Jason and incriminate Seb would most likely be the man himself or someone close to him. And who would be closer than a son? Two of the men there had fathers who could have been the judge we're looking for.'

'You're discounting Patterson?'

'Not completely. But I think he's unlikely. The solicitor is probably right, we'd never get Sir Philip to trial so his son wouldn't need to do anything so extreme to cover for him.'

'Then we still have Ferguson and his team at the house. If they could turn anything else up, it would be a game-changer.'

'I agree but it's a long shot. Wouldn't you have destroyed it all if it was you? Andrew told us he saw his father destroying photographs and film. All we can hope is that Sir Philip forgot about some of it, or his dementia took hold before he had time to destroy everything.'

As if on cue, a knock on the door was followed by Ferguson walking into the office.

'We found them.' He looked exhausted but sounded triumphant as he flopped down on a chair without being invited to sit.

'Have you been working all night, Mark?' Gawn said.

'Yes. But it was worth it. We've found a whole heap of old photo albums and some cine film.' He couldn't keep the excitement from his voice.

'Where are they?'

'They're in the general office. I left Walter sorting through the albums to divvy them out. Erin's phoning round trying to see where she can find a Super 8 projector.'

'A what?' Maxwell said.

'Old technology, Paul. Long before video cameras and camera phones. Care to join us, ma'am?'

'Try to stop me.'

* * *

They had started with the albums while they waited for a cine projector to arrive. Nearly twenty in total. Covered in the dust of the years. Some of them were really old. The fashions suggested pre-war, some even First World War with their sepia images. There were more recent black and white photographs too. Lots of holiday snaps; some posed studio portraits and a few school photographs. Gradually more up-to-date colour photos started to appear. There were some posed wedding pictures, a few of a little family group who they guessed were Sir Philip, his wife and baby Andrew. Judging by the ladies' clothes the pictures carried on into the sixties and seventies and reached up to the 1990s. There was a large formal photo of Andrew standing stiffly in front of a bookcase in what was very obviously a brand-new school uniform. Gawn recognised it, the same school Seb had attended as a scholarship boy.

Just when they were beginning to think that the albums were a dead end, a slim envelope creased and greying with age fell out of a flap at the back of the album Logan was leafing through.

'Leave it!' Ferguson shouted. He lifted it gingerly before anyone else could handle it. Wearing gloves, he looked inside and extracted six negatives.

'What are those?' Grant asked.

'You wouldn't remember the joys of taking photographs and not knowing how they had turned out until you got them printed off at the chemist. These are negatives. Pre-digital photography technology, young man.' Logan smiled benignly at his junior colleague.

'Yes. We found a couple of old cameras and some developing equipment in the attic too. Sir Philip must have been a bit of an amateur photographer back in the day,' Ferguson informed them as he lifted the negatives carefully one by one, holding them up to the light and squinting to get an idea of what was on them. Gawn saw the expression on his face change. 'Christ.' He looked across at her. 'I think I need to see if we can get any fingerprints off these first and then I'll get them printed and bring you copies. You'll want to see them.'

She didn't really need to, but she asked anyway. 'Bad?'

'Very.'

Chapter 65

It was getting late. It had been a long day for everyone, but no one wanted to leave. No one wanted to go home. They all felt they were close to a major breakthrough and they wanted to be there. Gawn had suggested they go home and the team could pick it up in the morning but everyone knew she and Maxwell wouldn't be going anywhere.

Eventually, around eight o'clock a uniformed officer arrived carrying a battered cardboard box. It contained a cine projector.

'Sorry it took so long. I knew it was somewhere up in my roof space, but I had a bit of trouble finding it. It's been so long since we've used it. I hope it's still working alright.'

'Thank you for lending it to us, Sergeant,' Gawn said, gratefully.

Ferguson's team had found three small yellow plastic reels of cine film. They had already been checked for fingerprints. They had found prints belonging to several different people on them. Sir Philip would have to be fingerprinted to cross-check. And Andrew too and they were checking through the databases in case any of the others showed up in their records. Ferguson took charge and spooled the first reel on the projector. They had cleared a space on one blank white wall to use as a screen. A hush fell over the room as if they were at the cinema and the show was about to begin but no one was anticipating a pleasant experience. They had closed the venetian blinds and now turned the fluorescent lights off leaving only a few desk lamps to illuminate the room.

'Ready, ma'am?' He looked across at Gawn and she nodded. She was bracing herself.

In the end it was an anti-climax. The film, with no sound, was of a baby Andrew on a day out at Belfast Zoo with his parents. He was a toddler, taking his first giant steps, his proud parents taking turns to be in front of the camera with him. There was almost an audible communal sigh when the film came to an end. Ferguson spooled it back and then put the second reel on the projector. He had seen the negatives of the still photographs. They were still waiting for printed copies to be delivered but he knew what to expect.

The second film was more modern. This time it was Andrew and Julie's wedding day. Gawn recognised the outside of the church in one of the more upmarket Belfast suburbs, the crowd in their best clothes gathering for a group photograph on the front steps. It must have been quite the social occasion. Dee switched the main lights back on while Ferguson worked to set up the third film. Gawn had hoped for footage of the parties taken in the bedroom with the hidden camera. But surely no one would have been stupid enough to leave that sort of evidence lying around? The third film would be much of the same. Perhaps a film of Andrew's children. They would just have to depend on the still photographs.

The lights were turned off again. Ferguson flicked the switch on the projector. The film started. Immediately it was clear this had been taken indoors. It was the inside of a room. Gawn was aware of herself leaning forward and holding her breath as she watched. Others were too. The camera panned around a bedroom.

'Freeze it!' Gawn commanded.

The cameraman had managed to catch his own reflection in a cheval mirror in the corner of the room. They all recognised Sir Philip from the albums and the cine film of a day out at the zoo.

'We've got him, ma'am.'

'Only for filming whatever happened but it shows he was involved. Go on, Mark. Let's see the rest.' Gawn noted to herself that this had not been filmed through the hole in the ceiling. Were there two cameras? Was someone else filming everything that happened too? Who and why?

As they watched the camera moved on. It was focused now on a naked girl spreadeagled on the bed. It wasn't Karen. This girl – she looked about mid-teens – was barely conscious. Her eyes were only partially open. Gawn would have loved to look away. She didn't want to see what she knew was going to happen to this girl, but she had to watch, had to know. Three naked men were all over her, pawing at her, biting at her like a pride of lions over a piece of meat. Gawn had heard of roasting but never seen it before. She heard Hill sniff back a sob as one of the men penetrated the mercifully almost comatose girl with a baton. So, Karen had not been the only one the truncheon had been used on. Gawn realised she was clenching her fists tightly, digging her nails into the palms of her hands. She was shaking with rage.

The film only lasted three minutes but when it ended and the reel flicked round on the machine making a rhythmic clicking noise as the end of the film hit against the body of the projector, it sounded so loud in the utter silence and stillness of the room that it was like a gunshot. No one spoke. No one moved. Then someone coughed and the spell was broken. Dee switched on the lights, and everyone changed position, fidgeted in their seats, coughed, wiped their hands across their eyes, shuffled papers at their desk. Something, anything to break the tension, the memory of what they had just witnessed. No one was unaffected. Even Logan, who claimed to have seen it all, looked paler, and Dee, the dour cynic, blew his nose noisily.

'We'll need you to get still prints of the men in that film, Mark. There were a few good images of their faces. Whoever they are, if they're still alive, I want the bastards.'

She clenched her teeth and then looked around the room as she spoke. 'I think we've all seen more than enough for one day. Go home. Be with your families. It can wait until the morning.'

'I'll have the other photos ready by then, ma'am, and the stills from the film.'

'Great. Thank you, Mark.'

'Go home, Paul, and hug Kerri and the kids.'

She retreated to her office and closed the door behind her. She had to concentrate on her breathing as she leaned back against the door pressing herself tightly into the hard wooden surface to stop herself crying. That poor girl, and God knew how many others. How could police have turned a blind eye to this? Some at least had. And how could nice respectable family men, pillars of society, have been involved in this and then gone home to their wives and children? God, this was such a sick world. How could anyone bring a child into it? She thought of Smyth's words to her that there was only so much of this work you could take, and she wondered if she was coming to her limit.

Chapter 66

She was back at her desk at seven next morning having managed only fitful sleep but from the look of the others, she wasn't the only one who'd had trouble sleeping. They all were in the office well before eight, even Logan was there. It seemed they wanted to get started as soon as possible. Ferguson had arrived with the photographs and McKeown and Hill had arranged them on the noticeboard. She had watched them working from Maxwell's office.

'They make a good team,' Gawn stated.

'They all do.'

Gawn and Maxwell walked over to the board. The pictures were graphic. They had five young women, including Karen, being sexually assaulted or raped. They had four men as well as Sir Philip, whose images were clear enough to be identifiable. Now all they needed was someone who was able to identify them.

'OK. I'll not say "good" morning but I want to thank you all for being here early and for all the work you've put in on this case. Let's see if we can close it and get some of these gentlemen today.' She enunciated the word gentlemen very slowly and carefully, showing exactly what she thought of them.

'We got a match on the DNA on the baton.'

'It was Karen?'

'Yes. But there were two others as well so if we had any victims who wanted to come forward, we could match them.'

'Do you think it's likely that anyone will want to come forward if we make an appeal? It's twenty years ago. They've probably come to terms with it, put it behind them,' suggested Logan.

'Are you bloody joking, Billy?' Hill spoke up. 'You would never put something like that behind you. You'd try to live with it, but you'd never forget. You couldn't. It would haunt you.'

'But if you've built a good life for yourself, got married, have a family, you wouldn't want all this to come out. You wouldn't want anyone to see you if you were the girl in that film.'

'Do you really think all those girls were able to forget and build a good life? I would bet one or more than one has been in trouble since then. Drugs, probably. Prostitution, maybe. Take the photos down to Vice, Billy, and see if they recognise anyone,' Gawn ordered.

The phone rang in Maxwell's office and he went to answer it.

'It's for you. Andrew Patterson,' he called to Gawn.

'Mr Patterson. Thank you for getting back to me. I hope you have news.' She had closed the door of Maxwell's office before lifting the receiver and speaking.

'My two fellow jurors have agreed to me giving you their names. They're Jonah Lunn.' Gawn knew him. At least, she knew of him. She'd never met him, but he was one of Seb's best friends and the person who had proposed Seb for the club. 'And Cameron Bristow.'

'Where do I know that name from?'

'You should know him. He's one of yours. A superintendent down the Ards Peninsula.'

'Were either of their fathers judges?'

'I don't know.'

'What about the man who you said had been a member twenty years ago?'

'I haven't managed to contact him yet. I think he's out of the country. He does a lot of business in Russia. I will keep trying, Chief Inspector. You should probably know that he was the one who pressed for Seb York to become a member. He'd been reading his books and raved about how brilliant they were and how he wanted to meet him.'

So that explained the sudden invitation to join. It had not been a coincidence. Gawn had never seriously considered that it was. Jonah had been used and Seb had been set up.

'And the record books?'

'I'll keep trying.'

'Thank you.'

He rang off.

She had wanted to tell him to try harder but at least they were making progress and they had something to work on with the photographs and film.

Gawn had decided not to be too heavy-handed in approaching the two men Patterson had named. Maxwell and Logan would go and have a quiet chat with Jonah Lunn, not bring him in for an interview. He was a journalist, a newspaper editor. He'd had a few clashes with police over the years, but the general consensus of opinion was he was a straight dealer. He wasn't afraid to cooperate with the police but he would need to be handled carefully. Maxwell would know how to approach him, get the information out of him. She decided to stay well away from it. Jonah was not only one of Seb's oldest friends but he was also the first person who knew about their relationship. She didn't want to complicate things by being there when he was questioned.

Meanwhile she had to figure out a way to approach Bristow. She didn't know him, had heard nothing about him, good or bad. Being Gawn, she decided to take the direct route and phoned his office to make an appointment to speak with him only to be told he was at Police Headquarters this morning. So, he was in the building. Convenient. For whom? Him or her? She didn't want him casually dropping into the office and having sight of the board with all the photographs on it. She had just walked in to ask Hill to move the board out of the way when a tall man in uniform walked in behind her. She had no doubt who he was. His superintendent's uniform was a giveaway, of course.

'Chief Inspector Girvin? I'm Cameron Bristow. I hear you'd like a word with me.'

He seemed perfectly at ease, but she noticed his eyes flicking towards the noticeboard as he waited for her response.

'Yes. Good morning, sir. I didn't expect you to come to us. Please, come into my office. Jo, maybe you'd come too?'

'I'd prefer to speak to you alone, Chief Inspector.'

She would have preferred a witness, but she would go along with him for now. She led the way to her office, offered coffee which he refused and once he had settled himself into a chair, sat down and looked him straight in the eye.

'I'm not going to beat about the bush, sir.'

'I didn't expect you to. Your reputation precedes you, Chief Inspector. Hit me with it. Your best shot.' She didn't know whether he had heard something and was making some kind of oblique reference to her striking Deirdre Mackie or it was merely a figure of speech. She was becoming paranoid, believing in all kinds of conspiracies and collusion. She didn't know who she could trust, who to believe.

'You're a member of the Raffles Club?'

'Yes. I make no secret of it. I've been a member for several years. I'm very proud of the excellent charity work we do.' He was sitting back comfortably in the seat and had folded his hands in his lap.

'And your father was a member before you.'

'Yes. He was.'

'And he was a judge?'

'Yes. For a couple of years. Look, Gawn, may I call you Gawn?'

'Of course, sir.' How could she refuse? There was something charismatic in his demeanour. It wasn't just the authority which came with his rank. He had stunning blue eyes which seemed to drill right through you, coupled with a charming smile which suggested a kind and generous spirit.

'Andrew told me what's going on. I suppose he felt he had to although I think he would have preferred to keep it secret. It can't be pleasant finding out your father was involved in something like this. My father is not perfect, but I am certain he was never involved with any sex parties or a cover-up of a girl's murder.'

'How can you be so sure?'

'You mean apart from knowing my father?'

She nodded.

'I said he was a judge but only for a couple of years. Why he didn't serve out the full five years was because of his health. He'd already become more or less an invalid when Karen Houston went missing and her body was found. He had his first heart attack the previous year and he was in hospital after another major one when she was killed. I remember clearly sitting reading all about the case to him while he was in his hospital bed. It was front-page news.'

'I see.' She was disappointed. If he was telling the truth, it was another possibility off the list. It should be easy enough to check what he had said about his father's health.

'And you're talking to Jonah Lunn as well.'

'Yes. You two are sons of previous jurors from that era and you were at the dinner on Monday night.'

'Of course, Jonah's father was a judge too, but we weren't the only ones there.'

'Andrew Patterson only told us about the two of you.'

'He probably didn't realise. He mightn't even have seen him. It was just by chance I ran into him in the hallway. And, of course, he's not a member of the club but his father was a judge.'

'Who?'

'Nicholas Hunter.'

Who was Nicholas Hunter and how had they missed him? Was he one of the waiters who had arrived at the very beginning? Well, they had photographs of them too.

'We photographed everyone arriving. Perhaps you could look through them and point him out.'

'Of course.'

She led him back into the office and let him peruse the photographs on the noticeboard. She noticed his slight hesitation as he passed the one of himself. Then he stopped a little further along and pointed.

'There. That's him.'

He was indicating the close protection police officer who had accompanied his VIP to the dinner. He had stayed outside with the car and the driver, hadn't he? No. She remembered. He had been inside part of the time and had come out carrying a box. He wouldn't have needed a box to carry out a knife, but he could easily have secreted a knife in his pocket when he was picking up whatever it was he had carried out.

'Jack, find out everything about Nicholas Hunter.'

'I hope this has been useful, Chief Inspector, and I hope you get your killer.' He smiled and shook her hand.

'Thank you, sir.'

Chapter 67

By the time Maxwell and Logan were back from talking to Jonah Lunn, Dee had already got information on Nicholas Hunter. He had just handed a printout to Gawn when the other two walked in.

'Any joy?' she asked.

'Nothing new or particularly useful. Only that one of the other club members pushed for Seb to be invited to join. Lunn said he'd put Seb's name forward months ago and nothing had happened until one of the other jurors, an older man called Anthony Middleton, started pushing for it. So Middleton might be worth looking into. But apparently he's out of the country at the minute. Does a lot of business in Russia. What about you?'

'We've had a visit from Superintendent Bristow.' Maxwell's eyebrows rose sharply. She pointed to a new picture on the board. It was a blow-up of Hunter standing by the side of the car. 'Meet PC Nicholas Hunter. Son of Edmund Falloon formerly known as Ned Falloon to his friends.'

'Edmund Falloon, the property developer and all-round gangster?'

'Yes. Friend of our chums from Bako among others. Which might tie him to Middleton with their links to Russia too. He's one of the Garda's most wanted. I believe they have a nickname for him in Dublin, "Psycho", so Dr K seems to have kept his crazy reputation. How they'd love to get him for something. And we would just love to help them.' She smiled.

'How did we miss Hunter?'

'His parents split up when he was a child. He took his mother's name. He joined the PSNI five years ago. His record is exemplary. No red flags. First class shot. He joined the Close Protection Unit last year. But obviously he's still in touch with good old dad and it looks like he's doing some favours for him now.'

'Like getting the knife and passing it on to Vassiliev.'

Hill was just pinning a photograph of Edmund Falloon on the board. She placed it side by side with one of the stills from the party film. Twenty years might separate them, but they were obviously the same person.

'Got him!' Maxwell punched his fist in the air in a victory gesture.

Gawn walked to the door and beckoned to him to follow her to her office.

Once the door had closed behind him, Gawn started speaking.

'I think we've got enough to get Falloon. We can get Hunter too, although his father will try to cover for him but if they find Vassiliev he'll finger Hunter for providing the murder weapon. That's what Maitland thinks anyway. My guess would be that the PPS won't move against Patterson, what with his age and health and maybe his connections. Valerie Houston knows the truth now and so does Louise Sloan. I'm not sure whether they're the better for it but that's not down to me.' She had already told Maxwell some of what had happened in Smyth's office. 'Whether Smyth and Mackie have anything to answer for, I'm not going to judge. Maybe she was right, in different circumstances to protect my loved ones or get justice for them, maybe I'd go outside the law too. I'm going to leave it up to you to finish it all off, Paul. Give them all we have, tied up in a nice, neat bow, and let the legal boys decide who's charged.'

As she had been speaking, her voice had got quieter and her manner had changed from the elation of identifying Falloon to a tired sense of defeat. It seemed all the fight had gone out of her. She looked incredibly sad and tired. Maxwell was about to speak, mouth open, but she held up her hand to stop him.

'I've had enough. At least for now, Paul. I probably came back too soon. It was supposed to be a simple little misper to help out Norman Smyth; a fitting ending to his career. Instead, it turned out to be a nasty murder with a lot of things about people I'd much prefer not to know, not to even have to think about. I've found out things about myself too. It came too close to home. It hurt Seb again and it hurt his family. I need to take time. I haven't been well. I need to reassess my priorities; what I want out of life. I'll probably be suspended. I hit a senior officer.'

At that admission, Maxwell's mouth had dropped open.

'She deserved it but that doesn't matter. It's not a defence. If she makes a complaint I'll probably lose my job. But you can do this, Paul. You can finish this case and you can run this unit. You don't need me.'

He was still trying to process what she was telling him when he was surprised as she moved across the room and put her arms around him and hugged him before she lifted her coat and walked out the door without looking back.

Chapter 68

It was good to put Belfast behind her and all that had happened over the last couple of weeks. Her conversation with Maxwell, the departure from Police HQ, the call into her apartment to change and pick up an overnight bag and the drive north all seemed like a dream; like it wasn't really happening. She promised herself no thoughts about work, about her future now she had struck a senior officer, now she had walked away from a case. Just being, being with Seb while he wrote and she knew, she hoped, he would insist on at least one romantic walk on the beach in the moonlight.

As she approached the front door of the apartment, she felt light-headed again just for a second and put it down to nerves at the thought of seeing him and the fact that she hadn't had anything to eat all day. This would be the first time since he had been arrested on the murder charge that they would have been together. She opened the door and walked in without knocking. He was behind the kitchen counter. The table was set for two with candles lit and a bottle of wine standing ready.

'What time is she arriving?'

'She just has. Paul phoned and told me you were on your way.'

His face broke into a huge smile, then he opened his arms wide and she walked across and stepped into his embrace. She thought he was never going to let her go and she didn't want him to. He could feel her body trembling beneath his hands. He wanted to hold her forever, just like this; protect her, just like this.

Maxwell had phoned him and warned him. He had told him as much about the case as he could reveal, and he had shared what Gawn had said to him before she left. Seb wasn't going to mention anything about her work until she was ready, until she was the one who brought it up. She seemed to be content just to be there with him. They ate the meal he had prepared in almost silence, but it wasn't an awkward silence, and then they had the walk on the beach she had hoped for. It was a still evening with barely a cloud in the sky. The water was black and smooth, and moonlight played over its surface. No one else was in sight. It was as if they were the only two people in the world. The sound of the waves gently caressing the shoreline as they moved in and out formed a gentle soundtrack to their almost silent walk. Neither of them wanted to speak, to risk spoiling such a perfect moment. It was enough that they were connected, their fingers interlocked in a tapestry of interdependence. They both realised now how much they needed each other.

When they returned to the apartment, he lit the log burner and made hot chocolate. She sat on a cushion at his feet, from time to time leaning her head against his knee. He watched her face crinkling into a frown as she sat cradling the mug in her hands and looking into the fire, seeing what images in the flames, he wondered.

'I'm tired, Seb. It's been a long day. I think I'll head to bed.'

'Should I come?' he asked hopefully.

'Not tonight.'

She kissed him lightly on the top of his head as she passed leaving him sitting with a book in front of the fire.

'Goodnight, darling.'

Later she heard him come to bed being so careful not to wake her. Almost instantly, or so it seemed to her who was struggling to clear her mind for sleep, his breathing slowed and deepened, and he gave a little snore. Gawn lay awake. She didn't want to get up and sit in the chair at the window, fearing what she might see this time. Instead, she turned in the bed and watched Seb in sleep. Strands of moonlight played across his face creating shadows on his skin. His long dark eyelashes fluttered for a second as he dreamt. Gawn wondered what he might be dreaming about. There was still so much she didn't know about this man who had the ability to make her so very happy. He challenged her to be a better, more empathetic person. She knew he was good for her. They were good together. The first time they had made love was an experience she would never forget. And now was she questioning her commitment to him? What did she want from him? What did she want for herself, for the rest of her life? All her adult life had been career-driven, first in the army, then the police. She achieved results and that got her the respect of her fellow officers and satisfaction for herself. She judged herself by how many cases she closed; how many criminals she put away. But just recently she had realised that was no longer enough for her. Seb said he wanted to make her happy. But did she deserve to be happy? If she was being honest with herself, she didn't think so. The shrinks had tried to convince her that surviving her injuries in Afghanistan while others died was not something to feel guilty about. That didn't really help. And, of course, they didn't know about Harrison, her former lover, and his role in it all and about Max, the baby she had given up for adoption. She didn't deserve to be happy.

She turned around in the bed. Drawing her knees up into a foetal position she closed her eyes and concentrated on her breathing. But rather than her own breathing, it was Seb's she was aware of when he turned in his sleep, his breath on the back of her neck like a feather just touching her skin. Eventually she fell asleep.

Chapter 69

Gawn was up at dawn. Seb heard her prowling around the living room and then he heard the front door quietly close. Surely she hadn't left again without saying anything to him but when he got up and looked out the window her car was still there. He showered, dressed and was making breakfast when she appeared hot and sweaty after a run along the beach. Her hair was dishevelled, blown by the wind, and her cheeks were red with the exercise. He noticed her eyes were sparkling too. Gawn was a woman of action. Today she had made a decision to do something.

'Coffee's ready. Do you want toast?'

'No. Just coffee's fine. Thanks.'

He poured her a cup and she took it with her as she disappeared into the bedroom. He heard the shower running and had to fight an impulse to go to her. One of the first times they had made love was in the shower but he didn't think she would be in a receptive mood if he suggested repeating the experience this morning. He had to be careful, not rush her. Give her time and give her space. He realised something was still troubling her.

'Right.' She came bouncing out of the bedroom. He looked up and almost didn't recognise her. She was wearing her oldest jeans, a bright yellow sweater which he hadn't seen her wear before but which fitted tightly in all the right places as far as Seb was concerned and her hair was held in two little plaits giving her an almost rustic look. She was trying… too hard. Trying to be light-hearted and carefree; trying to forget whatever she had seen; all that had happened during this last case. She had talked in her sleep. Photographs and films. Over and over again. And she had cried out too.

He decided to play along with whatever she had in mind.

'Are we going for the Dorothy from *The Wizard of Oz* look or is it more Elly May from *The Beverly Hillbillies*? Should I go and get a piece of straw to chew on?'

She came across and hit him playfully on the arm.

'I just thought I should be a little more casual, more touristy. There's a fair at the commune today. I noticed it on a poster when I was running. I thought we could go. I don't want to appear too official or formal. I don't want them to suspect I'm from the police.'

'We're not going undercover sleuthing, are we? How exciting! Do I need my deerstalker?' he teased.

She laughed. 'You haven't got a deerstalker. Have you?' Little would surprise her about Seb.

'Course I haven't, silly, but I could get one if you like, if you're into dressing up.' He smiled back. He hoped this was more like their old relationship; that this was what she really wanted.

They set out straight after breakfast. This time Seb drove. It didn't take long to get to the farm shop, but they were surprised to see how busy the car park was. What was even more surprising was to see blue and white flickering police tape marking off a long white building to the side of the shop and three police cars sitting, their roof lights flashing. They spotted DI Cairns and Gawn made to walk across to him only to be stopped by a constable.

'Sorry, dear, you can't go through here. Oh, it's you, ma'am,' he added, and they recognised him as one of the two constables who had answered their original 999 call.

'It's all right, Davey. Let them through,' Cairns called across.

'What's going on?' she said.

'We have a warrant to bring Dellman in for questioning. We matched DNA on Magda's body with the DNA profile the Yanks have come up with for Dellman. Unfortunately we just missed him with all the crowds. There's nothing for you to do here. Just enjoy your day.'

Reluctantly Gawn turned back and joined the groups of people milling all around. The farm shop was popular with locals. Couples, women by themselves and family groups were all coming and going carrying bags of fresh fruit and vegetables. The café area was busy too, but it was the field beside the shop that was busiest of all with tents and colourful pop-up gazebos, manned mostly by young men and women. There was a group of children enjoying pony rides. It looked like any church or country fair. Some of the crowd were munching on hot dogs even at this time of the morning. The children were enjoying sticky pink candy floss on little wooden sticks. There were games stalls and food stalls. It seemed like the most normal and unsuspicious of scenes. It was hard to imagine something awful might have gone on here. Seb spotted a Win-a-Teddy stall and headed straight for it dragging Gawn by the hand behind him. He had three chances to win a prize. Although he was no great darts player, Seb managed to score a bullseye. He chose a fluffy yellow teddy and immediately handed it to Gawn.

'For you, darling. What shall we call him? What do you think? How about Sherlock?'

She threw him an angry glare and thrust the teddy back into his hand. He merely linked her arm and guided her to another stall.

'Undercover, remember? We're supposed to be here having fun,' he mock-whispered.

They were standing at a handmade jewellery stall admiring the silver and copper bracelets when Gawn noticed a commotion. One of the police cars had already started its engine and was making a speedy exit from the car park throwing up stones from the loosely gravelled surface as its wheels spun trying to get traction. They spotted Cairns almost running to his car. Gawn took off without a word and Seb found himself running after her, the teddy clutched under his arm. They intercepted the inspector who was breathing heavily after his dash.

'Have you got him?'

'Chief Inspector, this isn't your case.'

'Where is he?'

'It's not your case,' Cairns repeated hopelessly.

'Give in gracefully, man. She's not going to give up,' Seb advised.

'His car has been spotted at Torr Head. The helicopter has him in sight and they think they're making for the cliffs at the Devil's Dip.'

'They?'

'He has one of the girls from the commune with him.'

'Lead the way,' she called as she headed to Seb's car.

'It's not your case,' Cairns repeated again, almost plaintively this time.

Seb merely shrugged at the man as he followed Gawn to the car.

Cairns drove and Gawn, now driving Seb's car, followed almost sitting on his back bumper as he negotiated the winding country lanes. The sky had been darkening and rain couldn't be far away. He had put on his headlights. The wind was getting stronger too. He could feel its gentle buffeting of the car and wondered what conditions would be like on the clifftop. Cairns was debating with himself how he could stop Gawn interfering whenever they reached Dellman but he wasn't sure he wanted to. Unofficially this was almost as much her case as his. She had been there from the beginning.

Fifteen minutes later, Gawn brought Seb's sports car to a stop directly behind Cairns' car. There were two other marked police cars already stationary blocking the narrow roadway and a policeman stood guard beside the blue VW which belonged to Dellman. One of the policemen approached Cairns and spoke to him pointing in the direction of the cliffs over a stretch of open field.

'He was spotted heading to the clifftop over that field,' Cairns announced.

'Right.' Gawn was already beginning to make her way through a gap in the hedge when Cairns grabbed her by the arm and drew her back.

'Where do you think you're going?'

She looked down at his hand still on her arm until he withdrew it. 'I have experience in negotiating with hostages and jumpers. Have you?' She looked him squarely in the eye, daring him to argue with her.

He would have liked to say yes but it wasn't true. Nothing like this had ever happened before in his career. He'd had training of course but a long time ago and truth be told he was nervous about facing the man in these circumstances.

'We have more men on their way and the coastguard will be here in less than ten minutes. A hostage negotiator is coming from Derry. We'll just wait.'

'In ten minutes Dellman could have escaped or jumped or pushed the girl off the cliff and how long do you think it's going to take a hostage negotiator to get here in these conditions?' A light rain had started and the wind was picking up. 'Do you think Dellman is just going to stand around and wait for him to arrive?'

It was a sheepish Cairns who was very aware this was well outside his experience and what she had said was correct. Maybe he should just let her take over. That would be the easier option for him.

'Just wait?' Her tone was scathing. 'I'm going over there. The only way you'll stop me is to arrest me.'

For one split second Seb thought he might actually do that and for one split second Cairns was tempted. He liked Gawn as a person, as much as he knew her. He wondered if anyone really knew her, even York. He respected her as a police officer and her record was outstanding, but it was his case and this could all go horribly wrong if anything happened to Dellman, the girl or to her. He reached into his car and lifted out a set of body armour which he held out to her.

'OK. We both go. You can do the talking.'

'There's no way I am approaching him wearing that.' She looked at it disdainfully. 'I don't want him to feel threatened. I'll be careful. You need to hang back. We can't spook him. I'll try to talk him in but if the worst happens you need to have men in position to grab him and the girl. But keep them out of sight.'

Cairns didn't like it but there wasn't the time to start a whole discussion. Anyway, he didn't think it would do any good. She was a woman who was used to taking charge and taking action in a crisis. He would go along with it. As he began to follow her, Seb set off too.

'Dr York, you can't come. This is an official police operation.'

'Try to stop me.' The look on his face told Cairns he would have to waste time either arguing or subduing the man if he wanted to prevent him going.

'I don't know who's worse – you or your wife. Keep quiet and keep still. You do nothing unless I say so. OK?'

Seb nodded. Cairns just hoped Seb was more likely to obey his orders than Gawn.

The three walked briskly across the field, Gawn striding out in front. They had no difficulty in spotting Dellman, his long white robes billowing out behind him as he stood near the edge of the cliff face. He reminded them all of an angel hovering over the water below; an angel of death. His arm was around the shoulder of a young woman. She glanced round and saw the three approaching. The look on her face showed them she was terrified. Gawn held her arm out when they were about twenty feet away from the edge of the cliff to signal them to stop.

'You two wait here and watch for my signal.'

'What's your signal?' Cairns asked.

'You'll know it when you see it.'

They looked at each other but both remained where they were. Gawn walked quietly but purposefully on until she was about ten feet away from the two figures perched perilously on the cliff edge looking out to sea. Dellman didn't seem to have noticed her so far. She stopped and spoke.

'Moon?' Her voice was soft and soothing. She didn't want to alarm him; wanted him to keep calm and not do anything in panic.

He turned round quickly, almost overbalancing and dragging the girl even closer to the edge. Cairns and Seb held their breath until he had regained his stance and turned to face her.

'Keep away. We'll jump.'

The girl had started to sob.

'OK. No problem. I'll not come any nearer. But you don't want to jump. I just want to help.' She kept her voice even and unchallenging.

'Help? Who are you? Are you police? What can you do to help me? What can anyone do to help me now?'

'You won't know that until we talk. What about letting your friend go and I'll come and stand with you, and we'll just talk. Just talk. Can I come a bit nearer? I don't want to have to shout. It's hard to hear you over the noise of the waves.' He didn't respond so she took that as acquiescence and moved to within six feet of him. 'I don't have much of a head for heights, Moon. I'm going to sit down. Why don't you join me then we can really talk?' Keeping six feet distance between them she moved until she was in line with him at the cliff edge and sat down. She dangled her legs over the edge.

Cairns heard Seb gasp as he watched her. Then the two men saw Dellman sit down beside her, not quite within touching distance. He had let go of the girl's hand and Gawn motioned to her to move back. She took a step back and then turned around and ran towards Cairns and Seb. Cairns caught her and handed her on to a constable. The inspector spoke quietly into his radio mic. Then he and Seb moved nearer trying to catch what Gawn and Dellman were saying.

Gawn watched a flock of birds wheeling in the air, catching thermals off the cliff face and rising into the darkening sky. A storm was moving in. She allowed her eyes to follow the birds as they swooped far down towards the waves crashing onto the rocks at the base of the cliff face and then pulling up sharply just as it seemed they would be dashed to pieces.

'That's freedom, isn't it?' A note of wistfulness sounded in her voice. 'Nothing but the air beneath you and above you. No cares, no worries, no demands. No one with expectations of you. Just total freedom from the chains of this life, the "surly bonds". To be able to reach "the high untrespassed sanctity of space", that would be something.'

'You know your poetry. Yes. I feel that here and now I could just reach out and touch the face of God.' He leaned forward slightly and reached out one hand to the sky in a gesture like a small child reaching up to grasp the hand of a parent. It made Seb, watching, think of ET.

'But that wouldn't solve your problems, Moon. You'd just be running away. Think of all the hurt you'd leave behind for other people; the people you love; the people you care about, who care about you. Your mess for them to clear up. How do you know you wouldn't take that with you wherever you would be?'

'But think of the freedom. You don't know what it's like to be constantly straining to reach a perfection which is unreachable; to long to experience the unfathomable.'

'Yes. I do.' Her voice was low and hesitant. There was a wistfulness in the tone and both Dellman and the two listeners behind her struggled to make her out. 'I know the despair of imperfection when no matter what you do, you'll never be satisfied; it's never good enough. *You're* never good enough. And I know all about the guilt of loss. In my dreams I see their faces. I can never reach them. I'm still here but they're gone. I ask why I survived. I know that pain of hopelessness. How I long for it all to end.'

He turned and looked her full in the face.

'Do you really mean that?'

She didn't rush her answer. It seemed that all three men were waiting, holding their breath to hear her response.

'I long to be at peace.'

'Then come with me.' He stood up and extended his hand towards her in invitation.

Cairns felt rather than saw Seb take a step forward. 'Wait,' he hissed. They watched mesmerised as Gawn stood up and reached out her hand towards the figure in white. They glimpsed a movement further along the cliff edge as two men snaked their way towards Dellman from behind. Just at the instant their hands met, Gawn grabbed Dellman's wrist and twisted it. He wasn't expecting it. It was the suddenness of the movement that caught him off guard as much as the force she put into it. She pulled him back away from the edge and it seemed almost simultaneously two burly men materialised out of nowhere and grabbed him, pinning him to the ground. Seb dashed forward and grabbed her by the shoulders.

'What the hell were you playing at? You could have been killed.'

She didn't answer. She seemed to need time to control her thoughts and feelings. Her eyes were shining with intense excitement. He thought she wasn't focusing on him. Seb could feel her whole body quivering. He realised she must be experiencing the type of adrenaline high junkies crave. Then she seemed to pull herself together.

'I knew exactly what I was doing. I was doing my job. I could see the two officers making their way over and I just had to time it right.'

Seb was angry. She had risked her life for a murderer. Maybe what she had said was true. Maybe she was tired of struggling; wanted her freedom from everything, including him. He turned his back to her and walked away.

Chapter 70

Cairns shook hands with Gawn, a smile of relief across his kindly face.

'Thank you, Chief Inspector. For all your help.' There was no doubt she had helped but working with her had been a challenge from beginning to end.

'I'm just glad you got him. Just make it stick and make sure no more girls like Magda can fall under his spell.'

'We will. He's already talking his head off. Apparently, he's ranting that she deserved to die. She killed his baby. He killed her because she got pregnant and then had an abortion without telling him.' He shook his head sadly before turning to Seb. 'Thank you too, Dr York, for lending us your wife.'

Seb noticed there was still that slight hesitation before the word 'wife'.

'I don't think either you or I had much choice in that.' Seb laughed. 'When she gets an idea into her head, I wouldn't even try to stop her.'

He was surprised when he turned round to see Gawn already striding away towards the car. He caught her up but didn't try to take her hand. He knew she liked to keep her professional and private life separate. She wouldn't want to be seen holding hands in front of the other ranks. Besides he was still angry with her. No matter how flippant or blasé she was about it, what she had just done was dangerous and unnecessary. They could have arrested him some other way or even let him take a dive off the cliff for all Seb cared. After all he was a murderer. Why should she risk her life for him?

He wondered what Gawn had thought of being referred to as his wife. He had come close so many times to proposing to her only for something to intervene. He knew he would like it but would she ever consider marrying him? He knew he sometimes came a poor second to her career and that was alright. He had reconciled himself to that. That was just Gawn and he loved her as she was – faults, flaws and weaknesses, the whole package.

When they reached his car, she didn't immediately open the door.

'Let's walk along the cliff. I need some fresh air.'

'Sure.'

They walked in silence for several minutes. Seb dug his hands deep into his pockets. He was determined not to be the first to speak but the more time passed, the more concerned he became. He had known something was wrong for weeks. He had sensed a change in her. Eventually he could stand it no longer. He came to an abrupt stop and blocked her way.

'I know what was going on back there, Gawn. I couldn't hear every word, but I know what you were talking to Dellman about. You were talking about killing yourself.'

'It's negotiation 101, Seb. Empathise with the suspect, gain his confidence. That's all.' She tried to reassure him but he wasn't going to give up that easily.

'What's wrong? There's something wrong. Whatever it is I'd rather know.'

She didn't speak. She seemed to be trying to think of how to tell him what she had on her mind.

'For God's sake,' he said, 'just tell me. Do you want to break up with me? Is that it? Do you want to move on?'

'Do you?'

'No. Of course not. I love you. God, what do I have to do to prove that to you?' He felt like shaking her. She could be so infuriating.

She still couldn't seem to find the words to tell him what was wrong.

'Is it Cairns calling you my wife? Do you hate the idea of being married to me? Is that it? We don't have to get married, you know. Not if you don't want to. Just tell me. I can't bear the not knowing. My mind's imagining all sorts of things. The truth couldn't be any worse than what I've been thinking.' He was getting desperate.

She looked up at him.

'I know you love me, Seb. You couldn't put up with all I've put you through if you didn't. I love you too. I can't think of not being with you; not having you in my life.'

Relief flooded through him.

'Well, if it isn't that, then what is it?'

Her head was bowed and she spoke so softly that at first he couldn't make out what she'd said. The sound of the waves crashing onto the rocks below and the seagulls whirling and squawking in the sky overhead had carried her words away.

She looked up and her eyes were searching his face for his reaction.

'What did you say?'

This time she shouted. 'I think I'm pregnant!' and then more softly, 'I'm pregnant.'

How did she expect him to react? Did he see fear in her eyes? What was she afraid of? That he wouldn't want the responsibility of a child with her? He closed his eyes for a second and bit his lip.

'I thought you were going to leave me. Instead you're giving me the best news I could ever get. I'm going to be a dad. We're going to be a family.' He had taken both her hands in his. 'How long have you known?'

'I've suspected for a few weeks.'

'A few weeks! Why didn't you tell me?' And then something in her face gave him his answer. He let go of her hands. 'You were going to have an abortion.' It was a statement, not a question.

She was pale and her voice was strained as she answered. 'No. Yes. No. But I couldn't do it, Seb.' Now she reached out and took his hand in hers. 'I thought about it. This is such an awful world to bring a child into. I've seen so many terrible things people are capable of. But I couldn't do it. Not to you and not to our baby. I just needed time to come to terms with it all. I'm so afraid.'

'What are you afraid of?'

'I don't know if I can do it, Seb. I don't think I can be a mother; not a good one anyway. I'm afraid I'll fail you and our baby.'

'Gawn, you're the bravest person I've ever met. You deal with dangerous criminals all the time. You save people's lives. You're beautiful and clever and kind and you care about people. You're bloody amazing.'

'But what about my job? How would we—'

She didn't get the chance to say anything more. He grabbed her and kissed her to stop her talking.

'You'll be a fantastic mother and,' – he moved her back so that he could see her face and she could see his – 'of course, it goes without saying I'll be a brilliant dad.' His face seemed to have exploded into one huge smile. His joy was contagious. She couldn't help smiling now too. 'All the other details we'll work out together. Together, darling.'

He took both her hands in his. He smiled even more broadly if that was possible and now she laughed too. Typical Seb. But she knew he was right. He would be a brilliant dad. Then he knelt down on one knee.

Cairns was still standing by his car. He had just finished radioing in details of the arrest. He looked across to the cliff edge and saw the two figures silhouetted in a ray of sunlight pushing through the storm clouds in a darkening sky.

'Thank you, Dr and *Mrs* York,' he said quietly to himself and smiled.

Epilogue

Gawn and Seb had just finished looking at the details of his flight to LA and photographs of the beachside apartment the studio had arranged for him and he had gone to fetch a new bottle of wine from her hall cupboard which he had requisitioned as a wine store. Gawn's phone rang.

'Gawn?' She was surprised to hear Maxwell's voice. Two weeks had passed since she had walked away leaving him to deal with the aftermath of the Houston case. Two weeks filled with plans for their wedding in the picturesque Norman church not far from the famous castle and within sight of her apartment. Murphy was so excited. She had asked that he walk her down the aisle and he had been measured for a tuxedo to match his uncle Seb's. Two weeks when she had tried, mostly successfully during her waking hours, not to think about Karen Houston and the other victims and to forget what she had seen in the photographs and film from Smyth's attic. Night-time was a different story.

She wondered what Maxwell could have to say to her; why he would be ringing her.

'How are you, Gawn?'

'I'm doing OK.' She wasn't going to mention the wedding. It was to be strictly family only.

'I thought you might like an update on the Houston case.' His voice held a hint of hesitancy as if he wasn't sure how she would react. Did she want an update? Yes. If they had got the bastards, perhaps it would help her to put it all behind her.

'Yes. That would be good, Paul. If it's good news,' she added.

'Oh, it's good alright.' She could hear a smile in his voice. 'We got Hunter more or less right away. He was held at a traffic stop near Strabane trying to cross the border. One of the PCs recognized him from their time at Garnerville together. He's playing dumb but we have enough on him to charge him as an accessory.'

'What about Vassiliev?'

'Maitland was right about him. The Guards picked him up at Dublin Airport with a ticket for Krakow in his pocket and ever since he's been singing like Pavarotti. Lots of good stuff about Falloon's business interests and other activities he's masterminded but from our point of view lots of details about how Falloon had Seb set up and ordered Sloan's killing. He can't tell them enough to try to help himself.'

Gawn could tell from his tone of voice how much he was enjoying being able to tell her all this.

'And Sir Philip?'

His answer didn't come straightaway. 'It looks like you were right about him. They probably won't charge him. His doctors say he's too ill to stand trial and, I'm sure, a lot of pressure is being put on to try to keep him out of it as much as possible.'

She was disappointed but not really surprised.

'There's something else you should know.'

She waited. What could it be? Had Mackie filed a complaint against her? Was she being investigated?

'Smyth spoke to me yesterday. He was in collecting his belongings from his office and he took me out to lunch. He said he was sorry to have missed you at his retirement party.' Gawn wondered if he'd seriously believed she would turn up to wish him well after all that had happened. 'He had something he wanted you to know but he said you probably wouldn't want to listen to him right now so he told me something for your ears only.' He waited. Her natural curiosity kicked in.

'What did he say?'

'Apparently the parties were known about at the time – he didn't specify exactly who knew but I got the impression it was people pretty high up – but were tolerated because they were serving a purpose.'

Gawn's brow furrowed. What sort of purpose could they have served other than to satisfy the desires of a group of sadists?

'Our friends who like to work in the dark used them to get information and, shall we say, to "encourage" some of the men to help them. The spyhole Ferguson's team identified was used for blackmail. The men who came to the parties all had positions of power and influence and they could be manipulated by the threat of the films being made public. He didn't say what for or how but if you think back to all that was happening around then, it's not hard to imagine. But then Falloon, or Dr K as they all knew him then, went too far. When Karen was killed, the spooks pulled the plug but not before they had stymied the original investigation of Karen's murder to cover their tracks. Smyth said Mackie's husband was collateral damage. They reckon he must have worked it all out and been coerced to keep quiet. Probably they'd threatened to hurt her or the children. She can't believe he would have sold out for money. Over the years she had tried to investigate it herself or convince someone to take it on but with no success. When Smyth happened to mention Jason Sloan and the coincidence of his disappearance she saw the opportunity to re-open the case.

Gawn had listened with increasing anger. People in authority had not only known about what was happening but had actually covered it up. She remembered the SUV behind them on the dual carriageway as they had driven towards Holywood and her fleeting thought of being followed as they passed the army barracks where she knew MI5 officers operated.

'Oh, by the way, it appears Falloon put pressure on one of his old mates who's a member of the Raffles Club to get Seb's nomination fast-tracked so they could frame him for Sloan's murder. Falloon'll fight it all, deny everything and he has the money to get the best lawyers but they'll get him eventually.' He sounded confident. Before Gawn had time to say anything, he went on, 'Sex Crimes have taken the case over from us now. They're working on identifying the other men from the photographs and film we found. I would imagine there are some very worried old men in Northern Ireland wondering when a knock is going to come to their door. It may take our boys some time but they'll get there. They won't be giving up.

'As for our friends from the Dark Side, well what can you say? Smyth said there's no chance of touching them. They'd just plead the Official Secrets Act to cover any material which might help us to identify who exactly was facilitating the parties. I said "us" but of course, it's not "us" anymore. Or is it?'

He waited. He obviously expected an answer but she didn't know what her answer would be.

'Was anything said about me hitting Mackie?'

'No. As far as everyone's concerned, you're on sick leave.'

Was she going back? She could or she could walk away for good. The door opened behind her and Seb walked in. 'I'll be in touch, Paul. Thank you for phoning and letting me know.'

He walked over with a glass of red wine he had just poured for himself in one hand and a white wine for her in the other. 'What was that?' he asked as he reached the glass into her hand.

'Nothing important. Not as important as our future.'

He raised his glass. 'To the future.'

Gawn wondered what it held for them.

'The future.'

List of characters

Detective Chief Inspector Gawn Girvin
Detective Inspector Thomas Cairns
Assistant Chief Constable Norman Smyth – Gawn's godfather
Jenny Norris – Gawn's friend, pathologist
Jason Sloan – missing person
Keith Sloan – Jason's older brother
Scott Alexander – Jason's friend
Albert Wright – Jason's friend
Ray Totten – Starlit nightclub bouncer
Karen Houston – murder victim
Valerie Houston – Karen's mother
Martin Houston – Karen's father
Julie Patterson – Karen's sister
Andrew Patterson – Julie's husband
Sir Philip Patterson – Andrew's father
Sarah-Anne Wakely – Karen's friend
Sebastian Jacob York/Jakey – Gawn's partner
Angela York – Seb's mother
Murphy – Seb's nephew
Alan Turner – Seb's friend
Jonah Lunn – Seb's friend
Big Sam/Samuel Legget – fixer
Gemma Loughlin – Big Sam's partner
Scott Irvine/Jock – local community policeman
Paul Esdale – barrister
Daniel Mosgrove – solicitor
Anton Vassiliev – gunman
Cameron Bristow – Raffles club member
Anthony Middleton – Raffles club member

Edmund Falloon – Raffles club member
Magda Gorecki – victim
Arthur Dellman – commune leader
DS Paul Maxwell
Kerri – Paul Maxwell's wife
DC Josephine Hill
ex-DS Walter Pepper
DI Jack Forbes
DC Erin McKeown
DC Jamie Grant
DC John Dee/Jack
Assistant Chief Constable Deirdre Mackie
Mark Ferguson – crime scene investigator
Sean Ferguson – Mark Ferguson's brother
Chief Inspector Davy Maitland
PC Nicholas Hunter

MORE IN THIS SERIES

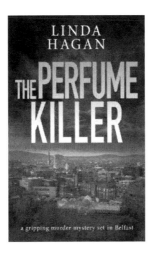

THE PERFUME KILLER (book 1)

Stumped in a multiple murder investigation, with the only clue being a perfume bottle top left at a crime scene, DCI Gawn Girvin must wait for a serial killer to make a wrong move. Unless she puts herself in the firing line…

Available free with Kindle Unlimited and in paperback!

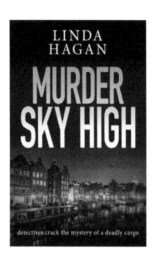

MURDER SKY HIGH (book 2)

When a plane passenger fails to reach his destination alive, Belfast police detective Gawn Girvin is tasked with understanding how he died. But determining who killed him begs the bigger question of why, and answering this leads the police to a dangerous encounter with a deadly foe.

Available free with Kindle Unlimited and in paperback!

OTHER TITLES OF INTEREST

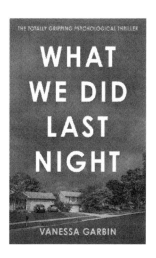

WHAT WE DID LAST NIGHT by Vanessa Garbin

When a group of close friends decide to hold a partner-swapping key party one night, it is meant to be "just a bit of fun". No obligations, but no strings attached. And anything that does happen will remain under wraps. But things quickly start to unravel, with utterly deadly consequences.

FREE with Kindle Unlimited and available in paperback.

PLANE DEAD by David Pearson

A plane lands at Dublin airport with a dead passenger –
poisoned, and for once not by the inflight menu. Detective
Fiona Moore is sure he's been murdered. But she'll have to
take on much of the investigation herself as her immediate
superior, DI Aidan Burke, has other things on his mind –
mainly the attractive Swedish co-pilot!

FREE with Kindle Unlimited and available in paperback.

Printed in Great Britain
by Amazon

69733901R00177